# The 99 BOYFRIENDS of MICAH SUMMERS

*the*

# 99

# BOYFRIENDS

— *of* —

# MICAH SUMMERS

## ADAM SASS

VIKING

VIKING
An imprint of Penguin Random House LLC, New York

First published in the United States of America by Viking,
an imprint of Penguin Random House LLC, 2022
First paperback edition published 2023

Created by Dovetail Fiction, a division of Working Partners Limited, 9 Kingsway,
4th Floor, London WC2B 6XF, England

Visit us online at PenguinRandomHouse.com.

Library of Congress Cataloging-in-Publication Data is available.

ISBN 9780593464793

1st Printing

Printed in the United States of America

LSCH

Edited by Kelsey Murphy
Design by Monique Sterling
Text set in Yoga Pro

For David, who fought hard for the right
boyfriend in this book

## Chapter 1
# BOY 100

How do I know it's love? Because I've already thrown up twice, and I haven't even asked him out yet. Although my friends could've done without that information, they agree that my anxiety-induced stomach issues provide the perfect excuse to skip school and ask out my first boy ever.

Who could focus on imaginary numbers or the Teapot Dome Scandal on a day like this? The signs that I should finally make my move are everywhere: the typical gray soup of overcast skies has finally broken apart over the Chicago skyline, giving way to a hopeful Tiffany blue. It's the first warm day we've had in half a year, which is perfect for my current mission because I can slip into my favorite black tank top that makes it look like I have ripped arms (twist: I don't!). I don't feel guilty skipping. I've already finished most of my finals, junior year is basically over, and half the seniors won't even be present today.

Like Andy McDermott.

I've been circling Andy all through May with the steely-eyed focus of a shark circling a drowning sailor. He'd been dating this girl in my pottery class for almost a year, but she cheated on him during spring break, they broke up, and then Andy started showing up at our school's LGBTQ+ club meetings.

As secretary of the club, the only meeting minutes I recorded that day were *OMIGAWD ANDY IS HERE*.

Hannah, my best friend (and best spy), managed to learn that Andy would be ditching class to go to Grant Park to record TikToks for his band. So that's where I'm headed, as fast as my penny board will take me.

The miniature hot-pink skateboard bucks under the weight of my overstuffed satchel, but I easily correct my balance. I am, after all, a little toothpick boy who is seventeen but looks twelve. Spring wind whips against my face as I glide across the rust-colored bridge between my home on the Gold Coast and the Loop downtown. When I reach the lake, I realize the entire city has chosen to play hooky: sailboat owners, bicyclists, joggers, picnickers—each of us desperate to take advantage of the first hint of warmth since October.

Yet the soothing wind does nothing to quiet the acid bubbling in my stomach.

Today is the day Micah Summers asks out his first boy, win or lose.

*It better not be lose!*

When I finally stop my board outside of a stone barrier leading into Grant Park, a stroke of luck finds me: Andy McDermott is already here. And he's alone. It's unfathomably rare to find Andy without his circle of intimidating friends.

Yet here he is without them, in line at a street-side hot dog cart.

Andy is a boy straight out of a fairy tale—but, like, the vaguely punk kind from *Descendants*. He has curly dark hair dyed aquamarine at the tips, a smattering of freckles over his lightly tanned cheeks, a stud earring, a flannel shirt tied around his waist, and silver rings on every finger. Ideal retro-music-video vibes.

Breathing steadily, I lick moisture back into my lips, clip my board to the back of my satchel, and join Andy in line.

He doesn't see me yet. My heart won't settle.

The hot dog vendor—a boisterous older white woman decked out in Chicago Bulls merch—waves Andy forward to take his order.

How am I supposed to start a conversation? Once I manage that, how do I ask him out in a way that's casual enough to not be off-putting, yet direct enough to avoid our date becoming a passionless friend hangout?

In real life, boys aren't fairy-tale princes; they're terrifying, unknowable creatures who hail from the woods of mystery.

No time to breathe. I leap to my phone for backup and text Hannah: Emergency! McDermott is in line ahead of me getting hot dogs. What do I do?

Her reply comes swiftly: Ask him out!

I nearly strangle my phone. Since seventh grade, Hannah has dated one pristine, popular boy after another—and she's always the one who gets asked out first—so I don't know why I think her advice will ever be applicable to me, a gay boy who hasn't even reached a middle schooler's dating level yet.

**Thank you, Hannah, but how?** I reply.

Just ask him if he wants to eat hot dogs together.
But, like, make it SOUND like "hot dog" is code for
something else.

**You're making jokes while I drown!**

Offer to buy his lunch!

At last, a concrete, actionable first step! Hannah is the queen.

"—run it through the garden," Andy tells the hot dog vendor in his coarse, husky voice.

"That'll be four fifty," the vendor says.

I lunge forward, credit card outstretched, before Andy finishes hunting for his wallet. "It'sonme," I blurt in a single, mishmashed syllable.

Andy staggers backward, shock etched across his scruffy face.

Oh no. I moved *too* quickly.

"Sorry!" I raise my arms in surrender for some unknowable reason. "It's, um, on me?"

Andy flutters long lashes, and his startled expression softens into a crafty smile. That's nice. Breath returns to my chest. "Oh, hey," he says. "Micah? From the school club thing, right?"

He recognizes me!

"Yes, uh . . ." I say, handing the vendor my card. My gaze leaps around wildly, landing on anything *but* Andy. The plan is breaking apart fast. To Andy, this twerpy little white kid he barely knows just jumped out of nowhere and isn't explaining why.

"Are you getting a dog, too, hon, or just buying his?" the woman asks.

The sidewalk is swirling. No way I could eat anything. "Just his," I mumble.

"Well, thanks," Andy says, his friendly tone powerless to relax me.

With ungodly effort, I meet his eyes—dark brown and flecked with gold. He's smiling.

It's too much attention. My stomach squeezes.

*Smile, Micah.* I obey. *Too much teeth!* I close my lips. *Now you look queasy.* I am queasy! Andy's smile begins to fade. *You're losing him!*

"I don't know what you're doing tonight," I blurt.

Andy's pierced eyebrow rises. "You . . . don't know what I'm doing tonight?"

The sentence was supposed to be *I don't know what you're doing tonight, but if you're free, do you want to go to a movie/dinner/whatever.* But of course, I chickened out on the important part, so I sound like a creep!

"Here's your card, sweetie," the vendor says before handing Andy a tinfoil-wrapped hot dog and bag of SunChips. A woman behind me nudges her children ahead to order, and Andy and I shuffle out of line together.

Literally what am I doing? Do I just follow him around all day like some sad ghost?

"I mean, if you aren't busy tonight . . . uh . . ." I stammer.

Mercifully, Andy knows where I'm going with this. Wincing

slightly, he leans closer. "Hey, Micah . . . I'm super flattered, but—"

"No worries!" I gasp. "Happy graduation, happy hot dog, bye!"

I sprint in the opposite direction with the intensity of a gazelle about to become a jaguar's lunch. I don't slow down until the toxic pool of acid inside me disappears.

My heart shrivels inside my chest. Once again, I couldn't do it.

As soon as I've safely put several blocks between Andy and myself, I drop my penny board and skate to Millennium Park—a bit touristy, but at least I can disappear into a crowd. Disappearing is what I need right now. After hopping off my penny board, I kick it into my arms and squat, cross-legged, a few yards from the Bean—a gigantic, reflective art installation of, well, a bean.

I open my satchel and pull out a charcoal pencil and Moleskine sketchbook. As soon as the textured paper hits my fingertips, the heat of my humiliation begins to simmer.

I put myself out there—*sort of*—but got shot down—*also sort of*.

That's really a bummer. Time to put the crush to bed and draw Andy out of my mind.

Beginning with wide, rough pencil strokes, I sketch Andy McDermott, but not as he is—how my crush made me feel. I exaggerate his features: his aqua-dipped hair becomes a shoulder-length mane; his eyes become glowing, golden moons; his flannel shirt becomes a torn, billowing, medieval tartan.

He's a pirate, like Westley in *The Princess Bride*. Or a wolf shifter from one of the romance novels I used to sneak from my mom's bedside table.

A wolf-pirate.

I add visual flourishes, like a nighttime forest scene tattooed down his left arm. A hoop earring instead of his stud. A pair of baby fangs peeking out beneath a thick mustache.

He looks nothing like the real Andy McDermott. In my fantasy, the wolf-pirate Andy whisks me away to his home deep inside a wicked forest. No need to ask him out and fumble my words—I am merely a wolf-pirate's willing captive. In this fantasy, I'm not a seventeen-year-old who's never even had a whiff of a date . . .

Unlike my friends, I never outgrew fairy tales, because I don't think they're silly or fake. To lonely little queer boys, they can seem just as real as anything else—more so because I control the story. In reality, I'm a wreck. I can't speak. I can't even look my crushes in the eyes. I control nothing. But in fairy tales, love can be as idealized as I want. I can be anyone.

When I draw, I'm me.

I open Instagram, and my heart lifts with renewed strength. Even though my art account—@InstaLovesInChicago—has been dormant all week while I finished finals, my follower count has grown by another thousand people. I'm almost to 50K! I try not to read comments, so I don't know if they're positive or negative, but just being reminded that this many people are seeing my art is everything I need after today's letdown.

*"I'm super flattered, but . . ."* I couldn't even let Andy finish his rejection, as if it would be less of a rejection if I stopped him halfway through. Whether the end of that sentence was *but I'm not interested* or *but I'm not ready yet after my breakup*, he doesn't share

my same feelings. Like a shoelace coming untied, the feeling I thought was love unravels into what it really is: a one-way infatuation. Love goes back and forth.

Oh well. Another miss for Micah Summers.

Like the ninety-nine other misses (or near-hits, as I optimistically call them), the ghost of my crush lives on in the romantic drawing of what might have been.

When I got this sketchbook for my birthday two years ago, it had 208 empty pages. To date, ninety-nine of them contain finished sketches of my Instaloves Boyfriends, each one kissed with a loving spritz of permanent Krylon adhesive.

Sealed. Posted to Instagram. Perfection.

Ninety-nine boyfriends.

Good thing nobody knows it's me behind the account. My family was on this reality show a few years ago (and *everyone* knows my dad), so the last thing I want is the whole internet knowing how many flopped crushes Micah Summers has endured. Making Instaloves anonymous keeps it about the art, not gossip. It's given me the space to play around and find my artistic voice.

I glance at my DM notifications—an endless column of unread messages from fans. In the tiny preview windows, they all ask variations on the same question:

Where is Boy 100?
When will you post Boy 100?
Boy 100 WHEN?

*When will my prince come?*

My chest sinks again. Ninety-nine crushes, and I've asked out zero.

All week, I thought Andy was Boy 100—the crush who finally becomes something more. But fate has decided Boy 100 is still out there, waiting for me like I'm waiting for him.

## Chapter 2
# THE PRINCE

The wolf-pirate smells that you're afraid, but your discomfort is something he cannot abide. "You don't have to say anything," he whispers. "I know a place we can go where it's just us." You look into his golden, animalistic eyes and instantly feel safe. This scruffy stranger knows exactly what you need. He knows how to be gentle with your feelings but fearless enough to make fun of you just the right amount.

You board his vessel and set sail for his family's ancient castle. Once there, you camp in the mountains. He serves you mulled cider in a ceramic mug he cast himself. A loyal wolfhound perches at your side.

I close Instagram without posting my drawing.

Andy's hands came out looking too big. They're not right.

Nothing's right!

Usually what makes my Instaloves feel so real is that I keep myself out of it. When you look at my drawings and read the caption, *you* are swept away. *You* live the fantasy. They're all based on my real crushes, but it's my job to exaggerate them so people feel what I feel. Yet this time, an invisible, heavy boot pushes against my stomach as Andy stares back from my sketchbook, his hands all misshapen. His allure is somehow missing.

Why did I get it wrong this time?

I sigh. This failed crush hurt. I thought I saw something in his eyes, something interested. Maybe I'm deluded. Maybe he *is* interested but still too raw from his breakup. Or he could've been open to dating if I hadn't blown it so spectacularly.

My phone buzzes with Hannah's text: Soooo??? When I text a thumbs-down, she replies, Meet us at Audrey's in 20 mins? Elliot will make your chai.

Elliot.

She is relentlessly trying to get me to be friends with that guy. Gays don't always need to be friends with other gays based on that trait alone! I want to text her back a sassy *No thx!* but she's being too nice. As I board across town, Chicago's inaugural hot summer day singes the hairs on my neck. God, I missed this toastiness. I'm sure by July, I'll be begging for October, but for now, this warmth is all I need to lift my spirits.

That and an Audrey's chai.

Audrey's Café is my newest obsession. Hannah brought it into my life at the perfect time, because I can no longer show my face around my previous haunt, Intelligentsia.

A former Instaloves Boyfriend—number 59—works there.

In fact, as I turn the corner toward Audrey's, Mr. 59 is in the Intelligentsia window changing signage to display their summer selections. I can almost see the number 59 pop over his head. He spots me crossing the street, his long, dark bangs flopping in front of his eyes. He smiles, but I'm too traumatized by my latest disaster to smile back. He tosses me a peace sign, and—miraculously—I'm able to return it as I zoom away.

Before heading inside Audrey's Café, a cozy French coffee shop, I pull out my sketchbook to take another look at the wolf-pirate Andy.

Tiny hairs frizzle on the back of my neck. I feel nothing. This boy, who I was certain would become the love of my life, sits in my sketchbook looking as foolish as I feel.

I want more than a flirty glance. I want a connection.

Boy 100 has to be special: a real date, not another disappointment. Andy wasn't it. Boy 100 can't just be a boy I fooled myself into thinking likes me because he gave me a half smile. The signals need to be stronger, and the feelings need to go both ways.

Surrounded by people happily sipping their lattes, I guide an X-Acto blade down the edge of my drawing. With a final *sliiiiiit*, I toss the wolf-pirate Andy into the trash.

"RIP," says Hannah. Almost out of a poof of smoke, my best friend—short, fashionable, and Black, with dark, always-radiant skin—appears beside me. Together, we gaze into the trash at my drawing of Andy.

"Who was that?" she asks.

Hannah doesn't even recognize Andy from the sketch, but the scents of mustard, freshly cooked onions, and Andy's musky cologne return to me. I sigh. "The boy of my dreams."

Hannah chuckles and hooks her arm in mine. "Ah, another one of those."

"Well, one day, I'll say it and it'll be true."

♡   ♡   ♡

Vanishing into Audrey's hectic crowds allows my humiliation to fade. These people don't know or care how horrifically I just embarrassed myself in front of Andy McDermott.

Deeper inside the brick-walled café, my sister, Maggie, waves to Hannah and me in a mob of other lost souls waiting for their lattes. She already ordered ours. Despite our family having enough money for an ample wardrobe, Maggie and I end up wearing the same things all the time like we're cartoon characters. With choppy chestnut hair and skin as pale white as a marble column, Maggie is dressed in her typical head-to-toe athleisure. I'm in my white gay uniform: fashionable joggers and a cheap black tank covered in paint smudges. Meanwhile, Hannah is far more style sensitive, dripping in yet another Instagrammable ensemble: jeweled, horn-rimmed glasses and a teal pencil skirt with matching short-sleeved blouse.

Hannah and I budge through a shoulder-to-shoulder crowd to wait against the bar with Maggie. "Why were you two outside staring into a trash can?" my sister asks.

"Another discarded Boy 100," Hannah says with a pitying glance.

Maggie's expression deflates. "What was wrong with that one? Just pick a crush already and post it. Your followers are gonna get bored waiting."

I stiffen. Maggie is headed into her second year of college for sports medicine—an artist and influencer she is not.

"What's that look for?" Maggie's lips tighten. "Oh, I should mind my own business?"

I shrug and wave my hands through the air as I search for the most delicate way to put this: "I'm trying to find The One. I can't 'just pick a crush already.'"

Maggie holds up "Fine, do it your way" hands, and Hannah sneaks farther down the counter to find her friend Elliot, a short, white, chubby barista with shaggy, hay-colored hair only a few shades darker than his complexion. He announces the next drink—"Cinnamon cold brew!"—while people complain about how long they've been waiting. Several of them loudly remember that cinnamon cold brew being ordered long after they ordered their much-easier-to-make drinks. Everyone is a coffee expert, apparently.

While Elliot mutters apologies and returns to his milk steamer, I spot my unmade chai among a line of cups that stretches down the bar all the way to the register.

Poor guy. The line is utterly endless, utterly hopeless.

Maggie turns to me with a crooked eyebrow. "Let me guess," she asks, "you threw away your sketch without letting Hannah or anyone else see it?"

I blow her a kiss, praying she doesn't pry the whole story out of me. Luckily, I didn't crush on Andy long enough for anyone but Hannah to know about it.

"I don't get it with you and not showing anyone your stuff," Maggie says.

"It's just a thing I'm weird about, okay?" I ask. "What did you think all those private art classes last year were about?"

Maggie shrugs. "I know, it's just been a while, and with Instaloves blowing up, I thought you got over that hurdle of showing people your stuff."

"Instaloves' followers don't know it's *me*."

Maggie and I have this argument at least once a month, so she either has selective amnesia, or she's trying to wear down my resolve like a hostage negotiator.

Hannah waves me over, so I leave Maggie to post her running stats to Instagram Stories. "Maggie getting under your skin?" Hannah asks with a hint of a smile.

"A liiiittle." I groan. "She won't let up about me not showing anyone my sketches."

"She just wants to toughen you up. Maybe get you to finally ask out one of those boys?"

Acid returns to my stomach, and I feel the blood leave my face. Hannah must have X-ray vision for when I'm Feeling a Certain Type of Way, because she takes my hand.

"Was it that bad?" she asks.

I sigh. "I couldn't do it. I almost did it, but . . . how am I ever gonna keep myself together around a boy to have a basic conversation? Like, my body *fully* rejected the whole situation."

Hannah rises on her tiptoes to kiss my forehead. A pleasant chill travels down my neck. "I'm sorry I don't have any advice," she says. "I'm not a chaser. I'm the chasee. Join me on this side!"

"I'm tryyyying."

We laugh and then groan. At least we have each other.

As we wait, Elliot's manager emerges from the kitchen behind him. She's an imperious, sunburned white woman in a crisp, neat button-down with her ponytail pulled back tightly, the way that balds ballerinas from traction alopecia. "Elliot, when's your break?" she asks.

"In ten minutes," he replies, never once pausing his breathless work. The manager says nothing. She surveys her remaining employees, but all of them look too harried to have the bandwidth to take over for Elliot.

"Uh, I could just skip my break and keep going," Elliot says, defeated.

"Thanks for being a team player," the manager says, giving Elliot's shoulder a chipper little squeeze like they're best girlfriends. Hannah throws death glares at the manager as she disappears into the kitchen without offering to help.

I wince at the endless crawl of drinks still to be made. I'm exhausted on Elliot's behalf. All these summer crowds, and we're not even at Taste of Chicago levels yet.

In just over a month, the historic lakeshore food festival will draw citizens out from under their air conditioners to feast on samples from some of the trendiest food-makers in the country (by law, Chicagoans do not recognize New York in this assessment). The Taste is fabulous if you're there to taste. However, if you work in food service, it's the stuff of nightmares, as it takes a sweltering, angry city and magically triples its population overnight.

The Taste is gonna drive poor Elliot nuts.

Although right now, he seems unshakable by this chaos. Or maybe he's just steady like that. I wouldn't know. He's newer in town. We go to different schools, so we mostly know each other as Hannah's *other* gay best friend. Frankly, I get enviously silent whenever his name comes up.

Not that he's ever done anything to deserve those feelings. Last summer, he and Hannah met interning at the same vet clinic. She couldn't emotionally handle all the sick and homeless pets, but it's Elliot's dream job, so he coached her through the hard stuff. It only took them a month to become as inseparable as she and I have been since birth.

Of Hannah's two best friends, he's the sweet one. He'd never dream of being weird about showing Hannah his artwork.

*That's probably why Elliot has a boyfriend, and you don't.*

My fingertips turn tingly and numb. To distract myself from today's rejection, I open Instaloves and scroll through my old sketches. There's Headphones Boy dancing by himself on the L and my story about the bohemian apartment in Boystown we would've shared, creating music and art every day. Then there's AP Bio Boy with the high-and-tight haircut, who bumped into me after his late basketball practice. In that post, I changed his sport of choice to skiing, and he swept me off to an Alpine chalet where he confidently schussed me around the mountain at twilight.

I started Instaloves for myself, but surprisingly, other people found my posts and connected with the anonymous, whimsical drawings. People seemed to *need* the fantasy, especially when the world isn't built around love like ours. Queers have to make our own magical stories from scratch, and I'm going to do whatever I can to help queer people dream.

A weary world deserves a little dreaming.

"Maybe Maggie's right," Hannah says. "Fish that old drawing out of the trash and give it a redo. I want you to keep your momentum. People are excited for Boy 100!" Her brassy voice carries so loudly, it can be heard over the whistle of Elliot's milk frother. A few people spin around with nosy interest.

"No so loud," I whisper, my neck retreating into my shoulders like a turtle. "I don't want Elliot to overhear it's me."

"Oh no . . ." Wincing, Hannah glances at Elliot as he free-pours a cappuccino. "I told him."

"*Hannah.*"

"I didn't know, like, zero people could know."

"What's wrong now, Baby Boo-Boo?" Maggie asks, rejoining us. My back tenses like a cat at her favorite nickname for me—as in *Crybaby Micah got another boo-boo.* I ignore her.

Elliot's hands move between drinks as gracefully as a dancer.

Without dropping speed, he glances at me and whispers, "It'll be our secret! Your Instaloves sketches are gorgeous—congrats."

Warmth rises in my cheeks. Reluctantly, I smile. "Thank you, Elliot."

"Brandon's the art critic, but I think they're awesome."

My smile dies. Translation: *I also told my boyfriend, and he thinks you're trash.*

I try not to growl. I guess it's fine if Sweet, Perfect, Never-Makes-a-Mistake Elliot knows.

He dumps ice into a tray of four large iced coffees, but as he calls out the order, the tray dips. He steadies it, heaves a sigh, and blows a curl out of his eyes. As he calls out the drinks again, a large, mustachioed man barges through the crowd and thrusts an open cup of coffee at him. "This is cold!" the man grunts, and Elliot flinches.

The tray tips again.

I hold my breath, but Elliot balances it.

"I'm sorry, sir," Elliot says patiently. "I can make you another one."

"And wait another thirty minutes?" The man scoffs at the crowd, as if he expects us to join him in attacking Elliot. "How about you make it right the first time?"

"I'll pour yours fresh right now. It'll take a sec—"

"Just refund me." Again, the man thrusts his coffee at Elliot.

Elliot gasps.

His hands twitch.

The coffee tray drops.

There's nothing to do but watch all four drinks plummet

to the floor, exploding one after the other like water balloons. Everyone leaps backward, including Elliot, who slaps his hands to his mouth as he surveys the aftermath: the area around the counter is a bloody battlefield of creamed coffee, ice cubes, and decapitated lids.

"I'm soaked!" the man with the mustache barks. I only see faint dark splashes on his pants. He's being a total drama queen.

Elliot was doing so well with the drinks; he was a blur of productivity. Now he's standing there in shock, everyone watching him angrily, all because this ogre barged into his space.

The manager emerges once again from the kitchen. Her nostrils flare at Elliot. "Clean it—I'm taking over bar." As she fastens her milk-stained apron, Elliot rushes to fetch a mop.

"That kid better pay my cleaning bill," the man shouts.

The manager nods as she steams milk. "We'll make it right, sir." Narrowing her eyes, she spins on Elliot, who is wheeling a mop bucket from the back. "Elliot, this is like the hundredth time with you. It's gonna have to start coming out of your check."

Elliot doesn't speak. His lower lip quivers as he huffs deliberately slow breaths.

My heart implodes for him. An hour ago, this was how I looked: silently begging the universe to make me disappear.

Anger rises in me like a balloon.

That cretin made Elliot spill those coffees, but now *Elliot* has to pay for it?

I step forward into the sea of spilled coffee and ice cubes, and I thrust two twenty-dollar bills at Mr. Mustache. "Hey, it was an accident. Get them cleaned on me. Take your bad attitude over there; see if they'll put up with you. Oh, and your coffee went cold because you put cream in it. That's what cream is supposed to do."

I swear, the man's mustache turns white as a smattering of customers applaud behind him. He snatches the bills from my hand and stalks off, muttering, "Millennials . . ."

"We're Gen Z, by the way!" I yell after him.

Hannah and Maggie watch me with surprise. I'm a little surprised at myself.

I just confronted a stranger! That's a first.

Elliot works too hard to be spoken to that way, and even if he wasn't working hard, he doesn't deserve that attitude. No one does. Elliot smiles in my direction before rounding the corner with a bucket and a WET FLOOR sign. "Thank you," he whispers as he mops.

"Gay solidarity," I whisper. "Don't worry about it."

"Prince Charming after all, huh?"

Prince?

As Elliot's compliment hits my ears, my fingertips buzz. My feet aren't fidgeting. No weight shifting back and forth. Strangely, my shoes are firmly planted on the ground.

I can't help smiling.

Just now, in a room full of people, I tapped into something strong. Confidence?

Suddenly, everything makes sense. I can't be the chasee like Hannah. If I wait for someone else to make the first move, I'll be waiting forever. I've got to be Prince Charming. I don't have to be nervous, dateless Micah Summers when I ask out Boy 100. I don't have to worry what people think of me. It's a role I can play.

Instaloves is me playing an anonymous role, so why can't I play someone else in my mind if it helps silence my nerves asking the next boy out? Not, like, pretending to be someone I'm not, just a little mental switch to get my confidence up.

Whoever you are, Boy 100, wherever you are, get ready to meet the prince!

# Chapter 3
# THE PUMPKIN

Two weeks following my disaster in Grant Park, the end of junior year has come (*Andy who??*). Every day since school let out, my new persona, Prince Charming, has been confidently asking out one boy after another! Except by "boy," I mean my reflection in the mirror.

As of today, I'm nowhere close to finding a Boy 100 who makes me want to make that big move. Boy 100 must be special, and they must be someone I successfully ask out. I can't go backward and keep living in my drawings. Asking out Andy McDermott was a disaster, but only because the answer wasn't the one I hoped for—I'm *so* close to a yes.

Sadly, these rules have left Instaloves without any fresh content for over three weeks! Maggie and Hannah insist I'm being too picky and that my Insta buzz window is closing.

Even though I haven't found him yet . . . I can't stop thinking about him.

Who he is. What he looks like.

I already have the feeling inside me. I just need to find the boy who matches the feeling.

To take my mind off the search, I enjoy an evening stroll into Old Town for art supplies. Old Town Chicago, with its tree-lined streets and squat, ancient brick homes—barely a skyscraper in sight—feels like the land of permanent autumn. All thoughts of boys vanish once I'm inside my favorite art supply store, Rhapsody in You, smelling the acrylic paint in the air and running my fingers along the aged shelves.

I pick up a new pack of charcoal pencils and a pocket-sized spiral notebook. The moment I leave the store, I label the notebook *Little Book of Firsts*. On the first page, I write *First Boy I Ever Asked Out* and leave a blank space next to it for a future date, when it occurs.

In my fingers, the small booklet thrums with a mystical power. It's going to be filled someday—first date, first kiss, first sleepover, on and on and on. My hunch was correct: as soon as I bought the booklet—acted with intention—the depressing feeling of *Will I ever ask out a boy again?* was replaced by hope.

It *will* happen.

My heart might explode, killing me as soon as I ask him, but it *will* happen.

Afterward, I continue on to a scenic L train trip around the Loop for some artistic inspiration. At sunset, there's no better time. As the train winds its way downtown, toward the river, I catch my own face beaming down at me from a banner ad.

Well, not *my* face. My father's.

JEREMY SUMMERS, THE KING OF CHICAGO! WNWC—THE GOAL!

Running into one of his billboards is basically like running into myself: we have the same brown eyes, Roman nose, and high, rose-hued cheekbones. Jeremy Summers is inescapable. His face pops up on trains, buses, park benches, sides of buildings, and autographed headshots hanging in every deli, pizza joint, and car wash he's ever wandered into.

It's probably my destiny to be Prince Charming. My dad is, after all, a king.

In the banner ad, his front tooth is blacked out, and a puffy bruise is painted under his right eye. It's intended to conjure up warm memories of his hockey heyday, which led to an Olympic silver medal in Vancouver, then a Wheaties box and a bronze medal in Sochi. All of that led to *Pass the Puck*, a one-season reality show that followed Jeremy Summers and his darling family.

Tragically, *Pass the Puck* was the genesis of Baby Boo-Boo. My sister's nickname for me caught on, even spawning a drinking game.

*Take a shot every time Micah cries over nothing!*

Hence my reluctance at letting anyone know I'm behind Instaloves. These fantasies could quickly turn pathetic in people's eyes if they knew who was drawing them.

The skyline outside my window blocks out all icky memories. You can't see starlight in Chicago, but at least we have glorious sunsets. It's the swooniest view in the city. Not dark enough outside to turn the windows into a mirror, but not so bright that we can't see through the glare. Just a train zigzagging through a labyrinth of skyscrapers as the setting sun cuts through the gaps between buildings. My shoulders drop, releasing tension I didn't realize was there.

Everyone on the train is beautiful. The orange-sherbet light improves everything it touches. In this light, faces glow and eyes sparkle with flecks of golden embers.

This would be the perfect time to run into . . .

*No, Micah, forget Boy 100 for one night!*

Our train approaches the stop at Harold Washington Library Center. With its redbrick façade and ornate, copper-green roof, the library is a piece of architecture as crisp and warm as a harvest apple.

A palace. What an ideal setting for . . .

*NO, Micah. Stop looking for him. Boy 100 will show up when he shows up.*

The creaking train whines to a stop and throws several standing passengers off-balance. I grip my seat's handrail and fix my bronze cashmere scarf. Despite the heat, I wear the scarf over my T-shirt to really sell that bohemian artist vibe. Besides, it's featherlight and soft against my neck. It also makes my light brown eyes pop like candy.

I look so cute tonight. WHAT IF I RAN INTO—

*I'm not gonna warn you again, Micah!*

Then the doors open.

And *he* walks in.

He's so tall he needs to duck slightly to get through the door, has the body of a man, but the face of a boy. A mop of curly black hair and round, pinchable, light olive cheeks.

The only word that comes to me is *fate*. I'm literally psychic. I felt the energy in the air. The *Little Book of Firsts* immediately worked magic!

As others shuffle inside, The Boy lugs two tote bags down the crowded aisle. The bags are so overflowing with library books, it's a struggle for him, even with his arms bulging beneath the sleeves of a black leather jacket. A jacket in the summer? We both suffer for fashion.

He's so helpless with those books, I have to smile.

"Long day. I promise I'm normally a lot stronger than this," The Boy says, his voice shockingly bass-y.

Was he talking to me? He glanced at me. He had to notice I was smiling.

*Do something, Micah!* My feet suddenly weigh a trillion pounds.

The Boy hoists both library bags like a professional weightlifter. His shimmering eyes lock onto mine. I force myself not to look away, but the vulnerability of holding his eye contact singes the hair on my forearms.

He grins, and his eyes vanish behind his full cheeks.

Without question, he is looking at me.

*Say something!* My lips are too chapped and dry.

A familiar churn begins in the pit of my stomach.

*Right now, you aren't dweeby Micah Summers who almost vomited on the last guy you tried to ask out. You are Prince Charming, and you can do ANYTHING!*

If I keep letting these moments slip away without opening

up, without risking the potential rejection situation, I'll never be ready. There are no bigger signals than the ones in this moment: I'm stuffed into a train next to a boy who looks like a goofier Prince Eric, who has already smiled at me several times. I have to act now.

"Take my seat!" I hear myself say it—way too loudly—as I jump up clumsily.

"Oh, no, dude, I've got it. It's not like I'm pregnant." The Boy stands almost a foot taller than me. The library bags in his hands are as high as my chest. What if I were a third thing he had to lift up and carry? I don't weigh much more than a bag of books. I bet he could do it.

I want him to do it.

"Well, I'm already up, so you should just take the seat—oop." A middle-aged Filipino woman in a neon-blue jogging suit slides behind me and takes the open seat before The Boy and I can politely argue any longer. Unbothered, she settles in with her paperback.

The Boy shrugs. "Look what you've done. Now we gotta talk with each other."

"Talking? Don't you hate that? *Oof!*" The rust bucket of a train booms to life again, and I'm jolted forward. My face collides directly with The Boy's tanned and muscular neck. I could die of humiliation on the spot. His right hand, still clutching one of the library bags, grabs my shoulder, and finally, my balance returns. Tingling electric shock waves pulse outward from the place where he touched me. His grip was strong but sure.

There was never even a chance he'd allow me to fall.

"Sorry." I laugh. A clean, aquatic scent follows me from my trip into his chest. I duck my face away. It almost hurts to look directly at him, especially after I just got a face full of his chest, like we're totally skipping to date number three.

He laughs back. Deep. His bass notes shake my eardrums. "Ah, the old 'Oops, the train made me fall into you' trick, huh?"

HE IS FLIRTING.

I take a deep, quiet breath and find his eyes again. "Well, don't mess with a classic."

I don't dare to blink. I need him to know I'm flirting back. The Boy holds my stare—no blinking on his end either. This is officially not a straight boy, not the sensitive straight boy who's sweet and jokey with gays—the kind who throws off gaydars everywhere. His moon-pool eyes are staring at me. His lips are slightly parted.

He's signaling.

My heart attack is imminent.

His playfulness, his warm, inviting energy makes looking at him and talking with him so easy. This has never happened before. This is what it feels like to be wanted.

Up close, The Boy's leather jacket isn't flat black at all. Crimson- and tangerine-colored threads weave in a delicate, intricate pattern across the sleeves. "Are those . . . vines?" I ask.

"Yeah, check it out." The Boy twists in place and flashes his broad back. The pattern is even clearer: a pumpkin. Swarms of leafy vines extend upward from the pumpkin before spilling down the jacket sleeves. It's as if he took autumn and made it punk.

"Cool! Pumpkin season starts in June for you?"

"Guess so." Chuckling, he faces me again. Dimples pop across those very pinchable cheeks of his. As our train bends around the Loop, a flare of sunset cuts through the buildings outside. The Boy and I are bathed in gold.

Like, okay, sun, I get your point.

This is Boy 100.

"Pumpkin season stuff usually looks kind of tacky," I say. "No offense to tacky things—I worship tacky—but this is really chic leather."

"Vegan leather. I wouldn't want you thinking less of me."

"I wouldn't dream of it."

"Nobody going *moo* was harmed in my pursuit of fashion. Except for this finger, which needed three stitches." Grunting, The Boy hoists his left bag of books up to present his open palm: a shallow divot indents the pad on his middle finger.

I nod, wide-eyed, at the jacket. "You made this?"

He grins.

He's an artist, too—a talented one. We stare at each other for a brutally long moment, the air between us hardening into a tether. A rubber band pulled so taut, it's about to snap. His lips move slightly, without making a sound, as if he wants to say something.

*Say it.*

*Say it so I don't have to.*

*Ask me for my number.*

*Tell me your name.*

The moment stretches too far. We waited too long. The train stops, and dozens of people rush out all around us. If he leaves with the crowd, if this is his stop, I'm going with him. I'll pretend it's my stop. I don't care.

But The Boy doesn't leave.

On the end of a strained huff, he lets his library bags drop to the train floor. "Hey, open seats!" he says to a newly empty row. He shoves the bags to the bench with two more grunts before waving me over. A simple wave, but it's the signal—he wants me to sit with him! He might as well have met me at the bottom of a grand staircase and kissed my hand.

I don't need to be told twice. Across three open seats, we spread out beside each other. There are way more empty spaces now that we're leaving the Loop and heading north. I don't have long to admire his mess of silky, black curls, though—his phone vibrates, and in that instant, worry splashes across his face. Dread. Bad news.

"Everything okay?" I ask. A lump clogs my throat.

"Sorry, I . . . I gotta take this. It's school housing, I've been waiting on this for a week—"

"Go, take it—"

"Sorry, I'm so rude—"

"Don't miss your call—"

"You're not getting off the train soon, are y—? Hey there!" Boy 100 takes his call, but he doesn't finish asking me this most important question. He shifts his back to me—the threaded pumpkin mosaic fully on display—and, in a low voice, continues his call.

The lump in my throat triples in size.

Do I just sit here, waiting for him? Does that make me look

uncool? I don't want him thinking I'm desperate. I also don't want him feeling pressured to get off the phone to hurry up and get back to making eyes at me.

Even though that would be amazing if he did.

However, if I get on my phone, I'll just look bored. Ugh. Why is my knee bouncing up and down? It's like I'm not even in control of it! I feel like I've had a hundred cold brews. I need something to distract myself that also makes me look carelessly interesting . . .

My hand floats toward my satchel. As soon as my fingers close around the cool, metal clasp, my knee settles. A live sketching! This will show I'm also an artist, so when he's off the phone, we'll already have another topic to discuss: my sketch of him. I've never shown a boy their own sketch before—it's always been sort of a postmortem crush thing. But embracing this fear will be part of the magic spell that finally breaks my bad luck.

"Sorry," Boy 100 mouths as a muffled voice jabbers on the other end of his call.

His pained expression, the disappointment, feeds my confidence. It's proof. He wants to talk to me, he wants my number, he wants to date me, he wants to kiss me.

*No, you idiot, he's going to tell you "I'm flattered, BUT . . ."*

If he says that, he says that, but I have to try.

I chuckle and shrug. "Don't worry," I mouth as I pull out my sketchbook and pencil. Boy 100's eyes shoot directly to my pad. He glances up, surprised, and smirks. I've impressed him. Eyeing me again, he returns to his call: "I'm doing temp summer housing for interns and . . . yeah . . . I was hoping to swap roommates since I already have a friend . . ."

As he quietly conducts business (he's so conscientious of the other passengers!), Boy 100 wriggles out of his leather jacket, which he then carefully folds and rests on top of a green canvas army bag. The sudden appearance of his wide, defined biceps almost makes the pencil slip between my fingers.

Wind. Knocked. Out. Of. Me.

I begin to sketch. At first, my hand travels choppily across the paper, but within moments, a familiar rhythm finds me. *Whoosh, whoosh, whoosh.* Like a pinwheel on a breeze, it flies out of me. Another sign of fate. In the drawing, Boy 100 stands triumphantly before a mannequin, over which he's draped a vegan leather suit he hand-stitched himself. Pumpkins, giant spools of thread, and massive sewing needles lie strewn about an old-timey cottage. Key details about Boy 100 remain, like his strong arms and curly hair, but I've exaggerated and smudged his face. He clumsily, boyishly, wrapped his long tailor's measuring tape around himself.

"Prince of Chicago!" a man hollers nearby, and my pencil nearly jolts out of my hand.

Gripping the handrail above me is a smiling old white man who looks like Danny DeVito from *It's Always Sunny in Philadelphia*, with his flyaway, balding hair and large glasses. As soon as he locks eyes on me, the man's bullfrog smile broadens, and he points his pinkie and index fingers at me in a "bull horns" gesture. "The Prince of Chicago!" he repeats.

My dad's diehard fans know my sister and me on sight. I smile back to the man, briefly checking on Boy 100, who is still swallowed in his phone call. "You're a fan of my dad?" I ask.

"Are you kidding?" DeVito snorts and shows me his phone

display: my dad's face on the cover art for his show—which airs on satellite radio and feeds to his podcast the next day. "If it wasn't for the King of Chicago, we would've never been rid of the Billy Goat curse! You're too young to remember—"

"Oh, I grew up hearing all about it."

According to legend, the Cubs hadn't won the pennant for generations due to some curse from a guy who brought his pet goat to a game and got thrown out. The curse was such a scourge that when the Cubs finally did win, everyone claimed it was because my dad secretly brokered a peace treaty between the Cubs' owner and the goat guy's surviving relatives.

My mom and I would be happy to never hear about that curse again, but it puts food on our table and keeps my paint supplies in stock.

As DeVito calls me "prince" again, I remember what Elliot called me, Prince Charming, and it all feels so . . . possible. I hop in place on the bench, my feet bouncing against the train floor, as my insides pulsate with an invisible motor. Boy 100 is right in front of me! All I have to do is ask him out. Maybe I'll fall on my face, but the universe wouldn't have aligned this perfectly just to make a fool out of me.

Okay, maybe it would—but I believe that won't happen this time!

"Thanks so much for your time," Boy 100 says on his call.

He's wrapping up!

"Thanks for listening to my dad," I rapidly tell DeVito.

The fan brightens even further. "Every single day! I'll get out of your hair." Delighted, he shuffles farther down the car, and I thank the universe for clearing him out on time so I can resume my wooing.

The Boy turns to me, grinning sheepishly. "Sorry about that."

*It's simple: Ask his name. Show him the sketch. Get his number.*

I can do this. My rib cage might shatter from my drumbeat heart, but I can do this. He wants me to ask him. I can give him the romantic, sweeping-him-off-his-feet moment that I wanted so badly from the ninety-nine others but never got. That's why the universe had all those connections fall flat, because it was preparing me for this!

"Everything turn out okay—?" I ask.

*SCREEEEEECH.*

My lower back spasms as I stagger forward in my seat, accidentally leaning into two standing passengers. Sometimes the L stops gradually, but this is not one of those times. As I mutter, "Sorry, sorry" to the disoriented passengers, Boy 100 pulls me away from them—and toward him—with a strong, gentle grip. We smile together.

"Damn train," he says. "You all right?"

"I'm fine. Just wasn't expecting—"

"Your sketchbook—" Boy 100 is already bending down before it hits me: my sketchbook had flown out of my hands and landed— brand-new-sketch-side up—on the train floor.

Fear races from my chest to my throat.

He's going to see. Will he like it?

Boy 100 has his own sketch in his hands, and he gazes at it, transfixed, before returning it to me. The look of recognition is all over his face. Even with the distorted details, he knows it's him.

I'm completely stripped naked. I feel soaking wet. Jagged, painful thoughts stab me: the urge to apologize and run away, to abandon that sketchbook and never touch it again.

We lock eyes, saying nothing.

I take the sketchbook from him.

A digitized voice overhead announces our train's latest stop, Washington and Wabash. Surprise erupts over Boy 100's soft features as he says, "Crap, this is my stop."

"Mine too!" I lie.

"Really?" He smiles, relieved. "Let's book it!" He gestures to his bags of library books.

"Dork." I chuckle.

As Boy 100 sprints out of the train, I spot it: his handmade pumpkin jacket, abandoned on the filthy L floor. I scoop it up and follow him out, but his tall-person strides have put him a yard ahead of me. As swarms of new passengers rush inside, I fight against the swelling crowd, my heart pounding so hard it actually hurts. Boy 100 hops out onto the platform. There's too many people. But I'm almost there . . .

My heel slips against the floor, and I'm almost pulled into the splits before catching the nearest pole. Whew. Close one, but nothing can get between me and Boy 100.

"Prince of Chicago, you all right?" Mr. DeVito's hand grips my arm, and I face my father's concerned fan. "You had a nasty spill there."

"No, I . . ." I stammer.

"*DOORS CLOSING*," says the voice overhead, as I watch the automated doors shut between me and Boy 100.

My heart rips cleanly out of my chest. That's the only explanation for this searing pain.

I hesitated only for a second, but that's all it took.

"Wait!" I shout. "Hey, open the doors!"

On the other side of the windows, The Boy's lips move rapidly—he's trying to tell me something, but I can't hear a thing. I shake my head and point wildly at my ear.

This is a nightmare. Short, shallow breaths squeeze my chest.

We haven't moved yet. There's still time. Where's that button or cord that'll let them know that I need the doors to open? I could pry the doors apart—like the jaws of a dragon standing between the valiant prince and his distressed damsel.

But these jaws are closed too tight to find a grip.

Out on the platform, Boy 100 fidgets in place, worry creasing his brow. He knows what I know: it's too late to tell each other the thing we need more than anything in the world—our names. He mouths one final word, something that—sadly—I can understand: "SORRY." With that, another jolt shakes the train floor beneath me. We pull away from the station. Faster and faster, my dream man shrinks out of sight.

He's gone.

My father's fan asks carefully, guiltily, "You okay?"

I turn to him, my chest weighing a thousand pounds. "That was my stop."

# Chapter 4
# THE DECREE

I lost him.

I found Boy 100, and then I lost him.

At the very next stop, I take my once-in-a-lifetime dream boy's pumpkin jacket and bolt onto the platform. Without stopping to catch my breath, I run back to where he and I were separated by fate and closing doors.

There's no one else here but a young violinist. Boy 100 didn't wait for me.

A sweet, mournful violin tune echoes through the platform's cavernous, empty space between brick buildings and a canopy of steel girders. Playing just for me.

I spend an hour doubling back and combing the side streets, hoping for some sign of him, some clue of where he ran off to, but I find nothing. Purple twilight falls. Cafés switch on their patio lamps.

How could the universe let this happen? Drop this boy into my lap, align all the stars to bring us together so perfectly, and then let one screwup ruin everything?

What was his name? Why didn't I ask him his name?

After all my crushes failed, this one felt like it was supposed to be my fairy tale.

*Fairy tale . . .*

A new feeling arrives in my chest, battering away the heaviness that had settled there since those doors shut in our faces. Strength. This is my fairy tale, like the ones I've always written about. I'm the prince, and in a way, I've got a kingdom at my disposal.

Instaloves.

I spread Boy 100's jacket across an empty bench, the magnificent pumpkin design on the back facing up, and sketch it. Every vine, every stitched detail, has a mystical, fairy-dust glow in the light of these bistro lamps. Then, with my heart turning to lead, I sketch Boy 100 wearing the jacket. Just glimpses, all from memory—his curls, his cheeks—anything specific enough to identify him. When I'm done, I snap a picture and upload it to Instagram. Instaloves has only ever featured properly scanned sketches, but this is a Boy 100 emergency, so we're going to break from tradition.

I hit share and take a deep breath.

Our connection was real. The way he stared at me, ready for me to ask him out. His smile that made his round cheeks even rounder . . . A heavy ache returns to my chest.

I need reinforcements.

BOY 100, WHERE ARE YOU? Friends, I've only ever been anonymous here (that isn't changing today!), but I just met Boy 100 on the Brown Line by the Harold Washington Library. We flirted, and I was about to ask him out. In a twist of fate, I missed my chance. We were supposed to get out at the same stop at Washington/Wabash, but when he stepped out, I went back to get this jacket he left behind. The doors closed in our faces, and the train pulled away. I can't find him. I don't even know his name, but he IS Boy 100. If you're one of those silly people like me who believes in fate and signs and fairy-tale endings, please share this post and help me find him!

♡ ♡ ♡

Audrey's Café has quieted down from the after-work rush, otherwise we never would have snagged these leather armchairs by the window—much sought-after real estate. The chairs rest beside a tall, aging bookstack and fireplace. When it's lit during the winter, there's no warmer place to be in the city. Surrounded by cozy coffee house bossa nova, I spread Boy 100's pumpkin jacket across our circular café table. Hannah and Maggie press their noses to the vegan hide and inhale the fresh faux leather, not realizing they're smooshing train germs onto their faces. Behind the girls, I spy Elliot on the outside patio wiping off the A-frame chalkboard.

"That jacket was on the floor of the Brown Line," I finally admit.

Hannah and Maggie recoil, dropping the jacket to the table in horror. Glaring evilly, Maggie dabs hand sanitizer across her nose. "I'm sorry this boy ran away before he could find out what a little jerkoff you are."

"Maybe he already messaged you?" Hannah asks, applying sanitizer to her own nose.

"No, I've been checking," I groan, checking my DMs one more time for luck:

It's me! I wanted to ask you out, but I got scared.

Yo, it was nice talking to you, but I don't feel the same way. Can I get my coat back?

That's so cool that I'm Boy 100! I felt the same spark between us! I'm not comfortable enough to meet IRL yet, but if you send me your used socks, I'll Venmo you thirty bucks. What shoe size are you?

Clowns. Imposters. In the two hours since I shared that post, I've become a lightning rod for every queer pathological liar in the Chicago city limits. On top of that, I even got a message from someone who lives in Hungary! Hello! I said we met earlier this evening on the L and you are presently in Hungary?

"You really found Boy 100?" Elliot asks, lugging in the café's chalkboard.

"Yes, it was totally fate." I grasp Boy 100's magnificent, hand-made jacket by both sleeves. I can almost feel those strong arms inside. I was so close . . .

"So it'll be fate that you'll find him again." Elliot smiles, his hair wilting across his round face. I smile back. His cheer is infectious.

"What do we think?" I ask, holding up the jacket like a piece of evidence. "Go through his pockets for clues? Or is that invading his privacy?"

"No more of an invasion than sketching him on the L," Maggie says.

I point a warning finger at her. "I'm sorry I pulled you away from another night of bickering on the couch with Manda, but if you're just gonna attack me . . ."

As Maggie rolls her eyes, Hannah thrusts both hands inside the jacket's front pockets and says, "Whoops, this fell out of his pocket!" My breath stops as she pulls out a small, white scrap. I snatch it from her like it's a golden ticket.

"A library card." I turn the flimsy plastic card in my shaking hands. Those brimming bags of books he was lugging around . . . With another gorilla-sized grip on my heart, I remember the last words he said to me. *Let's book it!* A beautiful, dorky moment cut brutally short.

"He's a reader?" Hannah asks, alight.

"The lamination is worn out," I say, waving the flimsy card. On the front of the card, a smudged name has long since faded. On the back is an illegible scrawl of a signature. I gently touch the smudged name as if I could excavate it from the past like dinosaur bones. I think I can make out an *R*. Or is it an *H*?

"A big reader." Hannah dances in her seat. "I'm getting very investeeeeeed. Is there a name on the card?"

"The card is too old. His name's rubbed off!" I grunt, kicking a vacant chair. The squeak draws all eyes to me. Under the table, Hannah gently squeezes my knee. She doesn't need to look at me to get her signal across: *Be cool. I know this sucks.*

We return to the utter lack of details on the library card, and I sigh.

"Well, Mr. Intrusive," Maggie says, "account numbers have names attached to them. Why don't you go to the library and look him up?"

I gasp. "A clue!"

"I'm happy the boring relationship person could help." Maggie shakes scone crumbs from a pastry bag into her open mouth.

Moments ago, the road to finding Boy 100 was clouded in a thick, impenetrable fog, but now . . . I have a clue. Hope explodes in me like a firecracker. I can find him. We'll go to the library, look up Boy 100's name from his card, and I'll finally be able to ask him out.

In less than twenty-four hours, I'll get my chance back again!

I carefully slide my small arms inside the large jacket, and even though I'm swimming in it, it feels correct. The hairs on my arms stand on end.

"So, if we're going to find Mr. Fate, I need to ask you your least favorite question," Hannah says, looking me sternly in the eye. "Can you please show us the sketch?"

Instinctively, my fists clench beneath the table.

Three hopeful, waiting faces stare back at me.

This goes against every impulse in my body, but . . . it's that serious. This is Boy 100. It's a day to break the rules, especially if it means a better chance of finding him.

Since Elliot was so kind with his fate comment, I hand him the sketch first. He, Maggie, and Hannah hungrily crowd around my drawing; none of them are used to me being this forth-coming.

"A designer?" Hannah asks, tapping the drawing's hair. "You and curls."

"Arms," Maggie mutters, as hypnotized as I was by Boy 100's most winning feature.

"How long did it take you to draw this?" Elliot asks.

"Like ten minutes," I say.

An impressed smile spreads across his face. "You're kidding."

"It's just a sketch. I'm gonna clean it up." Blood rushes to my cheeks. That's enough sharing. Abort! I pluck my sketchbook from Maggie's hands, and she rolls her eyes.

"I always wondered how you managed to sketch these guys in such a short train ride," Elliot says, leaning against his chalk-board. "I can barely get through a page of a book!"

"Practice." I shrug. "It's not just trains. It's parks. Classes. Wherever lightning strikes—"

Without warning, Elliot is gripped from behind. These customers are out of control! I launch out of my chair to help him, but then I recognize the attacker: Brandon Xue—our school's swim champ. He's a six-foot-tall Chinese boy, whose pearly arms are as chiseled as a Greek statue. He lifts his boyfriend in the air as if giving him the Heimlich. Elliot gasps in surprise before realizing who it is, which sends him into a fit of adorable, girlish squeals.

"Brandon, stahhhp," Elliot shrieks in a whisper. "I'm at work!"

The pure gay joy of Elliot and Brandon together lightens my shoulders. Somehow, Boy 100 feels closer than he did a second ago. Boy 100 could lift me in the air just as easily with his powerful arms. Maybe he'll surprise me as I'm painting the mural in my bedroom, which is as massive and intricate as a tapestry in a medieval castle. Two princes, happy at last.

I'm glad Elliot knows this joy. I never see Maggie and Manda laugh with each other like this; there's always so much tension and miscommunication between them.

As Elliot continues giggling and begs to be let go, his manager grunts from the bar: "Ahem!" Glaring, she dumps fresh coffee beans into the espresso hopper.

Elliot's joy vanishes. "Okay, put me down," he orders his boyfriend, and Brandon reluctantly obeys. It jabs my heart to watch them stop themselves.

"Oh, uh . . ." Elliot points at the sketchbook clutched protectively to my chest. "We're helping Micah find Boy 100!"

"Yeah, I saw your post," Brandon says, turning to me with

a sharklike expression. "So you really just ride the rails all day, picking out guys to follow like a serial killer?"

"No," I reply hotly.

"That's how Jack the Ripper did it. They say he was a bored rich guy, too—"

"Brandon—" Elliot gasps, mortified.

"Babe, I was kidding," Brandon moans, annoyed that we aren't finding him hilarious.

"Micah doesn't stalk anyone," Hannah says.

"It's *soft* stalking," Maggie adds.

My ears burn as I hastily repack my satchel to leave, but Hannah erupts in protest: "Hey, wait." She snatches Boy 100's jacket before I can reach it. "We're gonna find this boy, and he's going to be so happy to see you again."

I grin. "We'll hit the library in the morning?"

"Our quest begins."

Later, on our way out of Audrey's, Elliot tends bar and calls out, "Iced dirty chai for Prince Charming!" The smiling boy hands me my signature drink, on the house. After a moment of speechlessness, I thank him.

He winks and whispers, "Go get him!"

Smiling, I glance down at the *Little Book of Firsts*. Next to *First Boy I Ever Asked Out*, an empty space for the date waits hopefully. Will it be tomorrow? The answer to all these questions—and all my hopes and dreams—lies inside the Harold Washington Library.

## Chapter 5
# THE LIBRARY

I've been up since dawn. It feels like Christmas morning.

In a few hours, when the library is open, I could discover Boy 100's name. I'll find him online and finally ask him out. The way we were flirting, there's no *way* it would be a no!

As I boil over with possibility, my trembling fingers open Instaloves. Maybe he's already messaged. Yet of the hundreds of unopened DMs that piled up during the night, none of the profiles are him. Nothing. No beautiful boy with black curls and a smile that makes his eyes disappear.

That *smile* . . .

I turn on my bed to watch the sun rising over my view of Lake Michigan. In our penthouse, every wall is a panoramic, floor-to-ceiling window with a skyline view that stretches forever. We're so high above the surrounding buildings, there's no need for blinds for privacy.

Hannah isn't meeting me for an hour, so I occupy my anxious hands with a brush that's been soaking in turpentine. I approach the giant, half-finished mural, which has been outlined on muslin stretched across my bedroom's only solid wall. In it, dozens of regal couples—princes and princesses, pairings of every kind—dance around the edges of a golden ballroom, leaving a vacant space in the middle. Eventually, I'll paint something in this empty space. I'm not sure what yet, but it needs to be big enough to be the focal point.

Painting is trickier than black-and-white pencil sketches. When I had private lessons, color blending is what always tripped me up. Colors quickly become murky if I change my mind midway through (which is often) and want to darken or lighten a tone.

Blending? Hate it.

I toss out two cups of paint I experimented on but only ended up with something that looks like muddy mustard. My throat tightens. I don't like feeling like I'm bad at this.

Why is sketching so easy and painting so hard?

*Because it's a challenge, Micah. Pushing yourself out of your comfort zone—ever heard of it?*

With Instaloves, I feel so much closer to wrapping my mind around my true artistic voice, but this mural makes me feel a million miles away from it. They're both focusing on queerness and fairy tales, so what's the difference!

Is it just the medium?

Something I haven't voiced to anyone in my family is that I really want to go back to having professional painting instruction—the dream is to study at the Art Institute. Chicago's museum contains a legendary school, and I wouldn't even need to leave home or my friends. However, pushing yourself is easier said than done. Every time I imagine myself studying at the Art Institute, my heart flaps through my chest like a powerful eagle, my breathing chops into little bits, and I can't think of anything else until I shove it all away.

*You're doing it again, Micah. Breathe and work.*

Clean colors, clean lines. Let's do this.

Abandoning the smooth, realistic style of my Instaloves drawings, I dab silver onto the muslin in staccato, almost violent jabs, creating a wavy texture. This texture isn't blended; the colors sit harshly beside each other in juxtaposition. It's a style my art history tutor called *painterly*—painting in a way that draws attention to the brushstrokes, intentionally making people aware of the artist's hand.

I exhale. There. That felt a little better.

After washing out the paint from my nails, I dress princely: a fitted, sailor-striped shirt and slender capris, topped off with Boy 100's oversized coat.

I hoped I could quickly slip into the kitchen for coffee and be gone, but it looks like everyone else in my family had the same idea. Four adults and one lionesque Maine Coon cat crowd around the long, marble island. My mom, Dr. Jane Summers, is short like me and wears a black-on-black pantsuit and oversized glasses like a younger Edna Mode. Where Dad gave me his olive undertones, Mom and Maggie share the same Morticia Addams paleness. They need the sun, yet it would destroy them. As a fresh pot brews, Mom grips the handle impatiently, ready to yank it the second it stops pouring. My dad, Maggie, and Maggie's girlfriend, Manda, hang back. My sister and her girlfriend are decked out in running clothes that have been printed with rows of coffee cups—this is Manda's doing; they frequently wear matching food-patterned clothes that she has made. It keeps Maggie vaguely stylish.

"Any chance I could be the second cup?" I whisper to Manda. "I gotta be somewhere."

Manda Choi is tall, Korean, and wears her pink-dipped hair in a French-knotted braid. Manda's skin always glimmers with a cool, silvery sheen. The best thing she ever did for my sister is teach her about retinol skincare. She's my go-to conspirator when my family is being too intense. Wincing, Manda whispers, "Fine by me, but your dad's ready to pounce on that pot."

"Off to the library, huh?" asks Dad, his ears clearly burning. Jeremy Summers—the King of Chicago—is as tall as I am short. Dad's DNA gifted me with his face and reclusive tendencies but then vanished to let Mom's DNA finish the rest of my construction. He slings his arm around Maggie's shoulder like they're old chums. The way he said *"Library, huh?"* . . .

He knows what's going on.

My stare hardens at Maggie. *"Yes*, the library," I snip.

Such a Daddy's girl, Maggie smiles smugly. "Okay, I told him. It's not like it's a secret what you're up to. You blasted it all over Instagram."

I glare, rapping my fingers angrily on the island. "But you always tell the story wrong to make me look like a weirdo."

She rolls her eyes. "I do not '*always*' do that."

"Micah, don't get upset," Dad says, smile gone. "It's exciting, your first date—"

I toss my hands in the air. "See? The story is already wrong. It's not a date."

Manda, ignoring this family snip-a-thon, downs a green smoothie while Maggie explains, "Dad, I told you Micah is trying to find the guy. They had a connection on the L, but got separated?"

"Ah, yeah!" He knocks on his skull. "Soup for brains. Sorry, Micah."

"Like *Cinderella*," Mom says, eyes locked on the coffee. "She told the story right, hon. We're all excited for you! I would've said something when you walked in, but I didn't want to bother you or jinx anything."

I smile as the rush of nerves slows within me. Mom gets me.

After she pours, Dad fills his WNWC mug and follows her out. While I stir creamer into my tumbler, Maggie playfully taps Manda's foot to get her attention: "Let's do something tonight."

"Awesome," Manda says brightly. "Netflix added another season of . . ."

I slurp my coffee too loud to overhear whatever zillionth show they plan on watching. Maggie's eyes flick toward me. "Well . . . maybe we could do something more exciting?"

Manda recoils slightly. "Didn't realize that was a boring idea."

"I didn't say *you* were boring."

The arguing has begun. They'll go a few rounds before Maggie caves and agrees that Manda's "let's just hang out like always" plan is fine. Manda is exactly the kind of laid-back stoner bro presence my sister needs to chill out her intensity, but they should be rock climbing or kayaking or *anything* besides more puttering around the house.

Romance is about imagination. If you want romance to be realistic and—well—boring, that's what it'll be. Boy 100 and I will always have this thrilling story about how we met! How I fought the odds to find him again. To me, that's worth all the nerves and doubt in the world.

♡　♡　♡

Later, those nerves get put to the test when Hannah and I meet at the L station.

The train. Back to the scene of my trauma.

The metal beast looms ahead, squealing as it pulls into the station. The train doors—those horrible, fate-altering doors—open to a car packed with morning commuters. I hesitate, but Hannah takes my hand. She winks. "Back on the horse."

Here we go. With this first step into the train car, my quest officially begins!

As we clamber toward the library, I apply ChapStick with a trembling hand. We're on the same train where I met Boy 100 so magically—except yesterday's golden sunset has been replaced with a pale morning blue.

Boy 100's absence is almost ghostly. None of these faces are him.

Hannah isn't bothered. She buoyantly bounces on her toes as the library stop approaches. She looks beat for beat as fresh as I am in a sunset-colored frock and cat-frame glasses. We're a dream team because we always put the same level of care into everything we do.

"I can't believe your soul mate quest is taking us to the library where I'm getting married," she says.

"Not until you're twenty-eight, though," I remind her.

"Of course. I'm waiting for my return of Saturn, or that's just asking for trouble. It has to be after I've already put out three bestsellers—"

"—so my relationship won't slow my productivity," I finish with her in unison.

Hannah doesn't believe in fate. She believes everything in life happens through sheer willpower and flawless day-plannering.

A bittersweet taste hits my mouth. I've felt this before in Hannah's presence.

Straights have so many dating options, it's hard not to take it personally when they're picky about their dates. Hannah has dated so many boys in our class—and like, good for her, she should do what she wants—I just wish I had that many options to choose from. To have so many boys lining up for me that I'd have that freedom of choice. Most of my options are already paired off, not out, not dating, or aren't sure what they're looking for yet.

Our pool is just . . . smaller. When I think of my ninety-nine boyfriends, it feels like I've reached the end of my possibilities. Like, I *have* to find Boy 100 because there won't be anyone else after him.

Sometimes, I just feel behind, like a little kid, and I wish Hannah understood that better.

I close my eyes and refocus my thoughts. I don't need ninety-nine boys. I just need one.

♡　♡　♡

In the library, I rush—one notch below a sprint—down the towering stacks. Head after head turns to Hannah and me on our way to a bullpen of librarians. Their quizzical stares say, *No one* normal *walks into a library at nine a.m. with this much excitement!*

Behind a polished, dark wood counter, four librarians fill their carts, while a fifth—a tall, sleepy-looking young man—waits to help us.

"Howdy!" I slap Boy 100's card on the counter. "So my family just moved—"

"Oh, congrats," the librarian says. His sincerity doesn't match his wary, catlike face.

"So many moving boxes, *ugh*. I never want to see another box again, right?"

"I wouldn't know. I've only lived in one place. If I don't get out of Homewood soon, I'm gonna lose it." He speaks in a bored, rambling monotone. Hannah and I stare back, our smiles silent and frozen. "How can I help you?"

Although we rehearsed these lines a thousand times on the train, I go blank. Hannah leans forward: "He's moving and needs to change his address."

"Yes!" I say, Hannah's assurance shaking me awake. "I need to look up my account on that card to see if I need to change my address. I've had to change it so many places, I can't remember if I've done this one or not."

The librarian sighs, clearly fantasizing about his future moving day.

"I knooow," I say with a *sorry about that* wince. The librarian, Hannah, and I linger in silence before he begins typing Boy 100's card account number.

My throat clamps shut. It's happening—my future boyfriend's name will be known in a matter of seconds. *Nathan? Eric? Isaac?* What is the name I'll sing from our palace's balcony? When I call his name—*Gregory? Frederic? Ludwig?*—it echoes over our sprawling view of the Alps. My voice alone has summoned him. Riding on the back of an enormous eagle, he swoops lower and lower, through crisp mountain wind, toward me.

Hannah squeezes my hand. "This is it!" she whispers.

"And the name on the account?" asks the librarian.

Hannah and I groan. I want to say, *That's what I want to know!*

I've been quiet too long. I blurt, "There's actually a few names it could be under, sooooo I don't know."

"Okay . . ." The librarian's hooded eyes narrow. "Want to give a shot at what one of them might be?"

"Sorry, like I said, I'm not super sure. It's not there in the computer?"

"You don't know one of the names it could be?"

"Um, what if you just gave me a last name to narrow it down?"

I'm blowing it. I lick my lips—they're as dry as a country road. Hannah withdraws into a stony silence. Our plan is flopping, and we know it. Worst of all, the librarian knows it. His eyes narrow until they're basically shut. "How about we start with 'What is your name?'"

I blank. Michael . . . Sommerset? Marcus Swiggins?

Hannah moans, "Ah, hell."

♡ ♡ ♡

The main library's doors burst open, and I rush into the outer rotunda, as flustered as a chicken as I stomp up a grand staircase. I don't know where I'm going, but I'm not ready to leave and give up yet. Hannah gently shuts the double doors behind us and follows me away from the scene of another of my many humiliations.

"It's just a library card," I hiss. "He acted like I was an identity thief. What was I gonna do, ring up a bunch of fines?"

"All right, keep your voice low," Hannah says.

"I am talking low! I wasn't yelling or—"

"You were starting to get upset. Do you want someone to record you, and then you become the internet's next villain?"

"I didn't get that bad—"

"Boy 100 will love that."

My head throbs. Boy 100's jacket weighs a trillion pounds. "Hannah, I lost him. I didn't ask him his name, and now I'll never . . ."

Hannah stops me at the edge of a large, glass-domed vestibule. She looks at me—into me—with those stern, warm eyes. Guilt stabs my lungs for thinking those unkind thoughts about her earlier. She's never put a single boyfriend ahead of me. Once, she even canceled on a date because I was spiraling during PE after I couldn't ask out Matthew, that sophomore with the cute snake necklace. We stayed up all night watching rom-coms in her room until I felt normal again.

I'm so ungrateful.

"It was different this time," I say, swallowing hard. "I was gonna ask him out; I was finally gonna do it. You know I'd plan the hell out of that date."

Hannah pokes my wet cheek. "You're still going to. Say it with me."

"I'm gonna find him." I exhale slowly, and my frustration dissipates. "Thanks, Hannah. I made you come all the way here for nothing—"

"We're not finished yet! I'm going back in to talk to another librarian."

"But they already saw us—" Hannah works swiftly, digging an enormously wide-brimmed, floppy hat out of her wicker bag. I gasp. "The say-something hat!"

A hat so large, people have to say something.

"That's right," she says. The hat swallows her whole. "I'm not that girl from before, no, no, I'm That Girl with the Hat."

"Your mind!"

Hannah swaps her glasses for a pair of large, bejeweled sunglasses. "*You* stay put." She adopts a lilting country accent. "My brother is very sick. He has library fines that need paying, and I've come here on this bright, sunny morning to make sure his balance is in order."

I stifle a laugh. "A mistress of disguise! What would I do without you?"

"Suffer." She lowers her sunglasses to wink and returns downstairs.

Grinning, I continue inside the domed vestibule with high, glass ceilings like a massive conservatory. The Winter Garden. A smattering of topiary arrangements dot the coolly lit space. The room is filled with rows of white chairs facing a podium that is draped in cream-colored satin, all framed by an ivory trellis.

A wedding. Just like the one Hannah wants.

It must already be over, because several workers have mounted a ladder and are disentangling garlands of flowers from the trellis. Yet romantic energy still crackles in the room. In the corner, a gilded A-frame holds a large, foam-core photograph of a bride and groom:

THE WEDDING OF JESSE PETERSEN & ALLYSON HICKS

A couple nuzzles each other in a slow dance. So cheesy. Then why is there all this pressure in my chest? Why am I clenching my teeth? Boiling hot tears race to my eyelids.

*Stop crying, Micah. Why are you like this?*

I'm lonely.

The clarity of the thought—the cold simplicity of it—startles me. I hope I didn't just say it out loud. I spin around to make sure the ladder men didn't just hear the silly queer boy say he was lonely to a photo of two strangers. They didn't hear—or they're too wrapped up in their work to care.

I am lonely.

I'm about to be a senior, but I've never dated anyone. Kissed anyone. If I go to college still in this *Never Been Kissed* situation, just bury me from embarrassment.

I distract myself with Instagram, but a swarm of private messages greet me, all variations of "I'm Boy 100! Who's Boy 100? Where's Boy 100?"

I'm trying to find out!

"Darling," Hannah says, reappearing behind me and pulling

off the say-something hat in defeat. She didn't get the name. Still, I smile and pull her into a side hug. Everything I learned about fighting for myself, I learned from Hannah.

She sighs. "The librarian wouldn't give me the name, but she *did* take my money for his library fines."

"Oh no!" I laugh. She joins in, and this levity finally clears the heaviness from my chest.

"Three bucks. You owe me a cake pop. Want to know what book your delinquent soul mate still has checked out?"

"They'd tell you what he's reading, but not his name?"

"*How to Teach Quantum Physics to Your Dog.*"

Of course he's a Dog Gay—an endearing goof, with that messy hair and jokey attitude. The Summers family are cat folk: independent, cautious people always on the move.

I envision Boy 100 and me volunteering at the vet clinic with Elliot, bathing stubborn pups as Boy 100 splashes me—even though he knows I *hate* getting wet. One of the unadopted dogs is so clumsy and sweet, we have no choice but to adopt him. The three of us go for long morning runs along the lake, which always end at Audrey's . . .

Back in reality, Boy 100's oversized jacket weighs down my shoulders. It almost feels like an embrace. When I readjust the jacket, I hear a soft crinkling. I press my hands to the jacket again. Another crinkle, this time from the breast pocket.

Something's in there.

It's a receipt.

Boy 100's receipt. My sweating fingers study it: no name or information about what he bought, but yesterday morning, he spent $598.71 at a place called the Dockside Farm Stand.

So much money to drop at a farm stand . . .

"What is it?" Hannah whispers. "You okay?"

Clutching the receipt, strength returns to my arms. I nod. "The quest isn't over. We've got our next clue!"

## Chapter 6
# THE FRIEND-IN-LAW

The moment we leave the library, we FaceTime Elliot. Hannah said he goes to this Dockside Farm Stand at least once a week to pick up orders for Audrey's. Alone in the café's storeroom, Elliot props his phone on a sink counter while he dumps steaming water into a pitcher of sticky syrup pumps. He whispers, "I know exactly who Boy 100 bought that stuff from!"

My legs turn to jelly. Hannah gleefully hugs my waist while we wait for the next train. "Elliot, who is it?" I ask through clasped hands. "Would they be working today?"

"Dockside Shirley," he says, shutting off the water. Nervous to be overheard, he brings his face way too close to his phone, so all we see is nose. "But she's only there early-early in the morning. If you don't mind waiting until tomorrow, I can introduce you! Shirley can be weird if you don't know her."

"Perfect. Thank you, thank you!" I spin happily on the platform. Everything is clicking into place. Startled commuters watch me spin once more with a less graceful landing.

"No more chai for you." Hannah laughs as she helps me regain my footing.

My joy at finding another lead cancels out my impatience at having to wait another sleep before finding Boy 100. Even though several days will have passed, he'll still remember me.

Won't he?

Confidence dribbles out of me as the rest of the day unfolds. Thank God it's Micah's Movie Night.

A monthly event, Micah's Movie Night brings together friends and family for a romantic comedy (the only genre allowed). We bring the TV from Maggie's room into the living room—which Mom has cordoned off as a screen-free space. To her, we paid for our panoramic view of the skyline, so why throw a screen in front of it? Yet on these special nights, even she can't deny the magic of watching a movie unfold against a backdrop of Chicago, lit up like a star field.

Dad makes the popcorn, Mom picks up mixed bags of candy from Dylan's Candy Bar, and I draw the name of the person who selects the movie. Maggie doesn't know a rom-com from a serial killer documentary, so I exclude her from the drawing tonight. I can't risk her picking something depressing like last time with *Marriage Story*. Adam Driver and ScarJo just scream-sobbed and pounded walls the whole movie.

From the moment the penthouse elevator doors open, our new guests Elliot and Brandon enter slowly, cautiously, like they just wandered into Oz. Elliot came straight from work; he's still in his Audrey's uniform of a black polo and khaki shorts. His eyes are dark-circled—it must be from a long morning shift after closing the night before.

I would fully riot, but he's beaming. Nothing gets him down.

"Thanks for coming!" I say, hugging Elliot as soon as he walks in. I even spare a hug for frenemy Brandon, whose head remains on a swivel for some reason. It's a day for putting the Old Micah behind me. New Micah is asking out strange boys, forging a bond with friend-in-law Elliot, and being gracious to the boy who called me Jack the Ripper.

"My shoes have oat-milk stains on them; is that okay?" Elliot asks privately.

I screw up my face. "No, gross." Worry flashes across his eyes, so I quickly stop kidding. "Of course it's okay! They're your shoes."

He laughs on a swell of relief. "Sorry. Just, uh . . . it's rich in here."

Foolishly, I protest, "No, it's . . ." I shrug. He's not wrong. "Well, yeah. Make yourself at home!"

Hannah brings Brandon into the kitchen, where my mom hands them each a candy bag. "Thanks," Brandon begins to say, but his words abandon him when my dad turns around from the popcorn maker to shake his hand. Starstruck, Brandon gasps, "Whoa, wow."

In the entryway, Elliot can't stop smiling as we watch Brandon fan out on my dad. "I never get a chance like this to drag him away from swimming," Elliot confesses. "His trainer has him on such an intense schedule. For Olympic swimming—did Hannah tell you?" I nod, even though she didn't. Before this week, I showed minimal interest in hearing about her *other best friend* Elliot, much less his boyfriend who doesn't like me. "Well, Brandon got so excited to meet your dad, he dropped everything. So thanks for a very rare date night."

I smack Elliot's shoulder. "Of course! You're helping me out so much with Dockside Shirley tomorrow—which I can't *wait* for—so just chill and have a good time away from those crappy customers!"

On another relieved laugh, Elliot says, "I may never leave. You'll have to throw me out."

Once everyone has their snacks, we migrate to the living room. On the sofa, Maggie and Manda spread out under a blanket Manda sewed *specifically* for movie nights—the entire thing is cashmere soft and printed to look like popcorn. Manda's creativity isn't some career goal, though, like mine. Her goal is to simply live life in a Wes Anderson movie. Next to them, Mom puts her feet up on the ottoman—her glasses resting at the tip of her nose as she scrolls through her iPad. Hannah, Elliot, and I congregate on the extra futons we pushed together.

While I'm happy Elliot and Brandon finally have a date night, it isn't much of a date for them. Kind of more of a date for Brandon and my dad, who haven't stopped giggling in the kitchen. "Did you get any popcorn?" Dad asks, noticing all the bowls have disappeared.

Brandon waves him off. "It's not on my plan."

Dad's grin explodes. "Ah, I remember that. Get your medals,

retire, and then make up for lost time." He slaps his belly, which is just a muscle tummy that he thinks is bigger than it is. He's worse than gay guys. But it is nice seeing Dad relive his Young Olympian Lifestyle.

Maybe I misjudged Brandon as much as I did Elliot . . .

Across the room, Elliot and I look at each other with bugged-out eyes. "Is your boyfriend flirting with my dad?" I ask.

"Is your dad flirting back?!" Elliot asks.

"He just likes attention," Mom says without looking up from her iPad.

Elliot leans in, conspiratorially, to whisper: "After you invited us over, Brandon was YouTubing clips from *Go to H.E. Double Hockey Sticks*."

This gets Mom's full attention. She looks up, her iPad dropping to her lap. Hannah and I are speechless. *Go to H.E. Double Hockey Sticks* was the first and last time a studio would pay my father money to act. In it, Dad played a lovable Satan who helps a suburban kid get better at hockey in exchange for his soul. That is, until Satan falls for the kid's single mom, played by Lauren Graham. ESPN crowned him Worst Athlete Actor of All Time.

Brandon must be the only person to watch that movie in years.

As Hannah, Elliot, and I giggle, an out-of-body feeling taps me on the head: Is Elliot my friend now? There's no awkward pauses. The three of us feel like we've been close forever.

This must be what Elliot does—last year, he and Hannah quickly escalated into besties, much to my chagrin. He just has that aura of goodness about him.

When the movie selection begins, everyone's names—sans Maggie's—are scrawled on scraps of paper. *Hunger Games*-style, I pluck a name from the bowl: "Hannah!"

Elliot applauds loudest as Hannah crawls from the futon to join me like she's accepting an Oscar. "Wow," she says, "I never thought I'd be up here after that long spring of Manda picks." Manda nods graciously, beginning the peaceful transition of power. "Because Micah is about to track down Boy 100"—Hannah crosses her fingers, and Elliot, Mom, and I join her—"I picked a movie that's about holding out for the right person, however long it takes: the 1987 cinema du Cher . . ." She twinkles her hands in the air. "*Moonstruck*!"

We erupt in cheers. I *knew* it!

On the futon, Elliot turns to me. "What's it about?"

A wicked cat inside me grins. I'm still the *best* best friend. "Oh, it's Hannah's favorite movie."

As Elliot's smile falters, guilt plucks my heart like a guitar. All right, I'll give the guy some pointers. "Cher is marrying the wrong guy," I whisper. "Then she falls in love with her fiancé's brother, who's *clearly* the right guy."

Elliot rests his chin on his arm. "What makes him the right guy?" he whispers.

I tap a finger to my lips. "It's complicated. The wrong guy is . . . boring. Doesn't challenge her. Doesn't know what's going on in her life or her head. The right guy is wild. Full of surprises." I point two fingers at my eyes. "The right guy is intense, but he sees her." I snap my fingers. "He has her clocked right away."

"Wow," Elliot says, mesmerized. "Is that how it felt when you met Boy 100?"

My breath stops. I didn't realize until just now how much I was talking about myself.

Smiling, I say, "Yeah. We only met once, but he's already turned my life upside down."

And tomorrow when Elliot takes me to meet Dockside Shirley, and we find out what Boy 100 bought from her, I'll be one step closer to meeting him again!

Elliot squeals with excitement and taps my hand. His touch is incredibly soft. "That's great!" he says. "I love that about Instaloves: these chance encounters and small moments that become something bigger. People need that. What's the thing you say? 'A weary world deserves a little dreaming.'"

I let out an inaudible gasp. I've never been quoted before.

As the movie's opening credits begin, Elliot whispers, "And you deserve it, too. We're gonna find him!"

The movie music is too loud, so I don't think he can hear my whispered "Thank you," but Elliot's words have me floating to the ceiling. The possibility of surprises every day. It could be tomorrow, or it could be the next, but finding Boy 100 *feels* just around the corner.

The quest is simply part of our legendary story.

# Chapter 7
# THE SQUIRE

*E*ven though movie night went late and Elliot had the farthest to travel home, he is already at the L station when Hannah and I arrive in the morning. I don't even think Sleepy Elliot exists. "One dirty chai for Prince Charming and his questing party," he says, thrusting a large tumbler toward me.

My heart lifts. Once again, it's nice to see him out of his Audrey's apron. He has on a robin's-egg blue tank top and black jeans with the knees torn open.

"Thank you!" I say. "Audrey's delivers to train platforms?" I take two sips before handing the tumbler to Hannah. She finishes texting and then chugs.

Elliot didn't have to do this—bringing this chai or helping me out. Is it pity? Can he sense my desperation? I've been going on and on about this boy I barely met, and queers have a sixth sense at spotting the telltale signs of gay loneliness: a prickly attitude, roller-coaster spirals, and highly delusional fantasizing.

I'm almost three for three on those.

"Which way, O Quest Leader?" I ask Elliot.

He performs a grand bow. "My liege, you are the quest leader. I am but a humble page."

Playing along with my silly fantasy? After this and last night, Elliot is racking up a lot of points toward becoming actual friend material.

He points confidently toward an overpass, and we hustle across the litter-strewn street. The final stretch before reaching the pier is a tangle of bridges, dead ends, and taxis desperately vying for a lakeside shortcut.

I should've worn better shoes. My lavender slippers are not the vibe for a long hike. However, I will gladly suffer, as each painful step brings me another step closer to destiny. Behind me, Hannah hits send on another lengthy text and hurries to keep up with us fast-walking gays. "That's the second free drink in a row he's made you," she whispers.

"I know," I whisper back. "It's nice having a guy on the inside at Audrey's."

"They aren't Starbucks. They don't allow employee comps, and he'd die before sneaking an extra drink. He bought those himself!"

"What? Why? I would've bought the chai."

"He's just sweet."

The tea curdles in my stomach. Elliot needs as much overtime as he can get. He has to rely mostly on scholarships for college and vet school, and there's only so much his dad can save. And Elliot is buying me chai? I'm lucky enough to have money from King of Chicago radio, but not everyone's dad was the star of *Go to H.E. Double Hockey Sticks*. Ugh. I don't want to make Elliot feel self-conscious about the freebies, though, so repaying him is out of the question. I open Venmo and, with a few strokes, whoosh fifty bucks to Audrey's digital tip jar.

Hannah returns to her phone, her turquoise nails a blur as she texts furiously with a relaxed, satisfied smile.

I toss her a little wave and ask, "Who is getting all that text love from you?"

She pulls back her phone defensively. "Nobody."

"Oh?" I circle her like an excited puppy. "Who is this nobody?!"

Hannah always discusses her dates. It's never news. So this must be someone she really *likes*. Elliot, an entire block ahead, jogs backward to us and asks, "Does Hannah have a boy on the hook now, too?"

Thank God both her best friends are in the dark on this.

"You two are bullies!" Hannah yells, but she can't stop smiling and texting.

"Is he a Taurus?" Elliot asks with a sly grin.

Hannah's expression hardens. "I don't mess with Taurus boys."

"Chorus boys, not Taurus boys," I say singsongily.

Hannah snaps and points appreciatively. "Make it a T-shirt."

She has a dewy glow that is not from her normal makeup routine. It's as if she's walking around with an invisible ring light on her.

"Hannah, I can't believe we're both finding The One at the same time!" I shriek as Elliot and I surround her.

"Well . . ." Hannah winces.

"What?"

"I don't know if he's The One yet . . ."

I round in front of Hannah, meet her eyes, and walk backward. "Okay, what was the feeling you first got when you met him?" I ask. "Were you head-to-toe tingly? When I met Boy 100, it was like the universe was throwing out signs. The sunlight made everything gold and—"

"It felt cool meeting him! I don't know." Hannah gives me a playful shove, and Elliot retreats as we approach the docks. His way of best friending seems to be to recognize when Hannah doesn't want to talk about something and give her space.

Fair. Emotionally intelligent. But is it right?

Hannah always deflects. *Enough about me!* will be on her tombstone.

She glances up from another text, and we exchange studying looks.

"All right, I'll drop it for now," I say as I apply ChapStick. "I wish you exciting, getting-to-know-you, getting-to-know-all-about-you vibes with this boy."

Hannah nods diplomatically, and I walk ahead to Elliot. I don't want to dampen her mood, but when he's The One, you know. There's no doubt. You can crush on a fun guy, you can think he's cute, but The One? You're either hit with lightning or you aren't.

Boy 100 hit me with so much lightning, he might as well have been Zeus.

And I'm Hera. Except without all of Zeus's cheating.

Under the last overpass, our view finally opens onto Lake Michigan and rows of tankers, crates, and loading docks. Elliot leads us into the Dockside Market's bustling thoroughfare, a sea of booths and shoppers with too many bags. The market workers are busy spacing out fruit trays, hanging roast chickens on spits, and giving floral bouquets a loving, dewy spritz.

When we finally meet the woman Elliot calls Dockside Shirley, she's younger than I expected—midthirties, probably—and she exudes a powerful energy for someone so small. Wide-eyed, dark-skinned, and beaming, Dockside Shirley wears a gardener's apron that drapes all the way past her ankles so that when she moves, she has to shuffle to avoid tripping.

Elliot and Shirley hug on sight, and he gets to business. "My friend needs your help. Would you recognize this boy who bought a bunch of stuff from you two days ago?"

Even though I'm already ready with my open sketchbook, my moist palms dampen the edges of the paper. It is so much easier to show people my work on Instagram than in person. Online, it's like *Whoosh, bye, I'll go hide now!* In person, there's so many instant judgments, judgments people don't know are showing on their faces.

But the artist catches every one of them.

Shirley has no judgments, however, as she inspects my drawing of Boy 100. She gazes at it, unblinking, as if it's a specimen in a jar. I hold my breath.

"You didn't get much detail in the face," she says.

"I draw faces abstractly, so they're more about the emotion

and not the person," I say, my tongue tripping on every other word. Elliot, Hannah, and Shirley stare silently. "Anyway, he would've been here the day before yesterday. And he's really cool. Charming. You know, um, easy to talk to? Wearing this jacket!" I twist around to show her the delicately threaded pumpkin design.

"That jacket does look familiar . . ." Shirley says, tugging off a pair of surgical gloves tinged with soil. Her farm stand holds an array of fruits, flowers, and open barrels of spices. Cinnamon and rosemary fill the tent. She fetches a slotted spoon and stirs each barrel as she thinks.

"He bought almost six hundred dollars' worth of stuff two days ago," Elliot says, hopping after Shirley. "Someone would've had to haul away half your produce to spend that much at once."

Shirley drifts over to a table of berries and douses them with a bottle marked SHIRLEY'S FRUIT WASH. We all wait in silence as she washes.

Please, *please* remember.

At the precise moment I open my lips, Shirley smiles and says, "He had curly, dark hair."

"Yes!" I gasp, staggering forward and knocking my knee against her cinnamon barrel.

"I remember him. Funny guy. With an old soul. Like Elliot."

"Well . . ." Elliot dips his head bashfully.

"What was his name?" I ask.

"I'm sorry, I don't know," Shirley says. "But what I can tell you is . . . one hundred twenty-five pomegranates."

Hannah stops texting. We glance at each other.

Shirley giggles to herself, as if it's a private joke. "Thought I'd leave you hanging there, sorry. He bought one hundred twenty-five pomegranates, one hundred bushels of grapes, and three hundred long-stemmed red roses."

Hannah, Elliot, and I exchange rapid, gleeful expressions.

Roses!

Boy 100, a dyed-in-the-wool romantic, bought a gadzooks number of roses—obviously for some grand romantic gesture! Warmth surges through my entire face. He's buying me roses!

Wait.

He bought the roses before we met. They're for someone else.

"Did he say what he wanted all that for?" The words fall from my dry, nervous lips.

Shirley nods. "Said it was for some art project."

Hallelujah!

So Boy 100 is an artist after all, just like me. Our home will be a place of constant creativity and affection. Drawing, painting, designing, sculpting, sewing. He and I will do it all! We won't sit around in front of the TV! There'll be too much innovation and excitement in our artistic home to let anything as ordinary as boredom creep into our lives.

I've never been surer of my future with Boy 100 than I am now.

"How did he get all those flowers and pomegranates out of here?" Elliot asks.

"He had them delivered."

I leap onto my tiptoes. "Oh my God—where?"

"I can't give out addresses," Shirley says. "But if I remember right, he asked to find the nearest culinary supply store. Maybe they can tell you more about him."

Like any good quest, our journey is far from finished. We have a new destination to reach! What an amazing story this will be when we tell people how we met!

Boy 100 comes clearer into view with each passing revelation:

Reader . . . jokey . . . pumpkin fan, so he loves fall, which means cozy sweaters . . . maybe he has a dog . . . probably cuddling up with a dog in his sweater . . . putting together some kind of a food-based art project . . .

A true artist with a unique point of view! Maybe he could help me unlock my true vision and solve the riddle of my mural.

I thank Shirley, and with that, my companions and I continue our quest back toward the Loop, where culinary supply stores await us.

"What if the roses are for an art installation?" I wonder aloud, my steps bouncing with excitement. "A giant Valentine's card made of flowers! Or is that basic?"

"Not if it's done cool," Elliot says. "Like if he uses the pomegranates for juice that's dripping off the roses like blood."

"Eek, very romantic!" Hannah laughs.

Each of these ideas sounds more exciting than the last, and the hypothesizing continues the whole way back downtown.

We are the fellowship of the jacket!

I can't believe what a tightly bound trio we've become over the last day, full of shared purpose and inside jokes about pomegranates, Taurus boys, and old rom-coms. Honestly, the thanks are due to Elliot, his great sense of humor and easygoing way of slipping into new situations as if he was always there. I wish I could be so comfortable with newness.

If I was, maybe I'd be a pro at asking boys out. And maybe if I didn't let everything embarrass me, I could show people my unfinished work and get some serious art training!

Well, I am who I am.

Closer to the Loop, Elliot runs a handheld fan between the three of us like a human oscillator. Hannah fans herself with her clutch, but I enjoy the heat, so I take another swig of our dirty chai, still piping hot inside the tumbler.

"Thanks for coming last night," I tell Elliot. "Let Brandon know my dad kept gushing about him after you left. He's got a new fan."

Through sweltering huffs, Elliot smiles. "That's great. Brandon works *so hard*, it was nice of your dad to give him his time."

"Please, he loves all that." I take another chug. "Hope you had a good time, too."

"Amazing!" He offers me the fan, but I wave him off. "Your house was, like, oh my God! So many windows! Doesn't it ever get hot?"

"They're temperature controlled, I think?" Honestly, I've never thought about it.

"Wow, fancy." He chuckles and smacks his forehead. "*Fancy. Way to sound like a hillbilly, Elliot.*" I start to say "No—" but Elliot continues: "I live in a penthouse, too, you know. Right above my dad's pizza place. Two-story building, but we're on top. I smell that dough baking as soon as I wake up."

"Aw, yummy," I say, "I'd love—"

But Elliot still isn't finished. "And it is hot. As. Hell. We found out the roof, um . . ." Elliot tries licking moisture into his lips. "It's black, so it's absorbing all the heat and funneling it into my bedroom. The roof is thin enough to do that but thick enough to meet building codes, I guess. Anyway, the landlord says AC units will blow our building's fuses, and he's gonna update the wiring—but, like, in seventy years probably, so we're just dealing."

Hannah briefly stops texting to cast me a worried glance.

I've been in Elliot's shoes before, and it hurts to see it happen in real time: you start talking, start revealing, and before you realize what you're doing, you're spilling all the stuff in your life you pretend isn't happening.

"Ever been so hot, you cry?" Elliot asks, wiping his forehead. "I run hot as it is, maybe 'cause I'm a thicker guy—"

"Hey." I stop him. Time for the prince to help. "Let's get water."

I order us an Uber, and in under five minutes, we're at a Jewel-Osco, and I've stocked up my quest companions with large coconut waters. The hydrating effect is instantaneous. Thoughts flow clearer. Outlooks are brighter.

While Hannah hops into Potbelly's to collect lunch for us, I run the handheld fan over Elliot while he finishes the coconut water. "Sorry," he says.

"*I'm* sorry," I say. "That AC thing sounds awful."

He shakes his head. "I just haven't lived with my dad since I was a kid, and I hate his damn place. My mom's gone, so I've been staying with my aunt in the country. It was nice enough there, but I wanted to come back to Chicago because . . ." He rolls his eyes at himself. "There was all this stuff I wanted to do. Somebody I wanted to be. But I had no idea how underwater my dad was until I got here. All my energy just goes to . . . keeping going."

If this was Hannah, I'd take her hand, but that feels wrong. Touch a shoulder? Hug? It's all too intimate for a new friend. Where do I put my hands??

"That's a lot to deal with—" is all I can muster before he stands.

"Enough about me," he says.

I laugh. "Hey, that's Hannah's line!"

"Oh my God, right?!" Elliot grabs my wrist. When he does it, it's not awkward.

"What's my line?" Hannah asks, exiting Potbelly's with three sandwiches.

"You never want to talk about yourself," I say.

"And for good reason—I'm surrounded by gossips!" She lobs us our sandwiches, and we bicker playfully about Hannah's secretive nature until we find a tree-shaded bench where we can eat. Settling back into our new trio's comfortable rhythm takes no effort at all.

After lunch, we hit one culinary supply store after another. The employees at Sur La Table and Williams-Sonoma never saw anyone matching the description of Boy 100. However, Rudy's Culinary Emporium produces a lead. Rudy himself stands before us, his hairy forearms crossed over a maroon bowling shirt. He chuckles. "Leather jacket, big guy, sure. He came back. He's over in blenders right now!"

Hannah, Elliot, and I rapidly glance at each other like excited birds.

"He's here," I gasp. "Right NOW?"

I almost distrust it, like I would've felt an enormous tectonic vibration if Boy 100 were in my vicinity. My heart batters against my rib cage. Elliot charges ahead toward the blender aisle, while I can only stumble forward like Bambi across a frozen lake.

I'm finally gonna get my second chance . . .

But the big, leather-jacketed man currently checking out blenders isn't Boy 100. A middle-aged, scraggly man wearing a floor-length, coffee-brown leather duster waits at the end of the aisle, choosing between two different Cuisinarts.

Our smiles drop, and Elliot and I sink into each other's shoulders like sad puppets.

Later, as we make a full circle up the bougie tourist trap stores on Michigan Avenue, the afternoon sun turns the heat up to full bake. "Just one more store and then we'll give it up," I promise my quest comrades. My words come out in strained huffs.

I can't believe they're still with me.

Elliot pumps his fists in the air. As Hannah dawdles behind us, I whisper, "Thanks for doing this, Elliot."

He slaps my shoulder and flashes me a twinkling smile. "No thanks necessary. It is my duty to buck up your courage as we do battle against this dragon we call 'asking out a boy.' I remain your humble squire."

Thank God he's as into playing characters as I am. The Prince gives me strength, just as the Squire feeds Elliot's energy. "I thought you said you were a page?" I ask.

Elliot twiddles invisible whiskers on his chin. "Perhaps they're the same thing?"

"I have no idea." We chuckle. "Let's pick 'squire.' I like squire."

My exhaustion vanishes. With a cool, soothing blast of energy from my squire's encouragement, the three of us approach Fiddlestick's Restaurant Goods as a single, sweating entity. Behind the counter, a round-faced, light-brown-skinned Latine man with a thin, angular mustache smiles cheerfully. Without pleasantries, I wearily extend my sketch of Boy 100 and say, "I'm looking for this boy. Tall. Loves dogs. Probably great at board games but isn't a show-off about it. He knows exactly who he is, and when he looks at you, it's like he knows exactly who you are, and you feel utterly seen and validated." I catch my breath. "Anyone like that here two days ago?"

The man speaks in a nasally purr: "Was he wearing that pumpkin jacket?"

Hannah and Elliot gasp, and I shout, "Yes!"

Like we're in a silent movie, the three of us reach for each other at the same time, entwining our arms in a mutant group hug. The man recalls Boy 100 with perfect clarity. "He knew exactly what he wanted. Really sure of himself, like you said. Picked up an order that he'd called ahead to place—"

"He plans ahead, amazing," I say, letting the man keep his rhythm.

"It was a hundred-quart stockpot. Paid for it and left."

"He works in a restaurant," Hannah says, openly theorizing to the room.

"No, Shirley said it was for an art project," Elliot counters. "He's making gallons of grape-pomegranate jam."

"How is that an art project?" Hannah asks. "And what were the roses for, then?"

"I don't know, but we'll find out! Micah, this is him. We've got him!"

I can't even pay attention to Elliot because a cold, gray knowing falls over me. I lock eyes with the man. "You can't tell me his name or where I can find him, can you?"

He smiles sweetly and shakes his head no.

Reality crashes in all around us, as this man becomes the next in a long line of dead ends.

The fellowship of the jacket must rest.

Hannah and Elliot exit onto the street, and I trudge behind them, Boy 100's jacket growing hot between my fingers. Shady trees beckon us farther up the street, but construction crews block our path.

"We should ask your dad to put out a call for this sweetheart the next time he does his radio show," Hannah says as we idle outside the store. Her kindness is going to crush me. I wish I could involve her in one dating story of mine that didn't end with a pitying look.

This was my last hope for finding Boy 100. Where else could we even look?

Everyone worked so hard to help me, but all I did was drag us into a dehydrated disaster.

Under the waning shadows of skyscrapers, I hold up Boy 100's lovely jacket with its embroidered fairy-tale pumpkin—a work of art gone to waste, just like our connection.

I sigh. "Okay, enough. You should both just go home."

Elliot clicks his tongue in shame, but Hannah nods, her face looking particularly bloodless. "I need a shower." She groans.

"Maybe you're right," I say with a dull laugh. "I should put out a message on my dad's podcast. Like, 'Hey, sports fans . . . ' "

On the stoop behind us, a young Latine woman with a buzzed head, dark brown complexion, and hot-pink lipstick smokes a vape pen. She wears the same teal employee vest as the man inside. Not only that, she's staring at us. After exhaling a cloud of grape-scented vapor, her eyes widen with joy. "Your dad's show?" she asks. "Prince of Chicago!"

Not another sports fan. I don't have time to pretend to not be Jeremy Summers's son, because the woman approaches quickly, her phone already drawn. On her screen is my Instagram post of Boy 100's jacket. "I thought I recognized that coat!" she said. "*You're* Instaloves?? So romantic. I wish someone would go through this much trouble for me."

I don't have time to plead with her to please keep my account secret before Elliot rushes forward, saying, "Isn't it?!" He turns between me and the Fiddlestick's employee. "You work here, right?"

The woman's smile falters. For an eternity, she weighs her next thought before whispering, "I've seen it here before. Your jacket." She tugs the sleeve. "He was here two days ago. I dropped his pot off to him this morning."

The air around me freezes. Hannah and Elliot become as still as statues.

"We were told he came here to pick it up," Hannah says on my behalf. I'm too thrilled to make a noise.

"He was gonna," the woman says, "but that pot was too awkward to carry, so I offered to deliver it for free if he didn't mind waiting till today."

My entire body clings to life as I whisper, "Where . . . ?"

"The Art Institute," she says with a hint of a smile, as if fully aware how monumental this information is to me.

As "Thank you" falls breathily out of my mouth, heavenly sunlight cuts across Elliot, Hannah, and this wonderful woman.

I know where he is.

## Chapter 8
# THE PALACE

The Art Institute.

A kingdom of creativity. The palace of my dreams. I always knew it would bring my artistic vision into clearer view, and where else would two artists begin their epic romance together?

It all fits. Boy 100's stop at Washington/Wabash—where fate slammed its doors between us—is blocks away from the Institute. His call with the temporary housing people must be about the school there. After some furious googling, I learn the Art Institute has a summer internship program for high school students. For a moment, I'm furious with myself for somehow not realizing I could've had the opportunity to be studying *right now* at the Art Institute—mastering paint blends, pushing my boundaries with this mural, crystalizing my vision with help from the top experts.

But then I read farther down the site—the internship is only for fashion designers.

If Boy 100's divine, hand-stitched pumpkin jacket is any indication, he already has a leg up on his competition!

Since we're way past the time Hannah needed to get back home, the fellowship of the jacket temporarily parts ways beneath a mighty tower—at a Cheesecake Factory underneath the John Hancock building. Hannah, Elliot, and I rest our exhausted feet on the staircase descending into the McUpscale strip mall where tourists and office folk eat lunch in the sun.

"It's one forty-five," Elliot says, checking his phone. "Regroup at Micah's at five for the final leg of the quest?"

"Yes!" Hannah and I blurt. My heart lifts like it's on top of a geyser.

Elliot whines dramatically as he stands. "All right, I gotta head to Target for a fan for my hot, terrible bedroom."

I jump to standing. "Sounds like another quest! Maybe we go with?"

Hannah fans herself as she stands. "Elliot, I love you, but I have *got* to shower."

My smile remains undefeated. I can be there for Elliot just as much as he's been there for me. "Okay, well, I'll go! It could be a battle. The AC section in Target gets vicious in the summer."

Elliot chuckles, his eyes dropping. "And what would the Prince in his temperature-controlled palace know about dog-fighting someone for the last window fan?"

Hannah laughs at the sick burn. Even though it feels like a dropkick to my chest, I know he's joking—but he's right.

"Well, I've seen it in TikToks," I play along. "Gotta stay in touch with the little people."

Elliot smirks; the ghost of the handsome man he's going to become appears before vanishing, leaving only the boy. "I'm going to go it alone this time. But thank you." He waves goodbye and turns away to face the dragons of Target by himself, while Hannah and I catch an Uber north to our building on the Gold Coast.

"See, I told you he was cool," she says on the ride. "Look at all that hanging out you missed because you were jealous."

"Yeah, yeah," I say. I hate when she's right.

Honestly, today was the most fun, least anxious day I've had in a million years. When Hannah departs the elevator in our building to her place on the fourteenth floor, a heaviness settles over my shoulders.

The fellowship of the jacket had been a distraction from the anxiety of my Boy 100 search. With friends around, it wasn't this insurmountable challenge. It was a shared quest for a greater cause of romance.

I press my palm to my chest and try breathing steadily. *Relax. You'll find him tonight and finally get the chance to ask him out.* If he says no—*he won't*—he's totally allowed to say no; I very easily could've misread the signs—*I didn't*—if I did, then at least I tried. I gave it my all. I'll give him back his jacket, wish him well, and return home to disappear forever under my covers.

The elevator opens home. The lowering sun beats heavily against the panoramic windows of my empty living room, but I don't feel an iota of heat above the preprogrammed, sensible seventy-four degrees. That same sun almost cooked our brains today, but in here, I would never know what it's doing to people out there.

It's good I'm getting out more.

Now that I'm cooler, I pull on Boy 100's jacket. Its weight, its scent, brings me back into the fantasy realm where I can flirt, catch a boy's interest, and be the best version of myself.

As I cross the living room toward my room, Lilith—our black-on-gray Maine Coon cat—prowls across my path, pausing briefly to hiss at me. This big ol' tigress is Maggie's cat, and I swear, she trained her to act this way to me.

Maggie is studying in her room. Outside her window is a full view of Lake Shore Drive, with its sandy surf and roller-bladers who look like busy ants from this height. She lies on her belly, a kinesiology textbook open and a chaotic array of school papers spread out in a blast radius in bed around her. Her hair is down, and for a change, she's in tattered gray sweats instead of her usual black-on-neon athleisure. She glances at me in her doorway. "How was the quest? Oh, I forgot to dunk on you about this earlier, but you're *wearing* this boy's jacket now, Hannibal Lecter?"

I clutch the jacket across my chest defensively. "It was a magical day! Sorry you weren't there to poke holes in my confidence, but I'm sure you had an exciting time here, too, fighting with Manda over some new dumbass thing."

Maggie flinches. She sits up quickly, messing up her piles of papers even more. "You need to stop joking about that. It hurts my feelings."

"And you need to be nicer to me. This is a big deal for me."

Maggie glares. "You don't think you and Boy 100 are ever gonna fight?"

"We won't!" I throw my arms in the air. "We'll be too busy having fun. People fight when they're bored." Huffing, I cross into her room before changing my mind and walking back out. But then I walk back in. "Which I'm constantly telling you, but you never listen to me because you think I'm a stupid kid who doesn't know anything."

The harder I rant, the more Maggie leans back into bed, an infuriating smirk on her face.

"What?" I demand.

"You actually *don't* know anything about dating, Baby Boo-Boo—"

"Why do you keep calling me that? Do you ever stop to think the reason I don't know anything about dating, why I can't ask someone out without pissing my pants, is because my sister— who is supposed to love me—made a complete joke out of me on national TV?"

I stop myself from yelling all of this through sheer willpower. Maggie's face *collapses*. She hops off the bed and walks to me. "I'm sorry. I try to toughen you up because . . . You live on Planet Fantasia, and if you start dating this boy—*when* you do—he's not going to be a fantasy. He's going to be a real boy, who will be a real pain in the ass sometimes."

"I'm ready for real!" My hard expression melts away. "Maggie, what if . . . ? What if Boy 100 thinks I'm a total creep for tracking him down like this? I drew his picture; I followed his trail all over the city, like . . . what if he's like, 'Get away from me, Obsessed!'?"

I can't see Maggie's reaction because I'm staring at my belly button. She pulls me into a hug, and my small body crumples like an empty bag of chips.

"What if Boy 100 doesn't want to be someone's first? He's so cool and makes jackets. He's probably had an LTR already."

Groaning, Maggie walks me over to her panoramic view of the lake, teeming with joy and activity, cyclists and sailors. "There's no timetable for dating," she says. "Not everybody wants to date. Not everybody can date. Not everybody *should* date. But if you want it, no one cares how long it took you to start."

The chopping waves in my heart settle back into a gentle rhythm.

We're brother and sister again.

Above Maggie's desk is a framed ad for *Pass the Puck*. In it, my dad—ten years younger, in his athletic prime—wears hockey pads and roars at the camera, evoking his wild man reputation. He literally looks like me if I were a foot taller and lost the baby-ish roundness to my cheeks (one day). In the ad, Mom stands with her back to Dad—all in black, the epitome of an Annoyed Glasses Wife Who Loves This Wacky Guy Anyway. Dad deadlifts seven-year-old me over his head with one hand and ten-year-old Maggie in his other hand. My sister is holding Dad's bronze and silver Olympic medals, while I pump the Stanley Cup over my own head (supported by wires they airbrushed out, of course). The enormous silver goblet is bigger than I am.

What a little twerp. He has no idea that all his favorite fairy-tale romances are about to come true for him.

♡   ♡   ♡

After I shower off the heat-drenched slime of the day, I hurl myself into the world of my mural. There's still another hour until we leave for the Art Institute, and I've got some stress to get out of my system first.

This mural is perpetually unfinished. With sharp, painterly brush swipes, I color in the dinner jackets of two dancing princes with canary yellow and aquamarine, my favorite colors. Each stroke is carefully considered. This isn't a sketch where I can just ball it up and start over, and my hands do not respond the same to a paintbrush as to a pencil.

There's no easy flow. No *flick-flick-flick* to easily shade in dimensions. A paintbrush is large and unwieldy in my sweating palm. The globule of paint, no matter how small, changes the entire design in irreversible ways.

I'm lucky I could have my own private instructor, free of judgments and other students' eyes, so I could learn to create, fumble, and re-create in peace.

This isn't easy—none of it is easy—but there is nothing more therapeutic than creation. The physical action of painting calms my rapid heart as I drive out all worries about Boy 100.

"Hey," a soft, familiar voice calls from behind me. I spin around, dropping my brush onto my paint trolley. I reach for the rip cord that drops a solid black curtain over my mural—a security measure against snooping family members who want to peek at my work.

But something stops me.

Elliot.

He's standing in my open doorway, wearing a fresh pair of salmon-colored shorts and a patterned, pastel top. And he's covering his eyes with both hands. People burst into my room all the time—my parents, Maggie, even Hannah—and all of them wish I'd stop being so weird about letting people see my work early.

But somehow, Elliot is here and knows to shut his eyes.

"I'm not looking," he says. "Hannah told me you don't like anyone seeing your work before it's done."

My mouth hangs slackly open. "How'd you get in?"

"You mean, how'd the riffraff get in?" He keeps his hands clasped over his eyes. "I crawled in through a mouse hole. I'm just here looking for cheese."

"That's not what I meant, I—"

"I'm just messing. Your sister let me in." His dimpled smile is all I can see beneath his hands.

"One sec!" I shuffle over to the curtain cord, and with one yank, the black curtain drops in front of my wall, disguising the mural. "Okay, you can look."

Elliot removes his hands, and his eyes go wide at my room's boundless view of Lake Michigan, stretching to the horizon just beneath the late-afternoon sun. He's momentarily speechless, like a kid in a museum staring up at a T. rex skeleton.

"Okay, I love your room. Werk."

Remembering how hot and miserable Elliot says his room is, I run my hand nervously through my hair. "Did you conquer the devils at Target?" I ask.

Elliot clutches his chest in mock despair. "They conquered me." He relaxes. "Those shelves were picked clean when I got there."

Ugh. My shoulders slump for him. Can't he catch a break? "I'm sorry. Is there anyone there we can talk to?"

"Who, like a manager?" He pokes my belly hard, laughing. "Youuuuuu little rich person!"

I hop backward in a fit of giggles. "No! I just mean, like . . . I don't know. There's nothing we can do?"

Elliot shrugs again, looking genuinely carefree over something I'd probably be a huge whiner about. "It's summer. Fans are gone. Our building won't allow AC units, and fans online are back-ordered. The end!" He claps once. "Okay, the quest. Hannah's mystery date wanted to move up their rendezvous to this afternoon. So she . . . can't make it to help for this part."

I receive this news like an arrow. The fellowship is breaking right before the end of the quest? Not only that, but Hannah told Elliot and not me?

Elliot throws up stopping hands and says, "She was nervous to tell you and bum you out." He's psychic—or maybe I'm just that easy to read. "Would you be super disappointed if it was just you and me finishing the quest by ourselves?"

I avert my eyes, embarrassed. I don't want Elliot thinking he's some sort of lesser companion. "Of course not! *You* don't mind? You've got the whole day off. Did you and Brandon have plans?"

Elliot winks. "What kind of squire would I be if I bailed before the finale?"

Maybe it's Elliot's assurance or his respect for my wishes, but with him by my side, it all feels possible. After the last two days, he's more than earned his place as a friend.

Elliot waits in the living room while I change out of my

art-splattered rags. I text Hannah, You totally could've told me you wanted to go out tonight! It's not all about me, and I'm SO happy for you!!! Good luck with your date who may or may not be The One haha.

No reply or typing bubbles. She must already be on the date.

While I stare at a closet full of overwhelming outfit choices for Quest's End, I distract myself by scrolling through an Amazon list of cooling units that aren't air conditioners. Most generic fans are back-ordered. It isn't until I google "Which is coldest?" that I find an industrial-strength floor fan that's as powerful as a jet engine, like the kind Beyoncé uses for that windy look. I ship two to my house, one for Elliot and one for me—it's exactly what I need to dry portions of my mural faster.

Once that's finished, I call to Elliot through my door: "Don't mind the cat. She hates everybody."

"I'm snuggling her right now!" Elliot says giddily. All I hear is Lilith emitting honeydew-sweet mews, which only Maggie has been able to pry out of that cat. This boy is gonna be quite a vet.

Elliot continues serenading Lilith. "Where was this baaaaaaby during the moviiiiiiie? Were you hidiiiing? Too many strangers, yeeeees." I finally ditch my rags for something more princely so we can depart to slay the dragon. This time, I don't mess up in the shoe department. I don faux-suede boots with cushioned insoles. Paired with my periwinkle shirt unbuttoned to midchest, I am a cool, confident ice princess.

When the fashion is right, I walk with less stiffness and laughter comes easier.

How will I ask him out? "Hey, Boy 100," I'll say. "Oh, how did

I find you? It wasn't easy, but I had to get this one-of-a-kind jacket back to you. Let's grab dinner."

For the twentieth time today, Elliot and I hop in an Uber that shepherds us to the Art Institute, which rests smack-dab between Millennium and Grant Park. Return to the scene of the dating crime, I must!

Commuter traffic starts clogging us up the closer we get to the parks, so I make the executive (princely) decision to bail out and make the final passage on foot. With the lake and park green-ery to our left, we weave silently around sidewalk tourist traffic. The prince and his squire, galloping with purpose and bravery toward the tower.

That is . . . until I spot the tower.

The Art Institute's residence hall, an actual tower carved out of marble and stone, rises ominously in the distance. Clutching Boy 100's pumpkin jacket to my chest, I crane my neck upward in awe. Elliot approaches from behind, as cautiously as Lilith. He *hmmm*s to himself as we both stare at our quest's final destination.

"My liege, would you be mad if I gave you some advice?" he asks.

Elliot really knows how to play along and make people around him feel comfortable. He isn't awkward or pandering to me with this quest talk, and there's still that wink of playfulness to him that I worried would vanish without our friend-in-law, Hannah.

With regality, I ask, "What is your advice, Squire Elliot?"

With a sigh, Elliot's expression grows serious, and he puts both hands—damn, they feel almost *too* soft—on my shoulders. I'm star-tled, but I don't move. His pale brown eyes lock on to mine, but in a way that's comforting and safe—as if I've always known him.

"Fear is a trap," he says, all playacting dropped. "If Boy 100 wants to date you, nothing's gonna stop that from happening. If, for any reason, it's a no, just remember: he's just some boy."

He may as well have slapped me.

"He's The One, I know it," I argue, but Elliot gently holds my gaze.

"No doubt!" He briefly casts his eyes to the sidewalk. Is he ashamed? "Before Brandon, I would do anything for any boy, no matter how crappy he made me feel. But when I met Brandon, he was so independent, I could finally calm down." A simple smile crosses Elliot's face, and it unwinds the tension that has built up in my neck. "The One is just one boy."

Elliot is good at this pep talk stuff.

When he lets go of my arms, it feels like my life preserver has disappeared. Thank God he's coming with me to the end.

We turn to the residence hall tower. An entire building of professional artists my age, working in a shrine to creativity when I can't even finish a single mural, and I'm about to walk right into that lion's den and ask out my first boy ever?

*Yes, you are, Micah. You've got the sexy outfit. You've got the popular Insta. You've got everyone rooting for you.*

This is it. Walk in there and OWN IT.

"Onward," I whisper. The moment we cross the threshold into the cement quad leading to the residence halls, I realize I have no clue how to get into the building. A few tall, college-age women pass us on their way out the security doors, but I can't just slip inside a residence. That's not princely.

"Design program interns are on the seventh floor," I say, wagging my phone display at Elliot. "Art Institute subreddit."

He nods, impressed. I scrunch my face. "It feels stalky to go inside."

Elliot frowns. "Yeah." He glances around the spookily empty quad. "Maybe we just hang out, pretend to be students, like a stakeout?"

I bite my lip. It's not another dead end. Just breathe and wait. We press on deeper into the quad, past bulletin boards advertising calls for still life models and performance artists, as well as a colorful poster for an end-of-term show for design interns. That's what Boy 100 is here for! The show isn't for another two months, but I snap a picture of the poster, in case the quest drags on that long and I literally need to come to this thing just to find him.

God. Imagine. *Remember me? From the train A MILLION MONTHS AGO??*

Elliot and I stroll through the quad, which is sleepy with school's-out-for-summer vibes. Just a few scant professors jetting from one building to the next. It's dinnertime, so maybe we snoop around the cafeteria? I thought I'd be able to ask *some* passersby if they'd seen Boy 100; I wasn't counting on absolutely no one being here.

"What should we do?" Elliot asks.

"I'm thinking," I say.

The quad is so quiet, we can hear the gentle, powerful whir of in-unit air conditioners buzz in windows up above. That churning, water turbine sound.

"Micah," Elliot whispers, his eyes flaring open.

Every hair on my neck stands at attention. The same crackling energy from the train before I saw Boy 100 for the first time.

A set of double doors opens at the farthest end of the quad, and my breath unexpectedly stops. A small South Asian girl with dark golden skin and severe bangs drags two brimming tote bags out of the room. My shoulders sink. Those look like the same totes Boy 100 had, but his were filled with books. Her totes are only filled with something dark and red I can't make out.

"Pomegranates," Elliot hisses.

"No way," I whisper as my feet turn ice-cold.

The girl is indeed carrying tote bags full of pomegranates. I'm not sure if there's all 125 of them, but those are his poms! I know it.

A tall boy with curly, black hair follows his friend out the double doors while lifting a hundred-quart pot in his powerful arms.

It's him.

*Duck behind Elliot, quickly!* My mind practically screams as I move slightly behind Elliot. *You weirdo, don't do that!*

Boy 100's back is to me. He doesn't see me. He and his friend lug the bags and pot toward the opposite end of the quad . . .

They're leaving, and fast.

*You won't get a third chance, Micah.*

Do I run after him and risk looking nuts? If I move too slowly, I could lose him again.

My shock dissolves, and I start moving. Elliot grabs my arm, and an open, hopeful look crosses his face. Like he wants to say something. "What is it?" I ask.

Elliot is lost for words. His lips part slightly, like he's scared. "Um . . . just go get him."

"As you wish," I whisper with a grand nod. He gives me a playful push, and before I know it, I'm walking ahead to my destiny. Faster and faster, I close the gap between myself and Boy 100. He's too distracted balancing his awkward pot to notice me.

It's even better this way.

The one magical moment in the story where he isn't paying attention, where I can just see him in front of me, real, until suddenly he turns those eyes on me, sees me, and everything begins. My life begins.

"I think you lost something," I announce to the quad filled with blooming, magnificent trees, my voice as grand as any Prince Charming that ever lived in stories.

Boy 100's friend spots me first. A knowing grin breaks across her face, and she smacks the small of his back with the kind of force that only a best friend can deliver. "It's him," she whispers.

He turns.

A black curl falls in front of his shimmering eyes. I hold the jacket out to him like a tribute. That familiar round-cheeked smirk greets me.

"You found me," he says, bass notes rumbling in my ears. "What took you so long?"

He's been waiting for me. Could he have been pining for me as much as I've been for him? His smile warms me like the sun as I laugh and step closer. "Sorry to keep you waiting."

"I can be very impatient." He sets down his pot, breaks away from his friend, and the gap between us shrinks to three feet . . . two feet . . . less than a foot. He's staring down at me again, the friendly giant and me beneath the trees and open sky.

"You didn't make it easy on me. The pomegranates, the pot. Oh, and by the way, you owe me three bucks for library fines on *How to Teach Quantum Physics to Your Dog*."

He laughs and shakes his head in disbelief. "We have some catching up to do."

"We do." Our eyes lock. "What's your name?"

"Grant."

*Grant, Grant, Grant, Grant, Grant*—it echoes between my ears. An almost royal name. It's perfect, it's fate, it's everything magical.

This is it.

Give him the sweep. The rock 'em, sock 'em Prince Charming, fairy-tale, princess-rescued-from-the-tower sweep.

"I'm Micah Summers. Do you want to get dinner with me?" Every millisecond he doesn't answer lasts for a century. I don't break eye contact.

Grant nods. "Yes," he says, smiling, "How about right now? I'm starving."

Every nerve ending in my body erupts with joy. From my fingers to my toes, from my skull to my stomach—everything frizzles with a strange electricity. Prince Charming came through. I actually did the thing and successfully asked out a boy!

"Sounds like a plan." I smile. "But first, I've had a few . . . hundred people lie to me and say this coat belongs to them." I unfold his jacket embroidered with pumpkins and vines. "I need to see if it fits. You know, to make sure it's really you."

Grant grins, those dimples flaring. "We must be thorough."

He turns his back to me to await his jacket coronation. I smile at Elliot. Without him, I couldn't have pushed through my terror to come here. Alone at the other end of the quad, Elliot returns my smile—not bright and big like usual. This one is smaller. Filled with emotion.

Cold air rushes through my limbs. Why does he look different?

"Do it," Elliot mouths, summoning a smile back to his face, which calms my racing heart. Grant splays out his arms, making his highly muscled back pop through his shirt as I approach with the pumpkin jacket. I slip one sleeve over his large, delicate hand. It's breathtaking to be this close to him. I clamp down on my tongue to stop myself making any weird, happy noises.

Then I pull on his other sleeve.

"A perfect fit," I say.

And it is.

## Chapter 9
# THE PROLOGUE

Y ES.

I asked a boy out, and he said yes.

I'd done it in my mind a million times with ninety-nine other boys, but my body wasn't prepared for the reality of hearing Grant say yes in that deep, reverberating bass voice of his. *Yes.* What a magical word. "Yes" swept like a broom through my mind, clearing it of every "no" I'd ever heard or imagined.

"Yes" is so in the air that I agreed to get dinner with him right *now*.

No prep, no grand romantic planning, no announcement on Instaloves, nothing!

"Let's grab a bite at Potage, nothing fancy," Grant says.

Nothing fancy! I wanted all fancy! This is our first date—my first date. No fancy?

With nothing more than a quick "Have fun!" Grant's friend hurries away as fast as she can with the totes of pomegranates.

"Eshana! What about the pot?" Grant shouts, pointing to his culinary store purchase. Excitement surges back into me—he's in the middle of something important. We'll have to delay this first date until tomorrow when I can *really* plan. I'm about to suggest that when his friend, Eshana, shouts back without looking: "Leave it! I'll come back for it as soon as I set these down!"

Grant turns to me with a relieved smile, but I've gone rigid again.

"I don't know if I should ditch my friend," I say, pointing at Elliot farther down the quad . . . but he isn't there. He left.

Glancing at my phone, I find a text waiting from Elliot: **Didn't want an awkward goodbye to ruin your FIRST DATE!!! Have a great time!!!**

"Elliot," I growl. He couldn't have stuck around one more minute?

All at once, I'm alone with Grant. He watches me, his hands stuffed in his pockets, his smile suddenly a little smaller. He senses the shift in my energy.

*Explain the situation, Micah!*

"So listen—" I start.

"Micah," he says, taking my arms. I can feel his strength even through this gentleness. Even though his lips—two fluffy, pink pillows—are parted, he doesn't kiss me. He's close, though. Too close. My throat shuts. "Don't stress," he repeats. "You probably want our first date to be this big thing you put a lot of energy into. Am I warm?"

"Very warm," I say. He's perfect. Absolutely a perfect psychic person, and all I want to do is fall asleep on his chest after a day of *much* toil and suspense.

Grant smirks victoriously. "But I'm starving and would like you to get a sandwich with me across the street. This is not our first date. Why don't we call this, uh . . . ?"

"An audition?"

"Eh, sounds stressful." He swirls his mouth as he thinks. "Interview? That's worse."

"Right . . ."

We stand in a comfortable silence beneath maple trees as a warm wind shakes loose whirlybirds that spin and spin and spin.

We're in a storybook. Our story. And what comes before the first chapter?

"A prologue," I offer, and Grant's eyes pop like fireworks.

He offers me his hooked arm to take, the fresh leather of his jacket whining as it bends. "Micah Summers, would you like to go on a prologue with me?"

Our first prologue!

At Le Petit Potage, we eat along the window counter facing the lush green entrance to the Art Institute's North Garden. As Grant attacks his sandwich in rapid, tiny bites, I swirl my spoon around my soup in hypnotic circles. "You didn't have to pay," I say, "I was gonna—"

Grant smiles. "Don't worry, Micah Summers. I've got the prologue; you can pay for the date."

"Deal!" I blow on my spoon to cool it. "What's your last name? So I can catch up to you."

"Rossi."

*(Micah Rossi . . . Micah Summers-Rossi . . . Micah Rossi-Summers . . . Welcome to the Summers-Rossi home, please remove your shoes . . . )*

I can't believe I have this sudden wealth of information on Grant Rossi after subsisting on crumbs and guesswork. Throughout our prologue, Grant confesses to me like I'm the CIA. He's the youngest of eight (!!!) siblings, has a niece who's going to be a freshman at his high school this fall, hates corn on the cob but loves corn chowder, thinks David Lynch is the most important painter of all time, and if he couldn't be an artist, he'd want to work at one of those Seadog speedboat tours of the city—which is like a regular boat tour if it was run by Guy Fieri.

As Grant says this, I laugh. "The very first Instaloves boyfriend I ever drew was a Seadog tour guide I thought was cute." In my fantasy drawing, the Seadog tour guide became the rugged captain of a clipper ship.

*"Really?"* Effortlessly casual, Grant leans back, throwing his arm onto the counter. Without the jacket to cloak his body, his bicep swells to the size of a small pumpkin. I'll need two hands to hold it. "I love those Seadog guys; they're so corny. Does all that woofing into the microphone do it for you?"

I slap my hands over my eyes. "Stop, oh my God. I never told anyone before."

His dimpled smile drops a quarter inch. "So how come you told me?"

I hold his gaze. It's strangely comfortable. "I just . . . You're easy to talk to."

As the sunset fades to periwinkle dust, our prologue dinner

reduces to crumb-filled wrappers and empty bowls. With Grant, time simply disappears. No brutal moment-to-moment negotiations in my head about what to say. I'm being myself, but for the first time in my life, that feels like enough.

"So," I say, tapping his ankle. "About our first date."

Grant rests his chin on his fist. "Didn't we just do the first date?" My terror must be splashed all over my face, because he immediately socks me in the shoulder. "Kidding!!"

His punch lands harder than I expect, but he used the exact amount of strength for it to be thrilling. In fact, he seems to be putting his hands on me any way he can, just shy of holding my hand. It's like he has to touch me. I bite my lip as R-rated thoughts swarm my mind.

*Easy, Micah. Gotta do Steps A through C before getting to Step D.*

"The first date," I repeat. He nods like an eager student. "Do you have anything going on tomorrow night?"

"Nope."

"Good answer."

"What are we doing?"

"I haven't decided yet." We study each other as Potage employees sweep around us. I reach out an open palm. "I'm gonna give you my number." He unlocks his phone and hands it over. He placed a sticker over the back so it looks like the Snow White Queen is holding the Apple logo.

A single butterfly flaps through my chest. I wish I could send a picture of his phone to Elliot—he'd know immediately that it was like the universe was winking at me!

I text my own number: Hey, Micah, it's Micah here with

Grant and then hand it back to him. I did it. I gave a boy my number—not just any boy, *the* boy. Grant texts me below the one I just sent myself: Hey, Micah, it's Grant here with Micah. Save this cutie's number, please? Please say yes?

Adorable. I respond, Yes!!

"I'll text you details of the date when I plan them," I say. With that, I follow Grant outside into the twilight. Across the street, outside the entrance to the North Garden, we agree to part ways for the night. He waits with me until my Uber arrives, but as soon as it pulls up, he stops my elbow. Under the glow of the street-lights, his shimmering eyes say what I've been afraid to admit: it's terrible splitting up again after our last separation was so painful.

"I can't believe I found you," I say.

He grins. "I'm here."

After a breathless moment, I smile too. "Yes, you are."

"What should I wear tomorrow?"

With my Uber's engine purring, I mentally race through options—what could match the concept I'm planning, which I haven't decided on yet. In the end, Grant always brings out the simplest truths in me: "Wear whatever you would if this was your last first date ever."

This time, I knocked the breath out of him.

"Okay," he says with a stunned smile. "See you tomorrow."

I jump into my Uber in a dizzy, gleeful haze as we zoom out of the Loop toward home. At the end of an enormously long day, I finally begin my *Little Book of Firsts*. Next to *First Boy I Ever Asked Out*, I scribble the date *06-09-22*.

I did it. I had no idea I had it in me to be this cool.

# Chapter 10
# THE ENCHANTED LADY

The search is over! Boy 100 has been found!

Like with Cinderella's glass slipper, the jacket was a perfect fit. The obstacles to finding him were many, but we didn't give up hope. And neither should you! A weary world deserves a little dreaming, and little surprises are always waiting for you just around the corner.

Where do Boy 100 and I go from here? We have our very first date tonight (EEK!), so watch this space, because our story is only just beginning . . .

Every atom in my body feels like it's awakened from a century of slumber.

Following the best sleep of my life, the First Date to End All First Dates pops into my head, fully formed. I dreamt of Grant and myself on the deck of a Seadog speedboat tour that was just for us, except instead of Chicago, we toured magnificent, fantastical shores full of mermaids and ancient, crumbling castles.

Our first date must be at sea!

Although, if I'm going to pull off this idea in time, I have to get cracking. I send four texts in a very vital order. First is to my dad: Don't know if you saw my Instaloves post, but my first date ever ever EVER is tonight! I really want this to be special. I've never asked you for this before, but could I use the Enchanted Lady tonight??

My dad has trust issues with me using his pour-over coffee brewer, so getting the family yacht is going to be a challenge. After several back-and-forths (and some side texts from my mom assuring me she'll be able to convince him), Dad agrees, on the condition that I meet him at the boat at five thirty to receive several lectures before he hands over the keys.

Victory!

My second text is to Hannah. I already have a dozen **Tell me EVERYTHING** texts waiting from her, but with my new confidence, I'm feeling a bit wicked: **I'll tell YOU everything when you tell me about last night's mystery man.**

**bye,** she responds.

I grin, flip over in bed onto my stomach, and message, **First Official Date tonight! My dad is letting me use the Enchanted Lady. Want to help decorate with me? I'll supply you with lunch and much tales from last night.**

Within seconds, she says, **fool. I would've done it for the lunch.**

Translation: you're not getting any mystery man stories out of me. Normally, Hannah treats me to every detail of her dates, down to their shoe size and GPA. The plot thickens with this new one.

A second later, she adds, **I'll be up in thirty!!! Let's crash that mfin' boat!!!**

Love Hannah. She never needs nudging to get into business mode. This is the grand First Date of mine we've been talking about planning for years. Actually, it was a contractual pinkie swear at our seventh-grade dance, a night I thought was going to be us hanging out like usual but ended with her first kiss on the dance floor. Her *Little Book of Firsts* began a while ago. Although I was happy for her, I never grasped the difference between us until that moment—like, really felt it. I could be as out as I wanted, but if I wanted a first kiss, it might take a while until other boys caught up. Afterward, I was in my feelings but couldn't recognize why. Hannah knew why, though. She understands everything. She walked right up to me in the library, wrapped her pinkie around mine, and promised to plan the hell out of my first date, whenever it happened.

Four-plus years later, it's finally happening.

On a surge of warmth, my third text goes to Elliot, who hasn't texted since last night: We did it!! Grant and I talked for hours; it was everything. I couldn't have done it without you! We have our first official date tonight—Hannah is coming upstairs to help plan. Are you working? I'd love to do a quest part 2 with my favorite trio if you're around?

Elliot's typing bubbles appear before I even finish messaging. I love a fellow eager texter! His response comes fast: Hiiiiiiiiii! Happy to continue questing! That sketch you posted, WOW. I'm already at work, but I'm off at noon if that's not too late?

The fellowship of the jacket lives on!

I begin to tell him to meet us at the Columbia Yacht Club but stop before hitting send. What I'm *not* going to do is be like, "When you're finished mopping up coffee grounds, walk half a mile to my luxury yacht to help me plan a romantic date and then you may go home to your sweltering apartment!"

Take your time! I reply. Go home, chill first, etc. Meet us at Scully & Sokol's (this bougie grocery store near Audrey's) around 3 if that's cool.

He responds with excitement, and I check on his heavy-duty fan I ordered. It hasn't shipped yet. Delayed a few weeks. I laugh to myself. Elliot teased me that I'd like to speak to a manager instead of merely accepting that sometimes in life there are limits.

Maybe there are, but if I'm able to help Elliot's living situation, shouldn't I try?

As I search my imagination for alternative cooling solutions for Elliot, I draft my fourth, final, and most important text: Grant. I type and delete a dozen messages, but nothing strikes the right tone. It must be effortlessly casual but also big. Important. It can't be something like *Hi*.

*Good morning, handsome?*

Is that stupid? It's stupid. Also, I'd like to save my first *Good morning, handsome* for when I turn over to wake him up in bed.

Are you trying to text me something cool, Micah Summers? Grant's text arrives.

My lips part. It's as if he's materialized in my room out of thin air.

How does he always know exactly what to say? As fast as I've ever texted anything, I reply, It was going to be a real winner, too, but now you'll just have to settle for me telling you the details of The First Date to End All First Dates.

I'm ready! he replies.

Columbia Yacht Club. 8pm. Look for the Enchanted Lady.

A long pause of typing follows, and my stomach twists with an ugly thought: This is too fancy. I'm such a brat having a yacht, and he's going to think I'm showing off. He's probably typing that this is too much and that we should reschedule for another night when he's not so busy (but we won't reschedule; he'll just text less and less until I get the picture and disappear).

Damn, he finally replies. You don't mess around. See you at 8! Don't forget to bring that magic sketchbook of yours. You should have something new to post tomorrow.

Brief. Flirty. Insightful. Meaningful.

Grant Rossi couldn't be more ideal if I'd invented him myself.

The day passes in a frenzy of preparation. As we raid every crafts store on the Gold Coast, I fill in Hannah on the previous night: running into Grant on the quad, the fitting of the jacket, the prologue date, how he kept touching me, how he seemed to sense my every thought the moment I thought it. With her arms full of plastic vines and flowers, Hannah gives me a watery-eyed hug. She's been waiting for this almost as long as I have.

"Remember," she whispers, wrapping her pinkie around mine. "I promised you it would happen."

I can't stop smiling as I squeeze her pinkie. "And I promised *you* all the details afterward."

She winks. "That's not a pinkie promise, that's a *blood oath*!"

When we meet up with Elliot at Scully & Sokol's, a rustic West Loop grocery store, he immediately launches into teasing: "Oh, so we're decorating your *yacht*, are we? You failed to mention that little detail, hmm?"

In the produce aisle, I implode with hot embarrassment. "I thought I said . . ."

Elliot pops the collar on his dark polo and clutches it to his throat like an Old Hollywood star's mink coat. "Just a small yacht, nothing too big. Something for the family."

Hannah spurts laughter into her hand, and Elliot is so hilarious, I can't stop myself giggling. "Help me with this date, and the yacht is yours and Brandon's anytime you want!"

Elliot whistles as he bags up a crate of strawberries. "Forget Brandon! If it's got AC, I've found my new summer home."

By the time we finish collecting everything on my list, we're almost an hour late meeting my dad. I whisper a silent promise to the gay gods to let his lecture be over quickly so we can get to decorating before eight!

My phone buzzes with a text. It's Grant.

In my current kaleidoscope of anxiety, my brain transforms his text into *I can't make it! This is a huge mistake. Goodbye!* One blink later, his true text emerges: Just went shopping for my Yacht Date outfit. What do you think?

Grant sends a stock image of a pompous old man in a sea captain's uniform, smoking a pipe and gazing into the sunset.

A smile floats onto my face. Perfection, I respond.

The sun hovers low over Lake Michigan by the time we reach the docks at Columbia Yacht Club. In the distance, Navy Pier's enormous Ferris Wheel has already switched on its multicolored lights. The setting is so idyllic, I can't wait until I stop rushing and can finally enjoy the fruits of my labors. Hannah, Elliot, and I haul baskets of food, flowers, and décor down the docks, which are like a taxi stand but with small, private yachts. There must be fifty yachts, nearly identical in side-by-side rows. "We're looking for the *Enchanted Lady*," I say, trying not to trip over my own feet as I hurry.

Hannah pirouettes in her blue-checkered skirt. "Look no further, darlings! The Enchanted Lady is right here!"

"Ooh, all aboard!" Elliot crows, slipping his arm into the crook of her elbow.

"You wish!" Hannah kicks at his ankles, but he dodges and steps away, laughing.

"That mystery man of yours wishes," I add as I fall back into step with her.

As expected, Hannah's smile drops. "Nice try, Mr. Summers,

but we will not be discussing the Mystery Man tonight. Tonight is about making your first date dreams come true!"

Smiling, Elliot taps his basket against my hip. "We're your *Cinderella* helper mice."

"I want to be Gus-Gus," Hannah proclaims. "I, too, like wearing just the one shirt."

The more we laugh, the more confidence grows in my chest like a house of cards, outwardly intact but easily toppled. This date must—and will—be legendary.

Finally, the *Enchanted Lady* appears. At first glance, no more identifiable than any of the other McYachts dotting the lake. Beautiful, but with an oppressive sameness. However, the closer I get to our boarding ramp, the more I'm reminded of its uniqueness: instead of having the same creamy-white color as the others, the *Enchanted Lady* is a light, robin's-egg blue. Its name is stenciled onto the side in a swirling font—blue as well, but in a deeper, sparkling cerulean.

"There's the prince now," Dad greets me from the vessel at the top of the ramp. When he's out of the house, he wears all black, like Mom—black V-neck and black, high-waisted ankle slacks, yet styled with white loafers. He's so recognizable that whenever he's in public, he has to be the Fashion Guy. When he's at home, however, he looks permanently at the gym.

"You get lost, pal?" he asks, tapping a blingy watch with a name I can't pronounce.

"We got held up at the store, sorry!" I shuffle up the ramp, Elliot and Hannah nearly stomping on my heels behind me. In our rush, we compete to show my dad how much we aren't slackers. He has this way of making you feel like you're never hustling hard enough.

Dad whistles. *"Fifty* minutes late, Little Prince."

He follows us inside the *Enchanted Lady, tsk-tsk*ing all the way. I fight snarky retorts. I'm stressed enough about tonight without also having to deal with Dad's time obsession.

The yacht, however, is worth my dad's hassling. Hannah and Elliot drop our bags onto a long dining table in the middle of a grand parlor. Sleek, modern armchairs with golden cashmere throws line the walls, which are wallpapered with a textured, merlot-colored pattern. Twin glass doors open onto an outer deck . . .

This is where Grant and I will stargaze after dinner, and possibly—hopefully—more.

My visibly agitated father is joined by his producer, Theresa, a cheerful Puerto Rican woman with warm bronze skin and dark hair in a long, straightened, Ariana Grande ponytail. She tilts her head at Elliot, who is hastily emptying our grocery bags in between awe-filled glances at the majestic room. "That for the kitchen?" she asks. "Actually, let's bring it down here, love."

Elliot doesn't seem annoyed to have to repack his bags. He's probably used to such about-face orders at Audrey's.

Hannah and I dig out string lights and garlands of plastic vines when Dad repeats, "Fifty minutes." Evidently, I haven't been apologetic enough. "You know who keeps me waiting that long, Theresa?"

As Theresa helps Elliot pack, she casually responds, "The world record for keeping Jeremy Summers waiting is the Cubs' new owner with twenty-six minutes."

"Uh-huh, and what did I do when he arrived?"

"You canceled."

"Like that!" Dad snaps his fingers. Hannah casts me an unblinking stare.

Sighing, I face him. "I'm sorry we were late. Thank you for waiting and trusting me with the *Enchanted Lady*. I'm nervous about tonight. My brain is on Jupiter, so I don't even know what time is, as a concept."

Dad's tough, angrily ruddy expression collapses. "Aw, come here." He yanks me into a hug. "I'm sorry, Micah. I got all worked up waiting for you. Your first date! When did you grow up? You must've done it in secret." He lets out a pained grunt. "Gahhh, I hate it."

Jeremy Summers has always been at war with his enemy, Time.

Elliot bows his head as he shuttles groceries into the yacht's kitchen. My dad blocks his path. "Whoa, there!" He extends a friendly palm. "I'm Jeremy Summers, Micah's dad."

Elliot attempts to shake Dad's hand through three grocery bags. "Yeah, I know, uh . . . Nice to see you . . ."

Dad plows ahead with his speech, oblivious that he already introduced himself the other night. "So you're the special guy. Hope you have fun tonight. Gonna need you both off the yacht and my son returned home by eleven, sharp. None of this 'lost track of time' stuff. I'm not a spying man, but I'm making you aware that this vessel is equipped with livestream cameras I *will* have access to. Now, there's visuals but no sound, so it is only spying *light*. Feel free to talk about whatever you want, but I will know if the *Enchanted Lady* is used for anything other than dinner.

Speaking of that, Micah, why is he cooking? I thought you were trying to impress him?"

This is just too good.

Hannah presses the plastic vines to her mouth to stop giggles from overtaking her. Sweet Elliot has been nodding politely the whole time. I set down my bags and clasp my hands together like a prim schoolteacher. "Well, Father, that's because you've got the wrong boy. This is Elliot. *Grant* is the date I'm meeting tonight."

Dad turns to Elliot, who appears to be trying to smile his way back into my father's memory. Dad can only blink stupidly and say, "I'm gonna go throw myself in this lake."

Over the next hour, we have too much to do. Hannah and I move like dancers, draping vines and fairy lights across every banister while Elliot stocks the belowdecks fridge. A few dozen candles later, Hannah and I transform the parlor into a woodland fairy oasis. When Grant arrives, it'll be like he's a woodcutter entering a magical clearing to find me . . . waiting for him.

The fairy tale isn't in my head anymore.

The time has come for everyone to leave me alone to await my fateful date. Hannah hides the empty baskets inside a cupboard and wishes me luck with a bone-crushing hug. "It's all happening!" she whispers merrily.

I do a little dance inside her hug. *"Finally."*

She separates from me with a stern look. "Now, in case your prince turns out to be a serial killer, you call me, and I'll be there in a second with various knives and karate moves." Chuckling, I give her a playful push, but she doesn't drop her mom face. "I won't be far. I'll be in Old Town on my own date."

"Mystery man, hmm?" I ask, steepling my fingers.

"No questions at this time, Micah!" With that, Hannah slips on her sunglasses, blows me a kiss, and departs. Not long after, my dad leaves with Theresa, who gives me an excited little wave. Halfway down the ramp to the dock, Dad turns back.

He doesn't say anything. He just looks at me, like he's taking it all in.

"Dad?" I ask.

He shakes his head, as if to wake himself. "Nothing. Have a nice date." He stomps down the ramp before turning back again. "Would it totally embarrass you if I say 'I love you'?"

I inhale sharply. "Um, yes."

Dad clicks his tongue. "Good thing I didn't say it then. Enjoy your date!"

Floating again with a warm numbness, I join Elliot below-decks. This is no amateur setup. A brand-new electric stovetop sits on a kitchen island. A dozen pieces of copper cookware hang overhead. Elliot leans against the stainless steel fridge, admiring his organizational masterpiece: every ingredient needed for tonight's meal of sweet crepes and savory galettes laid out in pristine order.

"Looks amazing!" I say from the doorway. My words echo through the empty space—it's just me and him left.

Smiling, Elliot runs his palm over the black glass stovetop. "It's pretty in here," he says. "I can just imagine little you running around this kitchen, driving your mom nuts."

The visual seems to give him so much joy, I don't have the heart to tell him I've been in this kitchen exactly two times in my life, and both instances were because I got lost.

"I better get going," he says, gazing lovingly at the table. "I'm just admiring the setup. I wish I could do something like this for Brandon, make it special like in the beginning. We haven't had a date-date in a while, you know?"

"You still can."

Elliot nods, miles away. "I wish he'd do something like this *for* me is more what I mean."

"You work so hard," I say. "You deserve a big, splashy, attention-fest date more than anybody." Elliot tries to smile through his seasick frown. The lower berth buzzes with stillness. "What's your favorite memory of all time with Brandon?"

As if sprinkled with pixie dust, Elliot's expression brightens. "He swam with me." Whatever Elliot's memory is, however positive, it instantly brings him to the edge of tears. "We'd been dating a few months, it was almost Christmastime, and he took me to this seafood place overlooking the river. Oh my God, I ate, like, my body weight in crab legs. The *butter*—anyway, he drove me to the pool where he trains. They gave him some after-hours key. He wanted to watch me swim. I was nervous about cramping— remember, I was *stuffed*, girl, so he . . ." Elliot laughs. "He swam with me, wrapped his arms around me like we were two little otters, and we backstroked for hours. I could've fallen asleep right there, my body trusted him so much."

I smile as an image gathers in my mind—Elliot and Brandon as cuddly, shirtless mermen. Where's my sketchbook when I need it?!

As quickly as Elliot's smile came, it darkens again. "Brandon's so busy with swim now. His *Olympic* trainer"—he rolls his eyes— "told him greatness and relationships don't mix."

I snort. "Well, he's wrong."

"Brandon told him to mind his business, but legit, I can never plan anything for us . . ."

Elliot gets lost staring at his shoes, and pity floods my chest. How could such a beautiful fairy-tale beginning end with Elliot feeling this disappointed? That's not what any queer person deserves. We have to make our own magic, and I won't let that magic abandon Elliot!

"Hang on to that swimming memory," I say, touching his shoulder. "You'll get back there. Little surprises happen every day, remember?" Nodding, Elliot brushes back a tear. "You and I are different from everybody else. We're not like people who think falling in love or staying in love isn't worth the effort. We did it for me, now let's do it for you and Brandon."

Elliot chews his lip. "Really?"

"Prince and Squire, together again to slay another dragon: the Busy Boyfriend."

Elliot's laughter slices through the quiet like a sword. I rise another three inches off the ground just seeing him smile again. He exhales. "That would be really cool, thank you."

I offer him a grand bow, and he returns it.

"Good luck, Micah," Elliot says with a hug. He doesn't look at me again as he leaves, not even when I say, "Talk to you tomorrow!"

Outside, summer thunder rolls in the distance. With Elliot's sudden departure, I'm alone and vulnerability returns. Welp. Nothing to do now but have my very first date!

Grant will be here in a matter of minutes.

## Chapter 11
# THE KNIGHT PRINCESS

*Once I'm alone, the real date prep begins.*

In the yacht's bathroom, I pluck three stray eyebrow hairs. Next, I spot-check myself with concealer and a warm-hued foundation so subtle I even fool myself. I skip my usual mascara—for time reasons, not because I'm self-conscious about wearing makeup on a date; he should know I mean business with these lashes! Then comes nails—everything gets a fresh clip and a fine buff, even my toenails because I don't know how revealing tonight is going to get, and Micah Summers is always prepared. I finish with the all-important Last Bathroom Break because I want to project to Grant that I am a luminous, eternally beautiful elf who has evolved beyond such filthy mortal needs as a bathroom.

No one goes to the bathroom in fairy tales.

I undress and carefully unpack my date costume—freshly ironed, high-ankled pants and a black shirt with a stiff, high collar that buttons across my throat. My Prince Charming shirt. It accentuates my shoulders and stiffens my posture, granting me an illusion of height . . . and an illusion of confidence.

With one last swipe of my horsehair brush, I'm perfect.

Exhaling into the mirror, I tell myself, "Just *breathe*, Micah."

"Micah?" calls a voice outside.

A spasm jolts up my spine as dread wallops me like a cannonball.

Grant is already *here*.

"SHIT," I mouth. Get rid of the evidence! As quietly as an ant coughing in church, I shove every item into the cabinet under the sink: tweezers, old socks, my sweaty shirt, setting powder, everything. I snatch my toothbrush from the makeup bag.

Oh my God, I forgot to brush my tongue. What if my breath is bad?

I go to turn on the faucet but stop myself. NO. If Grant hears running water, he'll think bathroom-related things are happening here. No water. Gum! I throw back an Ice Breaker and chew like the date depends on it.

"Micah?" that gorgeously deep voice calls again, louder this time. He's closer.

*Chew faster, dammit! Faster!*

If I chew any faster, I'm going to break my jaw. There can't be any evidence of the gum, so I open my makeup bag and hock the used gum inside. Gross. I spray myself—and the bathroom—with my tiny bottle of Jean Paul Gaultier that's shaped like a sailor's torso, take a deep breath, and open the door.

If I was out of breath before, Grant Rossi just snatched away the rest. His curly hair sparkles with even more shimmer; a silver bracelet hangs loosely off his muscular wrist; a matching silver chain necklace drapes over the dark, floral-print T-shirt stretched snugly over his chest; and his short sleeves are rolled up a quarter-turn to make his broad arms really pop.

A boy who knows aesthetics. An artist, like me.

"Grant, you're here," I say, adding a small gasp to pretend he startled me.

"I thought I was in the wrong place." He laughs. "I should've texted I was here, but I, uh, got excited. Sorry, did I catch you in the bathroom?"

My smile freezes. "Nope. Just checking my hair."

"Well, it's beautiful."

I absentmindedly pat the back of my neck. "Oh, God, no. Nothing like yours."

Grant moans uncertainly as he tugs a curl straight before letting it *boing* back into place. "It just bounces like this, no matter what I do. I hate it."

"I love it."

LORD HELP ME, I ALMOST SAID I LOVE YOU BY ACCIDENT.

We hang under the doorway, just looking at each other. The silence between us presses down on my ears. Grant licks his lower lip. It happens fast—only for a split second—but it's enough to drive out all my other thoughts. He could kiss me right now, and this date would immediately turn into a hookup, damn the dinner.

But what kind of fairy tale would that be? No—our first kiss can't come this soon.

"Hungry?" I ask.

He smiles. "Always."

The crepes get off to an awkward start. I drop splintery bits of eggshell into my batter, and I'm so keyed up about cooking this flawlessly that I freeze. I can't look up. All I see is the bowl of egg batter and Grant's hand floating over to take it.

"My mom showed me a great way of getting shells out," he says soothingly. My shoulders relax. I look up. His hand hovers over the bowl. "You trust me?"

I smirk, my confidence returning in dribbles. "We'll see."

*Splurt!* Grant plunges his entire hand into the egg batter and splashes around for the shell pieces like a bear snatching salmon out of a riverbed. Uncontrollable laughter shakes my body as yolk flings across the island, into the sink, and onto the cabinets. With hardly any batter left in the bowl, Grant pulls out the last of the shells and proudly shows me his hand, gloved in dripping yellow. "Got 'em all."

"Neat trick," I say between laughs.

He touches my chin with damp, sticky fingers. "See the mess I made?"

It's my turn to wet my lips. "Yep."

"Now you don't have to be so worried about doing everything right because you'll never mess up as much as me." I smile—my first natural, unplanned one of the evening. "Let's stumble through this together, okay?"

"I'd love to." I clasp my hand inside his messy one—new milestone achieved: first boy hand-holding. Shock waves course through my body. A handshake could never. This hand-holding is full of power and promise I've only imagined.

Soft. Tough. Safe. Dangerous. Innocent. Not-so-innocent. I'm breathless.

The first three crepes are a disaster. The yacht's kitchen becomes a war zone of butter splatters, strawberry spills, and a lingering haze in the air of What Is That Burning Smell? But with Grant, every mistake becomes a memory. Relieved laughter replaces every impulse my body has to generate anxiety.

Burnt butter? Who cares! Crepe fell apart? Sounds like yummy crepe scraps!

Once the kitchen is cleaned of yolk, we shuttle plates of over-stuffed crepes and galettes into the parlor. As I walk ahead, Grant teases me that my tremoring wrist doesn't look like it can hold my plate steady. Giggles shake me, making this balancing act even more treacherous.

"Don't drop it, don't drop it," he whispers. "Doooon't drop it."

"Stop it, I'm really gonna drop it," I beg through laughter.

Ugh, why is teasing the best *and* the worst?

As we eat in the fairy-lit glow of the forested parlor, rain begins to fall. Even the rain is perfect. The soft patter is a backing track behind the smooth bossa nova playlist Elliot compiled from his favorites at Audrey's Café.

Hannah, Elliot, and I are the romance dream team. We're

going to make something so special for Elliot and Brandon, it's gonna fix everything for them. That adorable merman Elliot will swim again!

Grant cuts into his galette with a slice as thin as a baby carrot. He takes each bite carefully. I've been eating pieces twice as wide.

I match my slices to his. I don't go to the bathroom, and I don't take beast-sized chomps.

When we finish our crepes, I pour coffee from a glass decanter, and Grant proudly shows off the project he's working on at the Art Institute. "I'll show you," he says, "but normally, I'd scream my head off if someone else saw my designs before they were ready."

"I'm the same way!" I shriek, hurrying over with his cup. "That's why I made Instaloves anonymous. Nobody gets it."

Grant opens his camera roll to a series of rough sketches. "Right? Like with my dad, it's like, hi, I don't peek in on you when you're in the middle of a surgery."

"Yeah! And you don't even have to show me, by the way—"

"Oh, you don't want to see?"

"No! I really want to. Just . . . you don't *have* to."

He smiles. Dimple Central. "Get over here."

Then he pats his knee. I almost drop my cup.

Do I get on his lap? Is that weird? What if he meant "over here" not "on here"? Is that weird of him to ask? I mean, I want to, but . . . these stupid Dad cameras are everywhere.

I opt to slide my chair until it's kissing his. Knee to knee. That's not *too* sexual.

*Micah, that's not even too sexual for nuns!*

Grant and I settle in, shoulder to shoulder, over his phone. "You smell nice," he says.

"You too," I say as his cinnamon-y scent finds me. "Mine's not too much?"

He laughs. "I like strong cologne. I'm Italian. We're aliens from Planet Cologne."

I can't catch my breath tonight. I really, *really* like him.

The sketches on Grant's phone are his concepts but drawn by a friend in the design program. The rough figure models a gown that gets more defined with each passing iteration. The figure feels gender-fluid, with a bulky, metallic top that softens into a long, trailing gown. "I call this the Knight Princess," he says, flicking through photos with his strong, handsome hand (I don't know how to explain why a hand can be handsome, but it just is!). "My design program is building up to a runway show, and this is my finale look."

My thoughts return to the poster Elliot and I found in the quad: the end-of-term design show in August. "So cool," I whisper. "The Knight Princess looks like it's right out of . . ."

"Fairy tales. I knew you'd appreciate it."

"Is this what you needed all those roses and poms for?"

"Uh-huh. I'm using key objects from fairy tales to naturally dye the fabric, like they would in those times. A total pain, but it makes it more magical, you know?"

"Totally. I thought about doing that to make my own paints for my mural."

"Mural?"

The word leapt out of my mouth before I had the chance to stop it.

A nauseous swell of jealousy punches my heart. Grant is showing off his big, ambitious project, and I can't even discuss my mural.

"Micah?" he asks with that studying look.

His gentle tone shakes me out of my thousand-yard stare. "I'm painting a mural," I admit. "I don't know what I want it to be yet. I have such a stronger vision for Instaloves, but I just don't for this mural. Maybe it's me. I wish I felt confident enough to tackle a project as big as yours, but I'm not."

"Not yet," he replies.

The invisible grip on my heart loosens. *Not yet.* What a kindness.

"I can't believe I told you that," I say. "We're on a first date, and that was totally too personal—"

"Hey." Grant closes his hand around mine. Not like Elliot's soft hand. His is tougher, stronger, and shoots warmth through my veins. "Stop worrying so much about what I think of you. I'm already impressed, and I'm not that great."

I laugh. "Shut up."

"I'm serious. I don't think the Knight Princess is a big enough idea yet, and it has to be ready in two months. You should see the stuff everyone else in the program is working on. Most of them are older, like college age, and then there's me . . . a high schooler who got lucky with his cute idea. I need to prove I deserve to be there."

My hand warms inside of Grant's. We have so much in common, even our fears.

"Maybe we can help each other," I say.

"Sounds like you and me are fate after all," he says, grinning.

Thunder rolls as rain slaps the deck outside. Grant doesn't look away from me. More importantly, he hasn't moved his hand yet. I order myself to keep breathing.

I can't even nod, I want to kiss him so badly.

Do we kiss? Now feels like the time to kiss.

Grant blinks first. Standing, he says, "Come with me somewhere." He holds out his hand, that pretty bracelet dangling off his wrist so gently. Dad said to be back home by eleven, but Grant wants me to come with him, and I won't let that chance slip away.

We dash into the storm—no umbrellas, no jackets. The only responsible thing I do is lock up the yacht, but once that key is in my pocket, my body surrenders to whatever Grants has in mind. He runs down the dock to the shore. I follow. In the rain, Grant's mop of curls flattens into a messy curtain around his face. We're already drenched, our darling date clothes clinging dangerously to our various curves and angles. The rain has vacuum-sealed Grant's shirt to his torso—and I want to tear it off him.

Every other thought but that one leaves my brain.

Lightning strobes over Lake Michigan. The Chicago skyline—my familiar, childhood skyline—illuminates in the night. A count of four-Mississippi later, thunder cracks slowly like Velcro being pulled apart.

Grant howls with laughter. My leg muscles burn to keep up with him as he barrels out of the Yacht Club lot. "I'm not as tall as you, wait up!" I shout through the storm. "Don't make me chase you through the city again!"

He spins to me on the road but doesn't slow down. He jogs backward and hollers, "I thought you liked chasing me!"

He's right.

Another thunderclap shakes the sky. Grant runs over and pulls me close. Rain spills down his face onto me. His lips shimmer in the moonlight. He lowers himself closer . . .

Then stops.

He grins. "We're kissing tonight, but not yet. Gotta do it right."

Relief strikes me as hard as the rain. "You better."

He pulls me onward through a monsoon that refuses to relent. We stroll, arms wrapped around each other's sopping waists, until we reach refuge under the awnings outside Michigan Avenue storefronts. Shoppers dash from doorways into waiting cabs and Ubers, shrieking happily as they cover their heads with their purchases.

Grant and I catch our breath, but we don't let go of each other.

Even holding his clothed waist feels risky. My head rests on his shoulder, almost tucked into the crook of his arm. "Should we get an umbrella somewhere?" I ask.

Grant laughs, his chest vibrating under my cheek. "Why? So we don't get wet?"

We travel uptown, from awning to awning, each footfall launching a pool of rainwater into the sky. Wherever he's leading me, he's too confident to be lost.

Finally, on a quieter street near Old Town, he guides me to the rear entrance of a brick warehouse. I wait—and tremble in the rain—at the foot of the fire escape while Grant talks to an elegantly dressed woman at the door. Whatever he's saying, she's laughing.

They know each other.

Anyone who meets Grant instantly falls in love with him.

The woman opens the rear entrance, and Grant leads me inside, his hand never leaving mine. In the darkened space, dreamy classical music fills the air. Ponderous, lighthearted strings. Clusters of people huddle together and stare at brick walls. Cerulean blue lights strobe against them. It has to be some kind of underground, cool people-only club.

Then I recognize it—*America Windows*.

Chagall's bright blue masterpiece of stained glass he gifted to the Art Institute.

An immersive projection splashes over the entire room. The swirling angels and menorahs from the piece are almost as big as me. Marvelous, miraculous splotches of yellow and white amid the vast waves of blue. We're surrounded by art. Swallowed by its enormity. The masterpiece itself dances across my open palm— the one Grant isn't clutching.

In the center of the room, he holds me.

No kissing, just a firm embrace as rain collects in droplets on the floor around us.

I don't worry about what's going to happen or what I should be doing. Instead, my chest is flooded with a curious, new emotion I can't name. But it feels like . . . adulthood. I'm not here with parents or friends. No one knows where I am.

Something new is happening. Something fun. Scary fun.

With a *whoosh* on the soundtrack and a whirl of color, the painting changes. The room brightens into shades of pink and powder blue. Monet's *Wheatstacks*. Another Art Institute selection.

"Do you like it?" Grant asks.

"Yes" is all I can say.

Powerful hands turn me to face him. Rain hangs from his eyelashes like morning dew. "I wanted to take you here on date two," he admits, his confidence departing. "But if I only had one shot tonight, I didn't want to miss showing you."

"There's gonna be a date two."

Grant looks away, but only for a moment. "I've got, like, a hex on me. I get ghosted. Or I pick a straight one. Or they leave. I'm not in the habit of assuming there'll be a date two."

Pink light swims over Grant as the painting changes again. He's boyish in this light. Those hurt eyes, begging me not to hurt him further.

"You're the first boy I ever asked out," I say, squeezing his hand. "At least you had the guts to do that."

He shakes his head. "Not in a while. In April, I told my friend I was done. I wasn't gonna get fooled again. That's why I didn't ask you out on the train." His eyes dart away in shame. After a hard swallow, he admits, "My friend sent me your post almost right after we got separated. The one where you were looking for me. I could've messaged you. I let you get away, and I'm sorry. I let you do that chasing because . . . I liked seeing someone going to a lot of trouble for me. Like you might stick around."

I hide the shock from my face. He's being so vulnerable, I can't betray that trust by getting angry, or even huffy. All that running around, doubt, and fear; my friends helping on the quest . . . None of it needed to happen. I could've met him *that* night.

But the chase—I loved the chase.

I want to be mad, but I can't. He looks so scared that we're already over.

"You didn't give up," he says, his bass-y voice cracking. "You're this fairy-tale-endings guy, and"—he stops to catch his breath—"I don't believe in that anymore."

I boost myself on tiptoes and close my lips over his.

Under the moody-bright projection of Hopper's *Nighthawks*, two artists share their first kiss, and hopefully, somewhere inside Grant, he starts to believe in fairy tales again.

## Chapter 12
# WISH GRANTED

Not twenty seconds after our first kiss, Grant asks me the unthinkable: "Be my boyfriend?" Fright is etched onto every crease in his face. It's the question I've been dying to ask all night but was preparing to wait months for the appropriate time, whatever that is. But here's Grant—the most genuine, heart-on-the-table boy I've ever met—just putting it out there immediately.

"Yes!" I shout over classical music. I don't want to leave a crumb of doubt.

Grant lets out a single, relieved laugh. "Really?"

"I've been wanting to ask you, but I've never done this before and didn't know how long it usually takes."

"I've asked dates right away. I've asked after months. It's never the right time."

Snorting, he glances away with a bitter sneer, but I guide him by his chin back into my eyes. "Never the right time, only the right guy."

He melts like caramel. We kiss again, his hands cupping my face. The second kiss is even more powerful than the first. During the first kiss, my senses couldn't keep up with the shock of so much newness. The second time around, the uniqueness of his kiss becomes clearer. His signature—the stronger scents: *cologne*, *strawberries*, and *wintermint*. These are ones he intended me to taste, but there's subtler notes underneath he did not intend: *sweat*, *salt*, and *spit*.

These scents run deeper. They're native to him.

"Are you gonna sketch this moment?" Grant asks, pressing his forehead to mine.

"Oh," I whisper. "I left my stuff on the *Enchanted Lady*."

The music changes from the reflective strings accompanying *Nighthawks* to a livelier tune matching the newest projection: the warm pub lights of Toulouse-Lautrec's *At the Moulin Rouge*. It's as if Audrey's magically erupted all around us!

"This needs to be our first picture as a couple," I say, opening my camera. Grant squats to meet my height until our cheeks are smooshed together, the *Moulin Rouge* wall framed perfectly above us. I snap the picture quickly—I want it to almost look like a candid. No typical Micah overthinking. No fixing our hair or blotting our sweat-and-rain-dampened faces.

Our smiles are relaxed and genuine.

Two boys—worn out from so many failed dates—have found each other and can finally rest. Their quest is complete. Their wishes were granted.

I want to post the picture to Instaloves. I won't be anonymous anymore.

Tonight is about breaking rules!

"You'd do that for me?" Grant asks as I load the picture. To answer his question, I kiss him again. My hands feel bloodless, slick from a cold fear sweat, but I'm undaunted. Grant's kiss has given me a reckless confidence, like when Hannah and I got drunk sneaking a bottle of her father's vintage cabernet.

"Yes," I say, and smile.

We decide that #WishGranted should be our official relationship hashtag. Cringeworthy, yes, but I've spent my whole life avoiding embarrassment. The new Micah is doing all the corny stuff I want to do. Accelerate into the awk!

I post our selfie to Instaloves with just #WishGranted and Grant's name. No flowery caption, just us: the fantasy come to life.

Grant laces his fingers into mine and leads me out the way we came. "I was hoping you'd like the gallery," he whispers into my hair.

"I love it," I whisper.

"We're going to make beautiful art together . . ."

I press my cheek to his neck and moan pleasantly. What a thought. We *will* make beautiful art together, collaborating on his Knight Princess design and maybe even my mural. After tonight, anything is possible!

When the rear door opens, it's as if he's brought me to another, more stunning gallery: the skyline, alight and sparkling in the rain—which has slowed to a scant drizzle. The city is the background, and we are its subjects, gliding down the stairs without any thoughts other than how we can put our hands on each other as soon as possible.

We barely make it to the street before Grant turns to me, his eyes so hypnotically fixed on me that they're almost swirling. I only have time to wet my lips. He walks me backward, presses me against the gallery's brick wall, and feasts on my lips.

He was gentler eating the crepe.

His stubble scrapes against my chin, and sharp, prickling pains alternate between each cotton-soft kiss. *Sharp. Soft. Sharp. Soft.*

It hurts . . . So why do I like it?

I grasp a handful of his curls and pull him deeper into my mouth. I can't catch my breath. My only chance at fresh air comes when I moan. I can't let go of his lips.

Grant runs his hands wildly over my back and torso, yet always staying above my waist. Good thing he's restraining himself, because we're in public, and I'm already hard.

I want to beg Grant to unzip me and touch it.

But I can't. Cinderella's prince never got a painful boner behind an art gallery!

Maybe he did and they just left out that part of the story. They don't tell you that when fairy tales come true, you also have to deal with the realities of your body—and every weird, embarrassing feeling that comes with it.

"Let's get back to the boat," Grant says between more coarse kisses.

"There's cameras on it." I unclasp my prince's collar to catch my breath. Like a vampire, Grant lunges for my freshly exposed throat to relocate his kissing. It feels weird and suction-y, but once again, oddly welcome. A tingly Pop Rocks sensation explodes at each kiss point.

I was supposed to be home by now.

I've been too nervous to look at my phone, even though it's been regularly buzzing the closer we get to midnight. I'm late. They're mad.

Oh well.

Finally, Grant comes up for air. "Come to my room," he says, millimeters from my lips. "*Please.* My roommate is gone the rest of the week."

If I don't stop him soon . . .

Soberly, I touch his chest. *Thwap-thwap-thwap-thwap-thwap,* raps his heartbeat against my hand. We watch each other, our breaths slowing together.

"It's been a night of firsts," I say. "But not for this. Not yet. Okay?" Grant nods bringing himself back to reality. We both smile. "Be my boyfriend?" I ask. Redundant, but I just like hearing the answer.

"Yeah," he breathes, delivering one last kiss to my cheek. He listened.

I creep inside my darkened penthouse, the only light coming from the city sprawl beyond the panoramic window. Bright, twinkling skyscraper lights flare into hazy starbursts in my exhausted eyes. I tiptoe to my room, but no one is awake to scold me.

No one but Maggie.

Her door opens soundlessly, and I gasp. She scans me up and down, Beats headphones swallowing her head. All her lights are on. Her laptop lies open on the bed, Lilith sprawled lazily beside it.

Is Maggie gonna tell me off?

Take pleasure in letting me know how pissed Dad was when I blew his curfew?

With a bright, cheerleading smile, she gives me a silent round of applause. For an eternal, beautiful minute, we dance together in her doorway while Lilith watches, unimpressed. Before crashing into my mattress for the night, I find my *Little Book of Firsts* on the nightstand and triumphantly claim my victory: *First Kiss—6-10-22*.

$$\heartsuit \quad \heartsuit \quad \heartsuit$$

In the morning, I'm not even sure I slept. I slap my hand around on the nightstand for my ChapStick, but it's not there. It must've rolled under the bed. Dammit, I need it. I can barely open my lips. My entire being is as dry as jerky. No thoughts penetrate my brain, which feels crispy, wispy, and coming apart from my head like chicken skin.

Somewhere in my room, my phone won't stop vibrating. The noise is muffled—it must be under the quilt. I probably dropped it in my haste to meet my pillow. I only had enough strength last night to remove my socks and shirt.

I smile weakly as I trace the stubble burns Grant left in a

harsh ring around my lips. It stings, but the pain is sweet. I still smell him.

His hair. His skin. Nothing I could put a name to, other than "Grant."

*Eau de Him.*

Ninety-nine boyfriends came and went through my life, but not a scrap of reality in the bunch. They were sweet, pleasant fairy tales, a cocoon that never let the joy travel beyond the mists of my imagination. Grant brought the fairy tale crashing into reality, and that reality—like water seeking its level—is filling every corner of my life with its inconvenient brutality, sparing nothing.

The kisses burned.

My curfew, annihilated.

My online anonymity, abandoned.

Where is my phone? Somewhere. Where is my ChapStick? Lost. What time is it? What day is it? Do I have somewhere to be? Is someone expecting me? I don't know. I don't care.

Something very big and wild has invaded my life, and I'm not the same Micah Summers I was yesterday. I won't ever be again.

Good.

My phone vibrates again as I stagger upright and remember how to use my legs. I have to sketch something. This need is stronger than finding water, using the bathroom, or thinking of the best way to text Grant *good morning* without looking needy. I haven't been able to stop thinking about his Knight Princess design—and how open he seemed for my artistic input.

Two artist boyfriends working on the same project? Dream of dreams!

The dinner was a blur, so his design only pops into my

memory in bits and pieces. I decide to work with the emotions it gave me: grand fantasy, strength from vulnerability, and deconstructing gender norms.

In the hopeless mess of my bedroom, I locate a spare pencil and an old sketchbook with a few empty pages in the back. Within seconds, I finish a rough outline of the Knight Princess 2.0.

Or, the Knight Princess by Grant Rossi (ft. Micah Summers).

With a few tweaks, Grant's concept becomes something only a goddess would wear: a metal-plated armored bodice accentuating a flowing gown that ends with a long, bride-like train made of a knight's chain mail. I combine a princess's tiara with a knight's helmet to create something fabulously mutant. The rim is loaded with jewels, and the face shields are no longer metal but dark velvet drapes.

Why is it so much easier to execute someone else's vision than to realize your own?

Even if this isn't exactly what fits Grant's vision, maybe it will inspire him.

Plus, it's a perfect morning-after conversation starter. A way to show him that I haven't stopped thinking about him without admitting to such a thing.

Now, where's that phone that won't shut up?

I search my tangled covers for the source of this constant vibration. I'm popular today! Probably a ton of texts from my friends wanting to know how it went—and from my dad, wanting to know what the hell I was thinking coming in so late. As my hand finally closes around the phone under the covers, my door opens with a knock.

Hannah creeps inside wearing a lavender beret, matching

knee-high boots, and holding two Audrey's to-go cups. "Thank youuuuuuu," I say as she hands me a cup.

"Fresh from Elliot," she says, plopping cross-legged onto my bed. "His treat." As I start to protest, she holds up a stopping hand. "I tried to pay. He insisted. It's his way of congratulating you on a fabulous first date."

Elliot is too pure. He really didn't have to.

Hannah sips before getting to business: "So Wish Granted. What a way to come out—again, I mean!"

I bashfully hide behind my empty cup. "You already saw?"

She recoils so quickly, she almost smacks my headboard. "Uh . . . yeah, we all saw."

I swish the hot chai around my mouth and confess: "Grant is . . . everythiiiing." The whole night feels like a dream of a dream. It couldn't really be happening to Micah Summers, the lovelorn Baby Boo-Boo with his head in the clouds and his eyes on his belly button.

"I need more details than this!" Hannah smacks my covers. "That pinkie promise also included the understanding that I'd be first to receive a full report." Before I can respond, Hannah's eyes widen in shock. She points right at me. "You got love bites on your neck!"

Oh no.

Ignoring millions of notifications of missed calls and texts, I open my front-facing camera and shriek. A faint rash covers my chin—Grant's stubble indeed tore me up. On top of that, two wide bruises pockmark my jawline and throat.

Hickeys.

I slap my hand over the marks, but it's too late: Hannah has seen everything. She pulls me into a joyous hug. "Ohhhhhh, I'm so happy, my best friend is so nasty!"

I howl laughter into her shoulder. "I really was! He was sweet and funny and handsome and confident and into me"—giggles overtake us—"and he asked me to be his boyfriend"—she gasps—"and we made out so long"—she cheers—"and he asked me to come over to his place, his dorm or whatever. Like, he was *begging* me, Hannah"—she squeals under breath—"but I, uh, I need more time, which he was such a gentleman about."

Hannah high-fives me to death.

I can't stop smiling. After years of hearing sexy stories like this from her, I finally have my own. The divide I placed between us after that dance has finally closed.

Insisting I fill in more details later, Hannah departs with a mysterious plea: "Call Grant before checking any other messages. Don't look at Instaloves until you talk to him. Trust me."

"Okay," I say, lobbing the empty chai into my waste bin. "But, why—?"

"Just trust me, bye!"

*Bizarre.*

I can't "just" cold-call Grant. There needs to be a text intro-duction . . . and my updated Knight Princess drawing is the perfect way to do it. I brush my hair, change into a fresh tank top, and then snap a photo of myself holding the design. *Yikes, those hickeys are rough.* Grant was hungry last night. I sing *"That boy is a monster"* under my breath as I FaceApp retouch the kiss rash and hickeys . . . as well as the sleepy circles under my eyes.

There! My picture has become impossibly fresh and so, so rested. How *does* she do it?

I text the pic to Grant with a simple, not overwhelmingly long message: gm Boy 100. Throw away this message if I'm being too forward, but I haven't stopped thinking about the Knight Princess and how you're trying to make it bigger. Here's a quick sketch I did of some ideas—like I said, maybe we can help each other? And if you don't need any more ideas rn, pls just enjoy this pic of my face.

What if he doesn't text back? What if he hates it? What if—?

I don't languish long.

The FaceTime call from Grant comes immediately. The thrill skyrocketing through my chest is soon replaced with a plummeting dread.

IF I PICK UP, HE WILL SEE MY GNAWED FACE AND KNOW I FIXED THE PIC.

*Well, Micah, he's the one who did the gnawing. Don't leave him hanging.*

I swirl my quilt around my hickeyed neck like a cozy lil' cape and answer the call: "That was fast, I—"

But Grant is too hyperactive to let me finish. "Oh my God, Micah, can you believe it?!"

He can barely catch his breath. He's walking outside—the video angle is low, like he's taking me on the go. Even from this unflattering angle, Grant remains the handsomest boy who ever lived. He even has a small hickey of his own on his neck, so I guess he's not the only beast.

"It's so exciting!" he huffs before waving to someone off-camera. "Hey, Elise!"

"Grant, oh my *God*," calls the faint voice of this Elise person. "What is *happening*?"

"I wish I could explain." Grant laughs. "I'm late for my one-on-one with Tamiko!"

"I'm buying you coffee later, and you're gonna tell me everything!"

"If I get done in time, sure!"

With that, Grant refuses to explain to Elise—or to me—what's happening that has him so keyed up. He pulls his screen into an extreme close-up and confesses, "Elise is the meanest person. She is so fake. Never had five seconds for me before, but now she's buying *me* coffee? Wow, I'm gonna enjoy this."

My fingers fidget worse by the second. What's happening? And is he not even going to mention my drawing? Was it rude of me to send?

"That sounds annoying," I say. "But yay, I'm so happy for you?"

"Graaaaaaaaaant!" another off-screen voice shouts as he hurries across the street.

After smiling and waving, he pulls me close again. "There's another one! You should've seen me yesterday on campus—big nobody. Now I'm like a local superhero, and my phone is blowing up—"

"Grant, stop walking!" I blurt. If I didn't interrupt him, I was going to explode.

He does as he's told. His camera angle becomes beautifully, peacefully normal. His cheeks flush rosily from rushing around in this heat. "Are you okay?" he asks.

"I'm sorry if I'm making you late for your meeting—"

"Don't worry. I can be a little late. I was just saying that to show up Elise."

I allow myself a deep breath. *Don't be anxious, Micah. Don't be snippy.* "First, I want to say that last night was amazing, and you look really cute."

"It was great! You look cute too. Really sexy. Is that a blanket around your neck . . . ?"

I cinch my quilt tighter. "Secondly, I'm sorry I sent that Knight Princess drawing without asking if you wanted my help—"

"I haven't sat down to look at it yet, but I'm excited! That was sweet of you. I'd love to work with you on creative ideas and stuff—and help you meet the right people at the Institute! I wanted to look at it once I'm able to give it the time you deserve."

The lines of tension gripping my forehead since the beginning of this chaotic call finally loosen. He wants to collaborate. He wants to help me realize my dreams. He thinks I deserve undivided attention. He thinks I'm sexy.

He . . . still hasn't explained himself.

"So," I ask, "why are you suddenly so popular that you've got all these meanies warming up to you?"

His eyes bug out. "What do you mean?! You haven't gotten any messages?"

"I've gotten a million messages but didn't read any of them. I just woke up."

Grant laughs devilishly. "Micah. Just read the messages." Like Hannah, Grant is behaving so cryptically. "Actually, wait. The texts might confuse you more. Open Instagram. Don't read any notifications. Just search the hashtag #WishGranted."

An even larger smile dawns on my face. Grant kisses me through the screen, and I kiss back. It's only been a day, but we have such a comfortable rhythm with each other, even these little screen kisses feel like we've known each other our whole lives.

This is what it's like when the universe puts two puzzle pieces together!

"Text me later," he says, and the call ends.

My heart is going to smash through my chest with one more minute of suspense.

My trembling fingers search the hashtag, and all at once, I'm bombarded with the picture I knew I was going to find: our selfie from last night. However, looking at it now, it's clear just how many people were waiting to hear how the Boy 100 story ended and to learn the identity of the mysterious celebrity's son behind it all. #WishGranted is everywhere. Our picture is everywhere. Countless people shared it: my celebrity supporters . . . my dad's radio station . . . several Olympians . . . the producer of Dad's Satan movie . . . But mainly, it looks to have gained the most steam from simply regular people giving the picture—and my Instaloves sketches—hundreds of thousands of shares on Instagram and TikTok.

Overnight, my Instaloves followers have doubled.

The original post is already in the millions.

Not only are we officially a couple, we're a famous couple.

## Chapter 13
# THE GIFTS

You're slipping. You're about to fall hundreds of feet to the rocks below.

But your dashing hero made it just in time. He reaches for you, asks you to take his hand, asks you to trust him. Do you?

Two weeks later, everything is different.

Grant and I have progressed from new boyfriends to serious ones. After sharing two of the most fiercely intimate moments of my life—once on the train when we met, the other as we held each other in the art gallery—thinking about him still sends goose bumps across my arms. I'm no longer afraid that whenever we say goodbye, he'll somehow change his mind and get over me. My trust in him grows with each date, and we're seeing each other every day: rock climbing (I didn't plummet to my death!), gorgeous patio lunches, making out, late nights discussing his Knight Princess design, more making out. While it feels fast, every moment is completely natural. Preordained. I have found my artistic twin. I'm not going to slow things down because society says so. It feels right, so I say faster—more.

Apparently, the internet agrees.

My fantasy sketches of Grant gain me hordes of new followers with each post. Sadly, there's been an unfortunate downside to Instaloves no longer being anonymous: these sketches are taking me five times as long to get right. I'm so much more *aware* of the eyes on my work now. I second-guess so many more choices. Instaloves has always been where I could charge ahead, fully creatively alive, and spit something out. What if being in a happy relationship erodes my vision, and Instaloves ends up as stifled as my mural?

That can't—and won't—happen, because Grant is an artist like me! I know in my gut that being with Grant—whatever temporary setbacks I'm feeling—will ultimately lead me to a truer, stronger artistic voice.

Whatever that is.

Despite all my nerves, my followers are still loving what I'm putting out, seeing me progress from a series of failed crushes to happily ever after. I set up a Wish Granted email and PO Box because my DMs broke from people sending their hard-luck love stories and thank-yous for keeping them believing. The gallery behind Immersive Art Institute even sent us a tower of goodies from Milk Bar for giving them so much free press. Their three-tiered strawberry shortcake smoothed things over with my dad, who agreed not to press charges on me after I came home way past curfew.

"Mail lady!" Mom hollers as she lugs grocery bags full of mail into the kitchen.

"I could've gotten those," I say, already riffling through piles of letters, cards, and boxes.

"I don't want anyone taking a picture of you grabbing fan mail," Mom says, exasperated. "If people know you personally pick it up, they'll show up in the lobby trying to get you!"

"Mom, that's really not helping my anxiety about going public."

As I open today's mail, Maggie, Manda, and the cat rush into the living room to see what new shenanigans have arrived. They're both in matching emerald green bathrobes that Manda had monogrammed with *M & M* on the pocket. Manda circles around me to happily ladle Crunch Berries into a bowl. When my sister finds the mail sacks, the color drains from her face. "*Still?*" she asks. "All these letters are for you? What are you, Santa?"

"It's about time we had a twink reboot of Santa," Manda says, picking up a thick stack of envelopes as she crunches dry cereal.

"Timothée Chalamet already beat me out for the part," I say, taking the envelopes back.

Manda frowns and says, "Aw," as my mother fidgets nervously. "I don't like everyone touching the letters," she says. "Put them aside until your dad and I figure out what to do."

"Why?" I ask, pulling the letters protectively to my chest.

"Why?" Mom snorts. "Anthrax. Poison. It could be a severed finger. You don't know!"

Maggie and I groan in unison. Manda's jaw hangs open, frozen in repulsion. "Mom," I say patiently, "they're just nice words from people who are really excited for me and Grant. You should read some of them—"

"I already do!"

"Then you should know how sweet they are." I corral the bags into my arms. "But I'll let you know if I find a toe."

Maggie and Manda share a stifled giggle as Mom's lips tighten. "You think I don't know *exactly* what it's like to have your exciting new relationship become famous?" she asks. "I was dating *the* Jeremy Summers. He'd been with models. Actresses. Then came me, the med student who didn't know one designer label from another. People were furious! Someone mailed me a pig fetus!"

"*Jesus*, Mom," I yelp.

In shock, Manda stops crunching, but Maggie just rolls her eyes. "That didn't happen."

"Ask your father!" Mom says, jabbing a finger as she leaves to her room. "Wish Granted is exciting. We are thrilled for you, but be careful. This is the Fame Monster. Right? Lady Gaga?"

"I guess?" I can't keep the flummoxed look from my face.

"Okay, we'll leave you to your pig fetuses," Manda says, carrying her bowl to Maggie. Looking like two old-timey dads in their silken robes, they lock elbows and traipse back to their room.

"Exciting day planned?" I ask Maggie.

"*Relaxing* day," my sister says, glancing back. "A relaxing day of pampering."

"Ah, another of those."

"You should try it with Grant sometime," Manda says through a mouth of crunchy cereal. "It can't be epic quests every day!"

With a final pitying glance, I stop myself from saying, "Wanna bet?" I'll let them have their seven millionth cozy day. Me and Grant have too many adventures ahead of us.

Despite all my high hopes, moody reclusiveness takes over the rest of my afternoon. The sun begins to set over Lake Michigan outside my panoramic window as I curl under my covers and read a link Hannah texted me. She and Elliot were interviewed by PopClique, a splashy pop culture blog, about their role in Wish Granted and keeping the identity behind Instaloves a secret.

Interviews *about* me? This is really getting big.

Is Maggie right? Is this *too* big for me to handle? I love that my art is getting recognized, and I know I need to get more comfortable sharing myself if I'm going to make it to the Art Institute and beyond . . . But does my body know that?

My stomach clenches the moment I tap the link:

## MEET THE MAGICAL MICE BEHIND WISH GRANTED'S FAIRY-TALE ENDING

An excerpt from the PopClique exclusive interview with the Fairy-Tale Prince of Chicago's Best Friends, Hannah Bergstrom and Elliot Tremaine.

**ELLIOT:** Micah is the prince with the big dreams, but we're the backbone. No matter what quest you're undertaking, you need friends believing in you to keep you moving! (laughs) We're sort of the best.

**HANNAH:** (laughs) Totally best. We really did see ourselves as the helper mice in this quest. Fairy tales have always been such a big part of Micah's life. Having him take on the real-life role of Prince Charming helped him believe this was all going to work out in the end.

**POPCLIQUE:** Micah didn't always believe he'd get his fairy-tale ending?

**ELLIOT:** It's romance. If you don't have doubts, you're fooling yourself! That's what people respond to about Instaloves: seeing this person fail ninety-nine times but win the hundredth. That's what I loved about it before I even knew Micah. To be like, "Here I am. I tried, it flopped, but I'm keeping going." Determination is everything!

I stop reading. My stomach acid won't allow me to go farther. Elliot thought I was a flop?

*No, dummy. He thought you were cool for dusting yourself off every time!*

I can't believe how different Elliot and Grant are. Grant felt so cursed by his relationship failures, he couldn't even reach out to me once he saw my Instagram post. But I can't picture anything in the world keeping Elliot down for long. I smile—he thinks we're the same type of person. Someone who doesn't stay down after a punch. I've never felt that cool or strong, but I guess I am. I never gave up on finding Grant.

Elliot is like this mirror that only reflects the most amazing version of you.

Seized with a new energy, I toss my phone aside and pick up my sketchbook.

I don't know what I'm going to sketch, but when I shut my eyes, my hand begins to move across the page. The moment I do, the image appears: Elliot and Brandon, swimming together on their magical date. Elliot's happy memory I asked him to cling to until we could reignite their spark. *Swish, swish, swish*—my hand flies across the page, and the fantasy emerges from Elliot's memory: he and Brandon become two mermaids! Brandon—tall and lean—carries Elliot—small and curvy—through the sea, backstroking together like a pair of lovable otters.

A grin blooms on my face.

Damn! This is the fastest a sketch has flown out of me in weeks. I guess I haven't lost my vision just yet. Thanks, Elliot.

I'll take a few extra days to color and give it that final polish before gifting it to Elliot. This sketch won't go to Instaloves—it's just for him. Hopefully, it'll make his happy memories easier to hang on to. If anyone deserves a fairy-tale ending, it's him.

♡  ♡  ♡

That night, Grant and I meet in his dorm for a hangout-slash-art session. Grant owes his revised design of the Knight Princess by the end of the week, which means major crunch time. I've brought along my sketchbook so I can update the Elliot mermaid—and doodle new concepts to help Grant.

Even though he's asked me twice to help with the Knight Princess (and after two weeks of being his official boyfriend), I continue to be filled with self-consciousness about becoming too pushy. But being here, in the Art Institute—the palace where I could one day learn from masters and push my painting boundaries—surges my confidence.

Grant's dorm is plain and beige, yet the moment I stepped inside, I felt an entire world waiting for me. Lo-fi beats fill the room as my boyfriend hunches over his desk, reframing silhouette lines on a Surface Studio tablet. I'm sprawled on his twin bed behind him, shading Elliot's mermaid fin with different violet tones. The wall above Grant's twin bed is covered in various Knight Princess sketches. Dozens of discarded versions. Taped in the center is a printout of the one I drew for him.

I smile. "Do you think my sketch will help? With the Knight Princess?"

Not looking up, Grant drafts another line on an armored bodice and asks, "Hmm? Oh, for sure! Honestly, it really helps having you here. I've been freaking out. There's been no time to even think about the Knight Princess all week. My head is exploding with this Wish Granted attention and . . . you." He glances back to shoot me a dimple. It's too powerful for me to look at directly, so I continue gazing at his sketches. "I've gotta keep my head in the game, because the show is six weeks away and suddenly everyone is dying to see what I'm working on."

"Oh yeah?"

"Oh my God, Wish Granted changed everything. Nobody cared about the Knight Princess before. Now everyone in my class wants lunch with me. It's a lot, but it's . . ." He sets down his pen and takes a calming breath. "It could be really good for me, you know? All this. I can finally stand out here."

"You deserve it! I'm here to help."

We share a soft smile, and I relax further into his bed. We both share the same fears of this really amazing, positive relationship slowing our creative motors down. And he's not nervous to share what's going on in his head. It comforts me knowing I comfort him.

"Actually"—Grant glances back—"never mind."

I sit straighter. "What?"

He bites his lip. "Well, I noticed that the two times you've posted pictures of us to Instaloves, it's done amazing numbers. Maybe . . . would you ever think about alternating sketches with pics of us working on designs? Maybe tagging the Institute too? It could be really good for both of us if the numbers keep taking off like they have been!"

My feet hit the ground as my back stiffens. "Oh . . ."

Grant must see the shock in my face, because he immediately waves me away. "Forget I said anything. It's your account!"

What I don't say is *You don't know me well yet, but I've already majorly changed my account once for you and that was nerve-racking enough!*

But I'm still figuring out what I want Instaloves to be now, so maybe my boundaries have to be pushed again.

"Actually, your idea makes a lot of sense," I say brightly. Buoyed by my agreement, Grant shifts around to face me. "I've been figuring out where I want to take Instaloves now that, you know, I'm not sketching crushes anymore. I'll play around with it!"

Beaming, Grant returns to work. He's perfect.

As he focuses, mine falters. My beautiful boyfriend is wearing a black tank top, the same as me, but his broad chest fills it out more impressively. I've never seen his arms and shoulders this bare before—smooth and round, but somehow soft-looking. These last two weeks have been filled with blissful kissing and petting, but it feels like we've been building up to something more. A new quest, one where both our anticipations have been growing.

Now that we're alone in his dorm, it feels right. I want to go further.

"Where's your roommate again?" I ask, shielding my erection with my sketchbook.

"Switzerland with her family," he says, eyes still on his work. His biceps pump as he draws—they're like giant car pistons. His joggers dip low, exposing a furry patch of skin above his ass. His feet—bare, smooth, and wide—fidget beneath his seat.

Let's make him forget his deadline.

"Hey," I say in a low, serious voice. As I hoped, my change in tone alerts him. He turns . . .

I'm spread across his bed, wiggling my toes. Right away, his gaze locks on to exactly what I want him to be looking at. His pen drops carelessly to the desk as his chest bounces with sharp, shallow breaths. That predatory gleam returns to his large, glistening eyes, so much like the lion who tried to devour me outside the art gallery when I wasn't ready.

But I'm ready now.

"Lock the door first," I order him. He powers down his Surface, and as he crosses the room to shut us in snugly, I notice he's already as hard as I am.

We need mood lighting. Candles would've been nice if I prepared, but I'm resourceful in a pinch. I toss a few of his roommate's throws over the bedside and desk lamps, casting an amber glow across the otherwise beige, penitentiary-like walls. Through the flickering darkness, Grant towers overhead, his powerful arms moments away from snatching me—although he looks as frightened as I feel, as if we're about to skydive.

"Have you ever done this before?" I ask.

"Yes," he admits on a shallow breath.

"You look nervous."

He swallows. "I've never done this with *you* before."

Well, if that isn't the most perfect thing he could've said.

I drag him down into a kiss. He peels off my tank and lowers me flat against the mattress. On my back, I breathe deeply, trying to quickly prepare myself for whatever is next. Terror briefly shoots through my chest: *He's going to be on top of me. He's such a big guy; is it going to hurt? His dick is going to be in me. What if it really hurts, and I need him to stop?*

The bedsprings creak as he mounts it. In the dim light, all I can see are his curls, his bare, built chest, and the lamplight flickering in his wet eyes.

"Do you have a curfew?" he whispers.

"I want to stay the night." It takes all my strength to make it a statement, not a question.

Grant crawls closer to me, and I can finally see his soft, dark features. "Don't worry, we're not going full enchilada right away." We erupt into giggles, and I can finally breathe. Grant boops my nose. "And don't worry if it doesn't happen tonight."

"No! I want to—"

"Oh, we're gonna have fun, but sometimes, it takes a few tries until your body is ready."

I nod, my trust in Grant blossoming by the second. He grinds into me, and I pump my hips into him. I momentarily stop breathing—whether from fear or anticipation, I can't tell.

"It'll hurt?" I ask.

He shakes his head. "Not this." His hands move down my torso and hook my waistband. "Just tap me if you get scared."

I smile. I'm safe with him.

Grant pries off my shorts, freeing me of my final layer of clothing—and the final layer of Old Micah. The second Grant's curly head disappears below my waist, I lose all fear about any of this hurting. Pleasure jolts through me, into me, and I arch my back to brace against the shock waves.

The fairy tales *definitely* don't cover this part, but honestly, they should. Romance is all about the trust fall, and in my short two weeks with Grant, this is the scariest and most rewarding trust fall we've faced! I want to go back in time and scream to scared little Old Micah about how much closer he's going to feel with Grant after this.

How was I *ever* worried about pain? There must be a

homophobic conspiracy at play to make a gay boy so worried!

When we finish, Grant and I agree to save the full enchilada for another night—not because I'm not ready but because I want to draw out these moments—this newness—as long as possible. I drop back to his mattress, spent, gasping for air, and wonderfully fuzzy-headed. At last, I have what I've always wanted: a handsome prince with a pillowy chest to rest my head on.

As Grant begins to snore, my soul floats above my body. He made sure I felt okay. He cared if I was too nervous. I'm important to him. Smiling to myself, his chest hairs tickling my nose, I let go of consciousness and everything that used to be.

## Chapter 14
# THE MOUSE

In the morning, waking up in a strange bed, on top of the warmest boy in history, is pleasantly disorienting. Grant's dark curls look even more beautiful when they're mussed free of product. His eyes flutter open, and my heart lifts realizing my opportunity is finally here:

"Good morning, handsome," I whisper.

*First Time Waking Up Next to a Boy*—one for the *Little Book*.

"Morning, cutie," he says, grinning. His bedsprings squeak as he unwraps his arm from under me and stretches his long frame like a cat. His hand slaps down onto a box of Milk Bar cookies like he's punching an alarm clock. He breaks a large cookie in two and feeds me half. "It's funny, eating in bed with you like this," Grant says, licking cookie bits off his thumb. I curl back to him. "When we made those crepes, I ate such little bites." His cheeks glow red.

"I was scared to scarf them in front of you because I know I can really wolf down a plate."

"Yeah?" I giggle.

"Ten people in my house growing up. You had to guard your meal and eat fast, or you'd be out of luck."

I bite my lower lip. "I noticed you cutting small pieces, so I cut mine smaller."

"Yeah?" Giggling, he rakes his fingers gently through my hair. I get five percent calmer.

"I'm happy you're comfortable eating how you want in front of me now. It sucks how we feel like we have to hide that on a date, like we're people who don't eat. Everybody eats."

"I know." His bass-y voice, so gentle and low, could lull me back to sleep.

"Also, this is embarrassing . . ." I cover my eyes. He pokes me in the small of my back until I answer. "I didn't go to the bathroom during our date. Any of our dates." Grant wheezes out a *puhhhh* laugh. "I didn't want you thinking that I go to the bathroom."

Grant screws up his face in disgust. "You go to the *bathroom*?"

"I know, it's a thing I do. It's horrible."

Groaning, he pokes my chest. "Get out of my bed! Disgusting little bathroom boy!"

"All right, I'll go," I moan, climbing out of his bed, hunched like a mortified dog.

"Where do you think you're going, toilet twink?" With one yank of his powerful arm, he pulls me back down to him. We giggle as his cheap bedsprings bounce beneath us.

Perfect boy is perfect.

We stare at each other, our noses a centimeter apart, as

morning sun rays cut through the room, illuminating the dust particles dancing midair.

With a tugging on my heart, I ask, "I feel safe with you. Do you feel safe with me?"

"What do you mean?" he asks. But I think he knows—his face hardens with worry.

"Do you still feel hexed? Did I break the curse?"

Grant's eyes glass over, as if he's mentally teleporting out of my arms, back in time, to whenever, wherever, and with whoever made him feel so cursed. Just as I begin to worry that I've put him off and ruined our First Morning Waking Up Together, he blinks and returns a soft smile. "If you can't break my curse, nobody can."

He kisses me.

While that sounded sweet, he didn't answer my question.

*His hurt runs deep, Micah. It's not gonna go away easily.*

My parents were livid when I didn't come home last night, but Maggie covered for me—at least partially—by lying that I'd told her where I was going to be. In reality, she checked the Family Finder app and saw that my location dot didn't leave the Art Institute all night. The following morning, my parents march into my room and ask bluntly if I'm having sex with Grant.

"We asked your sister the same questions when she started seeing Manda," Dad blurts, shielding his face as if I were going to hurl a pillow at him for his insolence.

As I attempt to vanish into my hands, Mom says, "You're old

enough to make your own choices. We just have three rules. One: we get to *meet him*. We'll arrange a day this week to have him over for dinner."

"Done," I say, hugging my knees to my chin. A million fireflies swarm my chest at the exciting—yet terrifying—concept of Grant being in my house, meeting my family.

"Two," Dad says. "You do not spend the night somewhere else without telling us again. And telling your sister doesn't count."

I dig my chin farther into my knees when my dad says "again." All I've been able to think about is being with Grant again, but his roommate came back this morning. We'll have to think of a new situation that works for us.

"Lastly," Mom says with a pointed tone. She clears her throat before continuing: "You are coming with me to your GP to discuss PrEP—"

"Aw, Jesus—" I drag my pillow over my face. Maybe I can smother myself sitting up.

"I am a doctor, and you are sexually active—"

"I can't talk to Dr. Walcott about this," I say into my pillow. She's been my doctor since I had chicken pox when I was four. How am I supposed to talk to her about my sexual activity and HIV prevention medication?

Mom removes the pillow from my face with two sharp tugs. "Well, you're a big boy choice-maker now, so you have to."

"What's PrEP?" Dad asks cluelessly. Maybe I could tunnel my way out of this room.

"I'll walk you through it later," Mom says, flitting him away with both hands. "Micah doesn't need to see your reaction."

On that blessing, they finally leave me alone. All in all, the talk could've been worse.

The next week flies by as June turns into July. Every moment I can, I spend with Grant—being with him feels like I'm living in some impossible dream. Although it's murder finding places where we can be private once his roommate is back, we still find pockets of time to be together. When the full enchilada finally happens, it is painful, but by that point, I feel so safe and trusting with Grant that I let him slowly guide me through it. He promises that each time, the pain gets less. It isn't even pain so much as a startling, funny feeling, having someone else connected inside of you.

But connected we are.

When my family meets Grant for dinner, he knocks it out of the park, despite his intense nerves. It feels really fast to be hitting all these milestones right away, but it also feels correct. Preordained. Grant and I have both been denied these firsts for so long, maybe the universe is playing a quick game of catch-up. My *Little Book of Firsts* explodes with new entries: *First time meeting my parents: 7-1-22*. I write the next date after it, even though it's still a week away: *First anniversary: 1 month! 7-7-22*. One month from the first time we met on the train—and I never thought I'd see him again.

Whatever I plan for this, it must be leveled up.

As Fourth of July approaches, Hannah texts me about making holiday plans to hang with Elliot. As his name appears on my phone, my smile gets a bittersweet edge: I haven't heard from Elliot nearly as often as I did during the quest. I've been so wrapped up in Grant, I forgot I promised Elliot that I'd help him whip together a special date with Brandon.

That's okay! he responds when I text my apologies. You're having so many adventures with Grant (and probably overwhelmed with all this attention). Everything you deserve. I'm doing clopens at Audrey's all holiday weekend (hehehe for the rich boys in the room, clopen means back-to-back closing and opening shifts). Stop by if you get time!

As usual, Elliot's kindhearted words solidify the ground under my feet again.

It's time for Elliot's fairy-tale ending.

As I shower, puzzle pieces of the Elliot-and-Brandon date begin snapping into place: *music . . . a picnic, but somehow bigger . . . something to convince Brandon to make room in his schedule . . . something where Elliot is center stage, not making food, but being served . . .*

The festival.

The Taste of Chicago festival begins after the holiday weekend. It spans both Millennium and Grant Park, there's tons of food, and my dad does a remote broadcast from a booth there every year. Elliot said Brandon dropped everything when he found out he was invited to my home to meet my dad. Maybe I can make that magic happen twice!

I text Elliot the broad strokes of the plan: a scavenger hunt for Brandon to follow throughout the Taste of Chicago, which will lead him to a surprise picnic lunch in Grant Park with Elliot and a live show from Jeremy Summers.

THAT WOULD BE AMAZING!!!! he responds, agreeable as ever.

As soon as you can, email me a list of your favorite memories with Brandon, I reply. No wrong answers. Just favorite foods, special things you've shared together, inside jokes. I'll use these to write the scavenger hunt clues.

I'll send it tonight! Thank you!!!

Elliot is working on the Fourth of July, as well as the day after, and my one-month anniversary with Grant is on the seventh, so we lock in the sixth for the big day.

Three days from now.

Do you really think we can get this together in time? he messages.

Watch me, I reply.

The day before Elliot's scavenger hunt date, I realize I'm off the hook for planning my one-month anniversary with Grant. I don't want you planning ANYTHING, Grant texts. It's my turn to woo you. I've been planning something all week! Okay, now forget I said anything.

Sitting on a barstool in Hannah's family kitchen, I smoosh my phone to my chest and throw my head back in literal ecstasy. What could Grant be planning that would require weeks of preparation? A trip? Is he designing me something?

Oh my God, if he's *making* me something!

Hannah's family condo is laid out identical to ours, just half the size and a few floors below. Potted palms, tropical accent pillows, and opaque, flowing drapes give the Bergstrom home the feeling of an expensive Miami hotel. Perched on a high stepladder, Hannah frantically fixes entries on a chalkboard that spans the width of her kitchen's back wall. The entries are divided by family members—*Mom*, *Dad*, *Hannah*, and *Red Velvet* (their dog), then categorized by duties—*Work*, *School*, *College Prep*, *Exercise*, *Self-Care*, *Spirituality*, and *Health*.

The chalkboard covers only a single day, and categories are broken down across each hour, many times in fifteen-minute increments. Hannah cleans the ghost of a chalk stain from her row in the self-care column. She extends the half-hour portion into a full hour. Previously, she'd written, *Plan Elliot's date*. With the extra time, she adds, *Museum*.

We didn't make any plans for a museum. Is this an excursion with her mystery man?

"Done," Hannah says. She hops down, a frantic glint in her eye. "Upstairs to your place."

I scramble off the barstool. "I thought we were meeting Elliot—"

"Fine, Audrey's!" She lowers to an intense whisper. "Let's just *go*."

"I hear whispering!" a deep, happy voice carries from the other room. Hannah shuts her eyes, grimly accepting her fate. Yann Bergstrom, Hannah's father, emerges into his grand kitchen from a set of swinging saloon doors leading into a separate chef's kitchen. Yann and his wife, Jean, are restaurateurs—older parents, they were both in their forties when they had Hannah. All four of our parents kept busy hours, so growing up, Maggie and I would pop downstairs to Hannah's for the gourmet ice pops Jean makes fresh every summer. The Summers children fell in love with flavors like rosemary lemonade and plum and sweet potato.

All Hannah ever wanted was a blue ICEE.

Yann carries out a platter of something pink, fresh from his test kitchen. He is tall and handsome, with a shaved head, a neatly manicured salt-and-pepper beard, and the same dark russet complexion as Hannah. They both share an affinity for fabulous eyewear. Yann wears oversized, rectangle-shaped Tom Ford frames, which almost fly off his nose as he slides between Hannah and me and our exit. "Micah, you can't leave until you try this." He thrusts the plate forward. "You're my test before the Taste."

Every summer, with the run-up to the Taste of Chicago—where trendy cafés, start-ups, and food trucks unleash samples of new and classic offerings—the Bergstrom home becomes a palace of anxiety. Hannah frequently jokes about wanting a summer place to get away from her parents during her least favorite time of the year.

Yann lowers his plate, which holds three elegantly laid slices of fruit sushi. "Frushi!" he says proudly. "Strawberry, pineapple, cantaloupe. Black raspberry reduction. Aaaaaaand roasted persimmon." I throw back a whole slice. Yann anxiously reaches for me too late. "No, no, you gotta savor it!"

"*Dad*," Hannah says. "He ate the thing. We gotta go."

"It was amazing!" I say, handing back the plate.

"Amazing . . ." Yann repeats in disbelief. "How was the mouthfeel?"

I raise my hand in praise. "Mouthfeel, ten out of ten."

"Nose-feel?"

"Nose-feel?" It's getting harder to maintain my enthusiasm.

"You are making things up again," Hannah snips.

"Miss Bergstrom, the aroma of a tasting is ninety percent of it." Yann stress eats the remaining two slices. "'Making things up again.' You know who *does* know what I'm talking about? The good people at TimeOut Chicago!"

As Hannah hurries me out, Yann follows, jabbering more information. "There's a new menu at this year's Taste, so, Hannah, we'd better see you helping at the booth—"

"I'll be there, don't worry!" she says, ready to slam the door behind us.

Before leaving, I give a quick nuzzle to Red Velvet, their fluffy Pomeranian, who likes hiding in the coat closet because raised voices make her nervous. She gets a quick kiss on the head, and then I leave her to her solace in the dark.

Red Velvet would also like a summer place to briefly escape from her family.

Coming over to Hannah's is stressful lately. The more I'm reminded of how helicopter-y her parents are, the more I worry she'll make good on her claim to move as far away from them as possible. She's only discussed it vaguely—creative writing programs at NYU or Iowa—but always refuses to talk further. I'd like to think she'd tell me if she were seriously contemplating something that far, but she's been Queen of Secrets lately. She still won't even tell me about this new boy.

What if next year is the last one for us together? What if she leaves, Elliot and I shockingly become close friends instead of friends-in-law, until one day, we turn to each other and go, "Remember Hannah?"

I grab her hand, and we swing our arms as we walk like when we were little.

It's enough to quiet my mind for now.

At Audrey's Café, the shop overflows with twice as many customers as usual, but Elliot seems to be weathering the storm. While Hannah and I squeeze into a corner bench, Elliot dashes between tables, delivering fresh pastries and sandwiches to guests. The moment someone leaves their seat, Elliot flies in to wipe it clean with a wet rag. His hands are so nimble—he cleans as fluidly as he crafts a row of hot drinks.

Elliot's manager, Priscilla, has been suspicious of us from the instant we sat down. She eyes us dangerously from beyond the steamer wands as she makes a row of lattes.

I've got too many eyes on me as it is. No one has overtly recognized me yet—thanks to my oversized sunglasses and sparkly bandana—but a group of girls stared on their way out, and a twenty-something queer couple kept flicking glances my way. The more I shrink back into my bench, the harder they squint.

It's been a while since I've dealt with this many looks from strangers. That prickly feeling on the back of my neck. When *Pass the Puck* was airing, whenever people stared, I'd freeze to the spot and disappear somewhere within myself.

But I'm not that kid anymore. I'm the Prince. Fearless.

"For Hannah," Elliot says, delivering her almond croissant and then pivoting to me with a tomato basil sandwich. "For Elizabeth Taylor."

"Eeeee, don't draw attention to me," I say mockingly. "How are you?"

"Me? Thriving," Elliot says.

The customers on the bench next to us leave. Elliot thanks them for coming, pulls a damp rag from his apron, and runs it over their table. Hannah cringes. "You keep it in your apron?"

"Hey, who's the burned-out barista here?" Elliot balances four dirty plates in the crook of his elbow. "There's no time to run back to the sanitizer bucket. By the time I got back, there'd already be someone sitting down. People just want to see the table wet."

Before he can finish, a young white family of four plops down.

We won't have Elliot long, so I get to business. I spin my sketchbook around for him to see the diagram of Taste booths I drew, along with a line tracing a crooked path throughout the event. It resembles a child's maze on a diner place mat.

"It's a scavenger hunt through the Taste," I say. "Each clue will lead Brandon to a different booth. The booths we chose all relate back to a happy memory you two have together that'll be worked into the clue. Thank you for emailing me the list of places."

"It was easy," Elliot says, rebalancing his plates. "It was nice, thinking about those memories again."

We smile. There. That feeling right there is why we're doing this.

Elliot is going to have an unforgettable weekend.

Behind the corner of my sunglasses, I catch Hannah's gaze flitting between Elliot and me. That look she gets when something juicy snags her attention—but what did she see?

I tap my sketchbook. "Everything ends at my dad's booth, where he's doing a live show—"

"Excuse me, this table is sticky," groans the man next to Hannah.

Hannah rolls her eyes, but Elliot handles the disruption with cool calm. "It's clean," he says, twirling his dishrag around his finger like a gunslinger. "Just finished it myself."

The man presses his fingers onto a syrupy patch along the table's edge. "Not *that* well," he says, Purell-ing his hands.

"Sorry 'bout that!" Elliot shrugs and wipes the sticky patch. He winks. "There you go!"

"That rag didn't look very clean," the man sneers.

"Sir, you can take my word for it—the rag came straight from the sanitary bucket. Your table is squeaky clean. Is there anything else I can do for you?"

"You can clean my table with a clean rag."

Elliot's smile freezes. He could attack this man at any minute. Yet where I would've exploded seven times before now, Elliot weathers it with strength. This is not his first big-talking tough customer, and it won't be his last.

"Sir, the table is clean," Elliot says. "We have a lot of customers to take care of, so unfortunately, I do need to leave you now. But how about one of our famous giant cinnamon rolls on the house? A sticky bun for a sticky table?"

Elliot shoots the man a finger gun, and he relaxes. Brightens even! "Well . . . that would be wonderful."

Murder behind his smile, Elliot cheerfully raps his knuckles on their table and shuffles away. While Hannah seethes, I dash to

Elliot and whisper, "Hey, charge me for that cinnamon roll."

He laughs and smacks my arm. "It's four bucks, Richie Rich. Best money I'll ever spend getting those assholes out of my life."

"*Agreed.*" I laugh, watching him stride behind the counter.

God, Elliot just *handles* things that would send me into a spiral.

By the time I return to our table, Hannah has repacked my satchel and is pushing through the crowd onto the increasingly busy patio. I follow her out. She hands me my bag and hisses, "My self-care hour is almost over, and I'm *not* spending it next to those people."

"Are you okay?" I ask.

"I'm okay." She nods with her eyes shut. "These people. The way they treat Elliot."

"I know. But we're gonna give him a great day tomorrow."

Breathing deeply, Hannah cups my face with those perfect nails—Summertime Teal. "I'm so happy you two are finally friends."

"Right?" I chuckle between her palms. "Life always has a twist."

Without warning, she smiles sadly. "Yeah. And I don't think it's done twisting."

"What do you mean?" Her serious tone flips my stomach again, and I want to yell at her to please knock it off speaking so mysteriously.

She laughs to herself. "Nothing. It's the Taste, my parents are being intense, and my brain is fried. Which reminds me: I've got"—she checks her phone—"thirty-one minutes left for self-care, so I'm off to meet my friend."

We hug. Slowly, warmth returns to my body.

"It's been a month," I whisper. "I'm your best friend. Can't you tell me his name?"

Effortlessly fashionable, Hannah quietly skips into the street and hails a cab within seconds. She's been hailing cabs for us since we figured out how to crack into our families' Apple Pay. Before leaping into the back seat, she turns to me. "Jackson," she says. "His name is Jackson, and that's all you're getting."

After Hannah's departure, I camp out at Audrey's patio as dusk turns to night and the warm string lights surround me in gold. I spend hours putting the final coloring touches on Elliot and Brandon's mermaid fantasy. I even got the tail fins to shimmer. Never has there been a gayer picture. Once I finish, I doodle the rest of my scavenger hunt plan for Elliot's Taste Date in purple and black ink. Something cute that he and Brandon can keep as a memento.

Finally, Elliot appears. He slumps into the chair opposite me with a groan. He's removed his apron, and his hair is once again sweat-plastered to his forehead. I know he's overworked, but Elliot is even more adorable when he's flushed and sweaty. Like, poor tuckered-out guy, someone needs to get him a nap.

I have the next best thing to cheer him up: I eagerly spin around the scavenger hunt diagram to show him, but he's massaging his entire face. "I'm sorry about that couple before," I say carefully. Maybe it's a bad time.

Laughing, Elliot shakes his head. "It's like that every day here; don't worry about it." He gulps ice water. "I'm so hot, and I have to go back to my hot room tonight."

I almost leap out of my seat at the opportunity to turn Elliot's frown around. "Oh, I wanted to surprise you, but I bought you a heavy-duty fan!"

At once, Elliot blinks and his eyes shine like gemstones. "You did?"

"Yes, um"—my fists clench, dreading this next part—"it's back-ordered. The holiday. But I'm tracking it, and it'll be here soon. When you get it, you'll need to wear a sweater to bed, you'll be so cold."

Elliot struggles to keep the smile on his face, which suddenly looks like it weighs a ton. "Thank you, but you don't have to buy me stuff. It kind of makes me feel embarrassed . . ."

My stomach drops. *Shit.* Does he think I'm buying him this to show off?

"I'm sorry," I say quickly. "It just seemed like you were giving up on your AC, and I . . . wanted to help. But I'll cancel the order!"

Elliot smiles through a painfully obvious tension headache. "You must think I need a lot of help. Coming to my rescue with customers. Buying me air conditioning. Fixing my broken relationship . . ."

"It's not broken!" I reach across the table to him, but he leans away.

"I have to get back." He shakes his head again, as if he's going to start screaming. "This *job*. It's not even enough to keep me here."

Elliot stops himself just as his mouth forms "here," but it's too late. My eyes widen. The terrible math calculates in my head. "Are you . . . leaving Chicago?"

He shrugs, holding back a mountain of anguish. "I might have to."

"Why?"

"Money. You see me doing all this; I work this much, and I can barely make the money I need for vet school. When would I even go to school if I got in? I haven't been able to keep up my intern hours at the clinic all summer. How's it all supposed to work?"

As Elliot stares at the passing cars, my insides feel like they've been caught in a slamming door.

Not Elliot. Our adventures were supposed to keep going.

With another horrific churn, an image of next summer swims to the surface: no Hannah or Elliot. The fellowship broken for good.

A lump forms in my throat. I don't want to ask such a vulnerable, selfish question, but this news is spinning my brain: "What about Brandon?"

Elliot stares through the grating in the table. "He won't miss me."

"That's not true! He loves you. Look, I think you're just super wiped from a bad day at work. You'll feel better after Brandon goes through the scavenger hunt tomorrow and finds you waiting for him."

With my entire central nervous system about to jump out of my body, I open my sketchbook to show Elliot his gift. His grim expression doesn't change as he takes in the image of backstroking mermaids, floating together in the sea. In a blink, his face brightens like a sunrise. His recognition is instantaneous. "My happy memory with Brandon!" he says, smacking me with the sketchbook. "I knew you were up to something asking me about that on the boat!"

Grinning foolishly and not knowing what to do with my hands, I smack his shoulder back. "It's a *yacht*, not a boat," I joke. "Get it right."

He rolls his eyes on another laugh. "Of course, how peasant of me."

I chew my lip. "It's your own private Instaloves. Something you could hang on to when times are tough. Until they get better?"

Elliot's giant grin falls, and silence crackles outside of Audrey's.

Ugh. Did I step wrong again? I wasn't trying to make him feel like a charity case.

But then . . . he wraps his arms around my shoulders. Electricity shoots down my limbs as Elliot's soft, clammy skin hugs my neck.

"Thank you for always trying," he whispers.

After Elliot leaves, I remain on the patio for another thirty minutes. Yet no amount of stress-sketching removes the plummeting terror from my chest. What if I lose Elliot's friendship just as we got to know each other? Am I going to walk past Audrey's someday, and he won't be there?

Unthinkable.

I anxiously google *How much is vet school?* but get wildly different results. It's a lot. Maybe I could talk to my dad. *Hey, Dad, I need thirty grand to pay for school for this boy who's not my boyfriend so he can stay in this expensive city and keep making chai for me!*

Maybe I should just listen to Elliot and not have my first instinct always be to throw money at a problem. I just need to be his friend and help him through this, whatever happens. The best way to encourage him to stay is to support his relationship with Brandon, and that is a very Micah mission.

Through the café window, Elliot moves in a tornado behind the espresso bar, laughing warmly as he hands people their orders. It's not an act with him. He really does emanate joy, with or without a heavy heart. He's even smiling genuinely as he makes the drinks. He's not on an assembly line of lattes, and he's not trying to beat some manager's clock. He's competing with himself. Gamifying it. Taking care with each one.

Exactly how he'd care for someone's dog or cat. Or snake or whatever. He'd love them all the way they're supposed to be loved.

He deserves that same care reflected back.

Just as I'm about to worry myself to death about Elliot, Grant arrives. My boyfriend—all dimples, curls, and long legs in short shorts—dashes across the crosswalk to meet me. His hug lifts me inches off the ground. The moment his hands connect with my body, anxiety leaves me like smoke into the wind.

"I have the rest of the night free," he says. "Wanna take me on a date?"

"Yeah, I think I do." We kiss. Each time we do, it's like the first one all over again.

He laces his fingers inside mine. I'm ready to go anywhere with him. As Grant walks me away from Audrey's, I glance back: beyond plumes of frother steam, Elliot watches us leave.

## Chapter 15

# THE SQUIRE CAPTURED

The Taste of Chicago is finally here, but my plans couldn't be unraveling fast enough. While Grant brushes his teeth, I'm curled in the fetal position on his bed, unable to tear my eyes away from a cursed image on my phone: Elliot, at his espresso bar, staring at Grant and me kissing with the saddest face anyone has ever seen. Whoever took this candid inside Audrey's has turned Elliot into a meme that is currently e v e r y w h e r e.

In my memory, he absolutely didn't look heartbroken—at least, not *this* bad. Nevertheless, the camera doesn't lie. Overnight, Elliot has become the new face of shattered dreams:

MY DATING MOOD

When he says he'll call you

tfw McDonald's ice cream machine is broken

This haunting photo has done so many laps around the internet that the memes have already become niche. In one picture, the caption above Grant and I reads, Old Rose letting go of her past And over Elliot's watery eyes: The necklace she dropped in the ocean.

I've seen eleven different versions already, even though I'm actively avoiding them.

"I'm FINE," Elliot says on FaceTime when I call him, but his dark-circled eyes tell a different story. "By the way, your mermaid sketch was incredible. I cried last night thinking about it."

While this news lightens the load sitting on my chest, I wish it was under better circumstances for Elliot. We've never FaceTimed before without Hannah—and it's surprisingly not weird—but I insisted on it. His texts felt so blank and far away, not like his usual exclamation-pointed enthusiasm. Selfishly, I needed to feel like we were okay and to let him know the picture didn't weird me out.

"Did you sleep okay?" I ask.

Elliot heaves a violent sigh. "I know I look dead. Brandon and I were fighting all night."

All wind is knocked from my lungs. "I'm so sorry."

"We resolved it eventually, after"—a yawn overtakes him—"three hours."

"At least it's fixed. So he believes you that you . . . you're not . . ."

*In love with me. That you're not in love with me.*

"That I'm not super-duper, incredibly jealous of you and Grant?" Elliot asks. "Yep, I think I fooled him. How about Grant? Did you have a nice night of romance? You didn't spend hours arguing over some stupid, paranoid crap after working all night?"

Guilt squeezes my stomach. "This has to be the worst."

"It's not great." Elliot runs a worn-out hand over his face. "You know, in the *hours* we talked about everything, Brandon never once asked me if I was okay. Never asked if I was embarrassed."

"Are you embarrassed?"

"They're going to have to invent a new word for how embarrassed I am."

I don't have the heart to tell Elliot that he's currently the spitting image of his heartbroken meme face. His misery ends *today*, and I'm personally seeing to it.

"Hey," I say sternly. Elliot breathes deeply and looks at me. "It's a stupid internet thing. People will forget about it tomorrow. You have nothing to be embarrassed about."

Elliot rolls from his side to his back and takes the phone with him as he loudly groans again. "Maybe it's for the best that we don't do this scavenger hunt today," he says. "Brandon is pissing me off. Priscilla texted me. Audrey's is totally slammed with the Taste, so I've gotta come in to cover breaks."

I lurch upright in Grant's bed, all business. "Elliot, you cannot go to work today. That's gonna make you feel so awful. People are gonna keep showing you those damn memes."

His eyes widen, frozen in terror. "I know. Like . . . I have no choice. I'm just doomed."

"Take a mental health day!"

Elliot's booming laughter blows out his speaker. "Sweet summer child, mental health days? Where do you think I work? Pixar? It's food service. Mental trauma *is* the gig."

I wave my hand—*nonsense!*—across the screen. "Then fake the flu. Do not go in. Are the tips even gonna be good today?"

He rolls his eyes. "These tourists don't tip." After another languishing sigh, he nods. "Okay, I'll text her that I'm having symptoms."

"Good. And I know Brandon let you down, but this scavenger hunt date is the perfect chance to turn everything around."

Elliot blinks and then smiles. "You really believe that?"

"You believed in my fairy tale, and now I'm lying in his bed. We're believers."

Elliot is close to having no reason left to stay in Chicago. I can't let losing Brandon be the last straw that causes him to slip away. This meme couldn't have come at a worse time, but I'm going to shepherd Elliot through this fire.

"Okay," he says, sitting up brightly. "Brandon already took the day off from training, which is a miracle, so let's do it. Where do I bring him?"

"You don't bring him anywhere. You popping up at the end is the surprise! Meet me in an hour at the Taste. Make up some story about where you're going—"

Just like that, Elliot flops face-first onto his pillow. "This is going to be *murder*."

"It won't!"

"How am I going to get him there, then? He'll just run back to training."

"He *won't* when Hannah calls him to meet her at the Taste to talk about your fight. It's perfect! She's working at her parents' booth all day, so he won't question why he has to meet her there."

Elliot shakes his head. "All Brandon is going to think is that I'm up to something. He's so suspicious, and now I'm gonna run off somewhere without explaining? I can't say I'm going to the café because I already called in sick, and if he shows up and Priscilla asks, 'How's Elliot's flu?' and he asks, 'What?' and then Hannah's asking for secret meetings? *Ugh.*"

I gently shush him. "Stop. Don't think. Just leave it to me. This is your quest!"

As Elliot hangs up to pry himself out of bed, I sprawl across Grant's mattress and let the dread consume me. I can't help feeling responsible, making my relationship as public and splashy as we have been. It still isn't fitting perfectly with my anxiety, posting pic after pic of myself as #RelationshipGoals. Whenever Grant and I are in public now, I just feel *eyes* on us—on me. Grant loves it, but I can't believe publicity is part of my life again; this exposure is exactly why Mom canceled our own reality show.

Now the same snare has caught Elliot.

"Was that Elliot?" Grant asks, emerging from his bathroom licking freshly scrubbed teeth. He's been at it for minutes.

"It was," I say.

"Is he all right?"

"No, but he will be." I hop up to kiss Grant's mouthful of spearmint. "He's had some setbacks lately, so he needs a win."

Grant kisses my cheek, but his eyes are heavy with a thought. "You know . . . I think he *really* likes you."

"No, he doesn't," I blurt, almost guiltily.

"I'm sorry everyone's laughing at your friend, but that picture is really sad. Like 'watching my man walk away with someone else' sad. I know that look. I perfected it before I met you."

The stinging pain of past rejections materializes in Grant's eyes.

I brush curls off his forehead. "Whether he's got a crush or not," I say, "I'm with you. You're not rejected anymore."

When Grant looks up, smiling. "You're a good friend to him."

Is Elliot pining over me? It's flattering, but I don't think so. I just think he's mentally at where I was a month ago: desperate for a touch of magic.

Well, with Grant, I may be Prince Charming, but I'm Elliot's fairy godmother.

## Chapter 16
# THE FESTIVAL

Dad is doing a live broadcast from the Taste of Chicago, so at least I have a slightly less hectic place to finalize Elliot and Brandon's romantic scavenger hunt. Wave after wave of humanity fills the street festival, which has engulfed over half a mile of park along the lake. Fifty booths, over thirty pop-ups, and dozens of food trucks eagerly hand out plates of piping-hot delights in exchange for prepaid tickets.

Also piping hot? Madame Sun.

It's only noon and already one hundred degrees. There isn't a drinking fountain in sight, but each booth offers bottles of water and Gatorade . . . if you have enough tickets, that is.

A sputtering overhead fan is the only thing remotely thinning the air inside the WNWC radio station booth. Just outside, the colossal Buckingham Fountain geysers into the air while desperate festivalgoers ladle its cool water onto their necks. The fountain's surrounding area has been cordoned off by the radio station, giving us plenty of space to set up a romantic picnic table behind the booth.

What's the point of having the King of Chicago's access if I can't help out a friend?

Elliot's salmon-colored "date night" V-neck is already soaked under the arms as we prepare his fancy table inside the booth. This will be the finale location of Brandon's scavenger hunt, and as soon as he's close, I'll text Elliot to open the tent and pull out his prepared picnic: a linen tablecloth, fresh flowers, and baguette sandwiches stuffed with brie, chicken, and apples.

Impossibly fresh, impossibly summer, impossibly charming.

It's been a ton of organizing, but what keeps my motor running is knowing that if Elliot's relationship with Brandon improves, he'll be less likely to move away.

I won't have to say goodbye to the friend who makes me feel like risks can pay off, the friend who sees through all my bullshit like an X-ray, the only person in my life who doesn't try to sneak a look at my art before I'm ready.

Plus, if Elliot stays, I'll get to see him become a vet. I don't want to miss that. That's worth all the quests in the world.

Elliot and I work in silence, since my dad is currently broadcasting live, ten feet away. Dad straddles a stool as he whips up the crowd, his voice thundering from giant speakers.

". . . a boiling hot afternoon here at the Taste. I am fricasseeing in this booth. Somebody's gonna serve me on a skewer today!" Dad eyeballs the sparkling cider bottles as I plop them into a cooler. "All right, over to DJ Gummi Worm. Stay cool, Chicago, and eat to the beat!"

The red light on Dad's mic goes dark, and DJ Gummi Worm's electronica beats take over. Dad's producer, Theresa—somehow not sweating to death in her flawless white polo—runs him a Gatorade. Dad crumples like a marionette. "That AC is *failing*."

"Someone's already on it," Theresa says. "You're doing great, but remember: it's 'Enjoy the eats and beats.'"

Dad gulps from the Gatorade. "Wait, what did I say?"

"'Eat to the beat.' You can't say that in a sponsored festival. It's trademarked by Disney."

Dad groans, almost spitting out his drink. "'Eat to the beat' is better."

"That's why they trademarked it."

Dad growls under his breath. "And are our lawyers concerned what'll happen if I pass out and die in this booth?" With that, he swiftly exits, whistling to Elliot and me on his way out. I zhuzh a small vase of flowers before following him. It's cooler outside than it was in the booth. As Elliot tries to fan away the dampness in his V-neck, I hand Dad a folded scrap of paper containing the final clue that will lead Brandon here. Hannah is already at the festival's farthest entrance, waiting to give Brandon his beginning instructions. In a minute, I'll join her so we can monitor Brandon's path through the Taste . . . which means leaving Elliot with Dad.

"Sorry to leave you in another bad AC situation," I tell Elliot.

Chuckling nervously, he swigs from his Gatorade. "My natural habitat!"

He's fidgeting. His voice sounds miles away. I've lived this anxiety a million times over; it's the dating anxiety of Please Let Today Go Well.

This isn't going to mess up, not on my watch. I hug Elliot tightly and whisper, "Forget that meme. Shake off those bad vibes with Brandon. You get a fresh start today."

"Thank you for making this happen." Elliot shakes his V-neck collar. "I feel slimy."

"You look great." I dig a spare black tank top out of my satchel. "Change into this. You won't sweat through it, and it'll make the date sexier."

"AMAZING." Faint with gratitude, Elliot strips off his V-neck. His chest is surprisingly furry. A thin trail of hair travels down the middle of his torso, all the way into . . .

Eyes are looking at me.

Dad's eyes. Mid-sip of his Gatorade, he watches me watch Elliot get dressed in the tank top. His eyebrows shoot up to his hairline, and he wags his finger.

My lips purse.

Dad is a professional minder of Other People's Business. Okay, so Elliot took off his top in front of me, and I stared for a beat too long. So *what*?

*So, one beat is a beat too long, Micah.*

Mercifully, Dad doesn't make an issue out of it and leads Elliot back inside the booth. "I'm sorry to hear about your meme."

"It's the last thing on my mind right now, believe me." Elliot laughs as they disappear back inside the hotbox. For the first time since that terrible meme dropped, lightness flows back into my body.

Elliot has a vital superpower. Like my dad, he has a special way of putting people at ease.

It's time for me to put Elliot at ease.

♡   ♡   ♡

Over text, I confirm with Hannah that she snuck away from her parents' booth to meet Brandon and that he has officially begun my scavenger hunt. The tap dancers in my stomach finally take a breather. Brandon actually took time away from training, showed up, and is playing along without plaguing Hannah with a ton of questions. According to her, he seemed almost giddy.

A true miracle. Maybe they'll work out after all.

My smile dips. It would be nice if Elliot ended up with someone he didn't have to hustle quite so hard with to have a good time, someone who admires him, someone who takes the time to make him feel special, someone who knows how lucky he is to be with a boy as genuinely good as Elliot.

But maybe that someone is still Brandon, and today is the start of a positive change.

I hoof my way from the fountain to the entrance of the festival by Millennium Park, moving as cautiously as a spy. My super dressed-down attire of a baggy, paint-splattered shirt and board shorts should make me not so easily identifiable as the Fairy-Tale Prince of Chicago here. I don't want Brandon to spot me in the crowd, and if someone makes a fuss, his suspicions will skyrocket.

Also, seeing me will only remind him that his boyfriend is on the internet mooning over my storybook romance, and I need to keep him on Elliot's side.

The crowds are so thick that minutes pass before I spot Brandon, looking very cute in a relaxed hoodie and pink shorts. He clutches two scraps of paper—one orange, the other neon blue—as he wanders around looking like a child who's lost his mom. I scamper backward and hide behind a giant oil drum that's been carved in half to use as an open pit barbeque. Curtains of smoke fly upward, as dense as fog, and hide me quite nicely.

Also, the scent of sizzling pork is irresistible.

It's too hot to eat, though. Every inch of my skin already feels like barbecue.

This means Brandon is two clues down, so that's good. I update Elliot on Brandon's progress, and he immediately replies with !!!!!!!!!!

After some contemplation, Brandon's next clue leads him to the booth for Lavish Sweets—the Bergstroms' bakery. Yann wears a carnation-pink apron over his business casual rolled-up sleeves. He delivers slices of blue icebox cake to the mob that has swarmed his booth—they can't get enough. I don't see Hannah anywhere. Maybe she stayed out after sneaking away to start Brandon on the hunt. She'll be back—it's *very* unlike her to break her parents' routine for long.

Brandon idles just beyond the crowd and stares at Yann with his brow crinkled anxiously.

He doesn't want to butt into the heavy line.

My teeth clench.

*Come on, Brandon, you've interrupted my conversations hundreds of times!*

Escaping my smokehouse hideaway, I creep behind another booth—Lao Sze Chuan—to get closer. Yann, a fellow towering man, spots Brandon in the crowd. "Back here!" Yann hollers with a smile. Relieved to be summoned, Brandon meets Hannah's mother, Jean, in back. A tiny woman with dark bronze skin, Jean fans herself with a handheld mister, and her eyes brighten as she hugs Brandon.

Elliot and Brandon have been over to Hannah's apartment plenty of times, so they get along like old friends. It's hard to believe Elliot was best friends with Hannah for months before we ever met. I heard all about him and how she thought we'd get along so well, blah, blah, blah. Who knew I'd be the next person gushing about Elliot?

He's very gushable.

After chatting for a minute, Jean slips Brandon my next clue on a scrap of hot-pink paper. He skips off reading the clue, which will lead him to the steel drum players by the beer hall.

**Thank you!** Elliot texts. **It's boiling over here. Your dad is ready to stage a walkout.**

**Hehehe don't worry,** I text. **Only a few clues left!**

Elliot sends the praying emoji.

This time, I don't follow Brandon. I remain crouched behind the steaming pans of Lao Sze Chuan because a romantic couple behind my booth is distracting me.

I hold my breath to stop my yelp of surprise.

It's Hannah and her mystery date! So that's where she went. Sneaky devil.

They picnic on a park bench, a pair of complete opposites. She is fully made-up in a flawless, cherry-red pencil skirt and strappy sandals. Jackson, a pretty boy, his face shining like bright copper in the harsh sun, is dressed like a stray cat. Black hair drapes down his back. He wears ripped-up Keds, ripped-up black jeans, and a sleeveless Mario Kart tee that is one wash cycle away from dissolving. Hannah, perfect as ever, eats a funnel cake with two napkins laid neatly across her lap. Jackson gobbles corn on the cob, leaving scant flecks of corn across his cheeks.

She points at the corn on his face. Not only doesn't he wipe it off, he kisses her.

They erupt into giggles.

Perpetually Instagram-ready Hannah Bergstrom has buttery corn niblets on her face, and she's laughing about it. I smile with her.

Hannah checks her phone. A full-body jolt forces her off the bench. She rapidly explains something—probably about being expected over at her parents' booth. He just waves goodbye, smiling, as unbothered as a human can be.

She dabs her face clean, smiles sadly, and then runs off.

My friend is totally smitten. It sucks that her parents keep her on such an intense schedule. Does she ever get serious time alone with Jackson, or are they just these fleeting half hours? The best night of my life was when Grant made me chase him in the rain to the Art Institute exhibit. It wasn't planned. It was just life, finally happening—before Wish Granted and all the hoopla. No one knew I was behind Instaloves. No eyes on us but each other.

I already miss that quiet time with Grant.

That's why Hannah is keeping Jackson a secret. It's just them.

Well, Hannah deserves more than these bite-sized half hours. I shuffle on crouched knees from behind the Jeni's Ice Creams stand and bolt down the thoroughfare of booths—parallel to

Hannah one row over. If I can just get two or three booths ahead, I can catch her before she cuts left and reaches her parents. I can't let her know I saw Jackson—this needs to remain her secret.

Far enough ahead, I pivot right, behind the Drunken Donut booth . . .

Hannah and I collide almost instantly. Her shriek dissolves into laughter when she recognizes me. Very Julia Roberts in *Pretty Woman*. As I grip my knees to catch my breath, Hannah calms herself by pressing a hand to the cherry-shaped pendant across her chest that exquisitely matches the cherries on her skirt.

"I thought you were mugging me." She laughs.

"Well, I still might want that necklace," I say, attempting to sound as casual as possible, as if I wasn't deliberately getting in her way. "Sorry, Brandon has got me running laps here."

Hannah's body scrunches with glee. "It's really gonna work! Yay for Elliot."

"I know!" On the end of a large gulp of air, I make my move.

*Okay, Micah: pull this off and you could be helping two relationships today.*

"It's important for Elliot to get these moments, you know?" I ask. "Brandon's time is so regimented, and that's great for him . . . not so great for Elliot." Hannah nods with a friend's understanding, but I don't think she's taken my hint yet. "Elliot is patient. He'd wait forever for Brandon. But after their date today, I hope Brandon realizes all the times like this they could've had but didn't. Missed opportunities, you know?"

"Sure," Hannah says. Her smile wilts like a forgotten plant. "You know me with my schedule. Always gotta be mentally on the clock and locked at Yann's and Jean's sides." She snorts. "God, am I the Brandon in this?"

I didn't even need to say it. She's the Brandon, and Jackson is the Elliot.

Her realization wallops her into silence.

All around us, the city finally takes a break. Grown adults smash gooey s'mores into their mouths, and kids clap as they wait for skewers from the street-meat carts. Whatever else is going on in our lives right now, we're here without worries, making memories.

I take Hannah's hands and swing them playfully. We stand in the middle of a busy thoroughfare, going *sway, sway, sway* like we have nowhere else to be.

"That first time I . . . you know, with Grant, I didn't tell anyone I'd be staying the night," I say. *Sway, sway, sway.* "I didn't look at my phone, I just . . . got lost with him."

"Did your dad get pissed?" Hannah asks, a vulnerable gleam catching her eyes.

I laugh. "Oh *yep*." *Sway, sway, sway.* "But he got over it."

She smiles. "Do you ever wonder why we get so worked up worrying about our parents?"

I shrug, her fingers still laced in mine. "No idea. But I do know that someday, I'll forget about how mad my dad was, but I'll *never* forget that night with Grant."

Hannah pulls me into a tight hug. "Senior year is coming like a truck, friend," she says. "It keeps hitting me how we might not have as much time left as we think we do."

I don't break the hug. I squeeze harder. I can't even think

about this right now, but I need to give Hannah one more nudge. "Then let's make the time we have left count."

Hannah nods as she steps back from the hug. She watches me with deep focus.

"Speaking of time," I say, checking my phone. "I have to find Brandon!"

Lost in a million thoughts, Hannah says, "Good luck with Elliot," and turns around the way she came. Is she going back to her parents' booth or to Jackson?

"Hey, aren't your parents this way?" I ask, pointing the opposite direction she's watching to be sure.

She glances back—one thought after another gridlocking her brain—and shakes her head. "No, I'm . . ." She points down the road, toward the picnic spot where she left Jackson. "I'm not going back to them today."

*YES!!*

As softly and quickly as possible, I haul ass the way I came, pivoting around the Drunken Donut, down the thoroughfare, and back into my hiding spot behind Jeni's Ice Creams.

Jackson hasn't budged from his bench. The stringy, laid-back boy continues savoring corn on the cob as Hannah returns from up the path, her smile still gone. *You did it, Hannah.* As she reaches the end of the path, where cement meets grass, she does something unthinkable. Something I haven't seen her do in all my years knowing her.

She removes her heels outside.

Barefoot, Hannah wades into the park lawn toward her secret boyfriend, Jackson, on his bench. His eyebrows jump when he sees her. She says something I can't hear. Once she's finished, Jackson pats Hannah's spot on the bench, she scoops up the funnel cake she left behind, and they eat together. A smile returns to my friend's face.

From my hiding place, I pump my fist and whisper, *"Yes!"*

One friend's fairy-tale romance has come true, one more to go.

To catch up with Brandon, I take a shortcut down the thoroughfare. To be safe, I head directly for the second-to-last clue spot between Connie's Pizza and the Stella Rosa wine garden. When Elliot began dating Brandon, they stole a pack of Brandon's sister's wine coolers, so Elliot chose that memory as one of the final clues.

Our sentimental plan seems to be working.

As I crouch behind the pizza booth, Brandon approaches the wine garden with glassy, tender eyes and rereads the top clue in his stack. Elliot's clue has struck a nostalgic chord somewhere deep inside him. Brandon whispers something to an older white woman with permed, dyed-red hair at the wine garden booth.

Beaming, she disappears beneath her table and reemerges with an expensive, shiny gold invitation. "The last one," she says, handing it over.

He thanks her and tears open the invitation. As he reads, he drifts farther from the wine garden . . . and closer to me.

I flinch but don't run.

He pauses to finish reading. He smiles warmly. Nostalgic with the memory.

I press a palm to my chest. I cannot believe I'm feeling happy for Brandon. But it's not about him. His happiness will trickle down to Elliot, who deserves a special day more than anyone else in existence.

The invitation has no clue; it simply invites Brandon to lunch at Buckingham Fountain. We timed everything perfectly. The fountain can be seen spewing into the air just around the next corner of booths!

Brandon dashes toward it.

"Dammit!" I whisper, and fumble my phone to text Elliot: He's coming right now!

No response. I hold my breath. Hopefully, Elliot is too busy preparing the table to reply.

I follow at a discreet distance. No way am I letting myself be seen now that we're at the tail end of my masterpiece of romantic engineering. This crowd is limiting my movement anyway. The closer to lunchtime we get, the more elbow-to-elbow humanity we have to deal with. I narrowly avoid meeting eyes with two girls, Lauren and Sarah, who I recognize from Grant's program, both dressed in ribboned bodices as if they were at a ren faire.

This is the busiest I've ever seen the festival. No booth is without a gigantic line.

Everyone gets to be a star today—especially Elliot.

When I arrive at the great fountain, the surprise has already occurred. Brandon is laughing into his hands as Elliot embraces him and directs him to their elegant picnic outside the radio tent. Brandon mouths "Oh my *God*" when he sees my dad applauding them.

The happy couple sits to eat. They kiss above the flowers.

I pump my fist again. "*Done*," I whisper.

Earlier, Elliot was more sweat than person. Now he's radiant.

He has Brandon. No fighting. No stolen moments. Just him and Brandon, savoring a special memory together.

"Rose for the Prince?" asks a voice. A long-stemmed rose is thrust in my face before I can turn around. It's a young, dark-haired Asian girl—so familiar—dressed in an old-fashioned blue frock with a white apron fastened over it. A matching blue ribbon in her hair.

She looks like . . . Belle from *Beauty and the Beast*.

Like, exactly like her.

I accept the rose, quietly thank her, and then make a *shh* motion. I don't need anyone around here calling me "Prince" and pulling focus from Elliot.

Belle isn't even halfway to the fountain when another stranger puts something in my face: a ruby-red apple. "Juicy, sweet apple for the Prince?" asks the stranger. For some reason, the young girl is putting on an old crone voice. She's draped in a long cloak, her face obscured by the hood.

When I take the apple, the witch shuffles away, hunched over.

My stomach twists. Something is happening.

"Tea for the Prince?" booms a tall, brassy Latine woman in a red-and-black gown. Thankfully, she has no tea in her hands, because I couldn't hold one more thing.

"What the hell is going on?" I ask.

"OFF WITH HIS HEAD!" she crows as her golden tiara jostles.

With a grand sweep of her hem, she departs toward the fountain . . .

Where dozens of costumed performers gather and swirl around each other.

Fairy-tale characters. They're all here: Belle. The Witch. The Queen of Hearts. A man with fluffy white rabbit ears. A Fairy Godmother. On and on. There must be over a dozen.

Whatever is happening . . . it's choreographed.

Brandon and Elliot gasp with delight at the impromptu street performance. Among the performers, Lauren and Sarah dance in their ribboned bodices. Maidens and peasant girls, right out of a storybook. My heart drops to my feet with a horrible understanding:

I've seen them before. They're all from Grant's design program.

*"May I have your attention, please?"* a painfully familiar, bass-y voice calls from a loudspeaker. It can't be coming from the radio tent; my dad is in the middle of calling out raffle winners.

So where is he? Where is Grant?

*"Today's festival is made even more special by a person who needs no introduction. A person who has changed my life for good. Who taught me to believe in fairy tales."*

My boyfriend's beautiful voice has never frightened me before, but it does now.

Please don't let this happen. Don't announce me in the middle of Elliot's date!

My *plans*, my beautiful plans!

"Are you doing this?" Brandon asks Elliot. He's still awe-struck and thinking this is all for them. Elliot is still delighted, but his smile is waning. He knows this wasn't my design, and he definitely knows I wouldn't surprise him like this.

With the blunt force impact of a truck smashing into a gate,

I realize what this is: it's Grant's surprise anniversary event. The thing he's been planning for weeks.

Choreographing. Costuming.

One. Day. Early.

*"This song is for my boyfriend, my Wish Granted, the Fairy-Tale Prince of Chicago . . ."*

GRANT, DON'T SAY MY NAME.

*"MICAH SUMMERS!"*

The nightmare descends.

My dad's broadcast is drowned out by a trio of boom boxes held overhead by three of Grant's classmates dressed in mermaid fins. Then the music begins: *percussion, strings, winds, words.* "Kiss the Girl" from *The Little Mermaid.* Unmistakable.

From behind the fountain, Grant appears—more handsome than ever, dangerously so now that I'm powerless to stop this spectacle. He's dressed like Prince Eric in a partially opened silk shirt. Grant and his Flash Mob of Doom croon along to the song, each of them looking me dead in the eye as they do.

I am frozen to the spot.

Too much attention.

Old Micah is back in full force. I'm eight years old all over again with film crews barging into my home. I deep breathe the tingling sensation out of my fingers.

My dad and DJ Gummi Worm crane their heads out of the tent, their mouths agape. Theresa covers her mouth with both hands. It's hard to tell from this distance if she's overcome with emotion or horror. I'm currently leaning horror, especially as the White Rabbit and Belle performers hustle Elliot and Brandon out of their chairs in some attempt to encourage audience participation.

They have no choice but to stand.

Elliot claps along to the beat, even as life abandons his face. Brandon stands there, wringing his napkin in both hands as if it were my throat.

When Grant finally reaches me—and the song reaches its thunderous climax—all eyes in the festival are on us. Scores of onlookers encircle us as they munch festival doughnuts, meat skewers, and pizza slices. Every hand that is not holding a plate is holding a phone.

Pictures. Videos. Broadcasting live.

We are the show.

The song ends. Grant—sweating, huffing, and luminous—says, "You made my wishes come true. My curse is broken. This is how you make me feel. Happy anniversary."

Those dimples. That curly, dripping hair.

Tension calcifies my body into a rigid, panicked shape, like how it must look seconds before you're destroyed by a bomb you know has already detonated.

The kingdom is watching.

We kiss. We have to.

The kingdom erupts in cheers and hollers.

Beyond Grant's shoulder, Elliot and Brandon watch—mere spectators as always in my big show. Elliot's face transforms once again into his crestfallen meme. Brandon's scowl hardens as he and I lock eyes.

Drawing an enormous breath, he bellows, "YOU F—!"

## Chapter 17
# THE BAD LUCK

When an aspiring Olympian calls you a word they have to bleep on TV while you have a mild panic attack surrounded by beloved Disney characters, I call that a rotten turn of events.

Belle, Rapunzel, and I huddle in terror by the fountain as Prince Eric—my boyfriend—descends on Brandon with the most red-hot fury I've ever seen. "What did you say to him?!" Grant bellows.

He's gonna fight him, oh my God.

The crowd gasps—and some whoop to cheer on the impending scrape.

Brandon fumes silently as he and Grant come nose to nose. Dad, Elliot, and I race toward the pair, each of us wearing a different emotion carved onto our faces: Dad, confused; Elliot, frantic; and me, terrified.

How could so much go so wrong so quickly?

Reaching Grant before any fighting begins is my only objective. I'll faint *after* I've stopped him. The back of my skull throbs, as I have the farthest distance to run.

"No, no, no!" Elliot and I plead to our boyfriends, who can only hear their own rage.

Outside the radio booth, DJ Gummi Worm and Theresa stare in disbelief. Grant's design friends scatter, while the festivalgoers crowd all of us inside a tighter and tighter circle.

My heart shrivels like a raisin.

There's cameras everywhere. Phones. So many phones.

"Simmer down!" Dad is the only one tall enough to separate Grant and Brandon, two large boys who have somehow grown larger in this last minute, like bears in attack position. For now, they have locked into a scowling-and-staring contest—but thankfully, nothing physical.

Elliot and I, their littler boyfriends, attempt a vain, heroic struggle to throw our arms between them. "This is Brandon, Elliot's boyfriend!" I say rapidly, as if Grant will suddenly switch off his temper and say, *"Oh! Why didn't you say so in the first place? Sorry, friend!"*

"I know who he is," Grant snarls, his chest heaving with an ominous intensity beneath his open princely shirt.

"There's no getting away from you two, is there?" Brandon asks, glowering.

Elliot's mouth hangs open—his eyes dart around the rapidly enclosing space, as if he's considering making a run for it. "Brandon, it's okay," he says, grasping for Brandon's arms. But

Brandon will accept no touch from him. Elliot looks so pulverized, I want to pull him into a hug, but that'll go over like lighting a match in an oil refinery. He gestures to me, speechless at first. "Micah was just helping—"

"Micah, Micah, Micah," Brandon says, heaving a full-bodied sigh. "ENOUGH."

There it is. The meme returned.

The whole internet saw in Elliot's face what Brandon has apparently been seeing for a while: his boyfriend crushing on someone else. Me?

No, Elliot is just exasperated with his own relationship that Brandon is determined to let self-destruct. He's with an impossible guy, so he's getting lonely and a little jealous of what Grant and I have, made even worse by the fact that Wish Granted is *so* public and in-your-face.

And we just did the most public, in-your-face damn thing of all time.

I can't think of that right now. I have to get us all out of this park before the TikTok videos start rolling out—*lol look at these gay messes attacking each other lmao.*

"Are we calm?" Dad asks, placing a firm—but careful—hand on Grant's shoulder. He knows cameras are on him, too, as much as they're on us.

"We're calm," Grant says, his eyes softening. "Just standing up for Micah."

My dad nods, channeling the fragile agreeability of a hostage negotiator: "Very admirable, but we're going to handle this without fighting. I think what we have here is a case of bad luck." Dad twists to Brandon, whose eyes are red and watery. "Micah set up this surprise date for his friends, which unfortunately coincided with Grant's surprise anniversary show—"

"Yeah, right," Brandon says, glaring at me. "You set up this whole date for us on a random day that just *happens* to be your anniversary?"

"Our anniversary is tomorrow!" I say, pushing my five-six body between these six-footers. "I don't know why he did this show today."

"I didn't realize Micah was doing something, and it was the only day everyone was available," Grant says defensively. He throws up his arms, like *Sue me!*

Brandon snorts. "I can't believe anything you two say. You did this just to steal more attention for yourself."

This is hell. Actually hell.

All these fairy-tale characters here, and not a single genie. I wish I'd never told anyone I was behind Instaloves. I wish Grant and I could've just enjoyed our pictures for ourselves, as a normal couple, without leaving behind all this wreckage in our publicity wake.

For Elliot's sake most of all. He grips the linen tablecloth of his abandoned, beautiful picnic. It'll take weeks to repair this damage—if it even can be repaired.

"I gotta get out of here," Brandon says, speeding out of the park without looking at Elliot. The crowd parts easily for him. After all, he's not the star of this show.

That's the problem.

Elliot—another nonstar—wears a frown that might become permanent if I don't do something soon. I'm halfway to him when his phone vibrates with a call. One look at the ID, and his shoulders collapse. He gazes up helplessly and shows me the display:

*Audrey's Café.*

Oh God. Oh no.

Someone saw Elliot here. News has already spread. He's supposed to be out sick.

Accepting his grim fate, Elliot takes the call: "Hey, Priscilla." As his manager most likely begins tearing into him, he summons the impossible energy to stand and collect his keys. "Yeah. Yeah, that was me. I'm coming in now. Sorry."

Like a ghost, Elliot walks out of the circle, which has already begun dispersing since there is obviously going to be no more screaming. The show is over.

There's no blood left in me. I couldn't have ruined Elliot's life more surgically if I tried.

Once everyone is gone, Dad lets Grant and me hide from other people's phones in the privacy of his non-air-conditioned booth. I don't even want to be here anymore, but I can't go home—or to Grant's room—until I've asked two important questions.

Grant sits under the broken fan, his shame crushing his bigness. This wide-eyed, curly-haired, vulnerable boy awaits my judgment. My dumping of him, like all the rest did.

I hold my phone with both hands—it gives me something to grip so I can get feeling back into my limbs . . . and it stops me from texting a billion apologies to Elliot (who will get them, just not right now).

"First of all, that was a really beautiful show," I say. "I'm so touched at the work and emotion you put into it."

"You liked it?" Grant's chin trembles, and my chin sympathetically trembles with him.

"I loved it. I just wish I could've enjoyed it." Grant shuts his eyes and nods, like *I know I messed up.* I rake my fingers through his beautiful tangle of curls, and he accepts my love like a dog being petted. "You really had no idea I was planning this for Elliot today?" I ask.

On a wet snort, tears streak down Grant's round cheeks like highway lines. Invisible fishing wire tugs painfully on my heart. How can he look so small? "I thought I heard something was going on," he says. "I heard you planning, but I thought it was a few more days away. I didn't want to mess up your cool thing, I promise."

"But why today?" I ask. "Why not tomorrow?"

He looks down at his feet. "I just got excited to do it. Our morning together was so amazing. You broke my curse."

Grant opens his arms like a child and envelops me in his broad wingspan. Hugging me only causes him to crumble further. He tries to speak, but his tears won't let him. I softly brush his curls until he quiets. Still holding Grant, I reach across the radio equipment to pull the cord that releases the booth's top flap. It falls, concealing the window that had been Dad's view of the fountain during his show. We need total privacy.

My anxiety disappears in the face of his distress. All I want is for him to be okay.

"Heyyy, what's wrong?" I ask.

"So much," he chokes out. "Everything."

"It's okay." I shush him as he buckles again. "I'm here. I'd love to hear what's going on."

Grant tries to take a deep breath, but his sadness hiccups chop it into a staccato rhythm. "This design show is turning me into a maniac. The deadline is in less than a month. I feel nuts. Design school scouts are coming, my professors and everybody are foaming at the mouth to see what Wish Granted comes up with, and my model dropped out yesterday."

"What, why?" I groan, careful to be sympathetic but not catastrophize.

Grant rolls furious, bloodshot eyes. "Got a better paying gig that weekend."

"I'm sorry. We'll find someone else."

Grant stares for a long, pregnant moment, his beautiful face so open and vulnerable. "I've been so scattered, I didn't know when you were doing Elliot's thing. Then I got here, had everyone dressed, and it was too late."

I stroke his arms. "You were amazing getting all those people together just for me."

"Oh God, they love showing off. Most of them already owned the costumes."

I laugh and continue stroking his arm. The longer I do it, the faster our connection returns. "I'm sorry it didn't end well. I was just trying to help Elliot not feel so overlooked."

"I'm sorry too," he whispers. "I'll make it up to him."

It's time to leave this heat before we drop dead. As I help Grant to his feet, I can't stop thinking about Elliot, who is out there alone with a spurned boyfriend and a furious boss. I don't know if either of us could make up for the damage we caused him.

# Chapter 18
# THE PARTNERSHIP

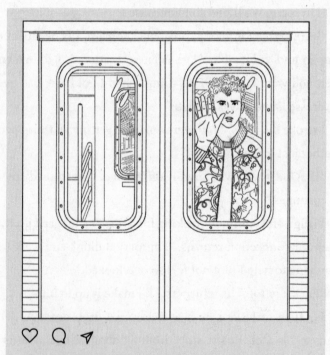

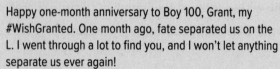

Happy one-month anniversary to Boy 100, Grant, my
#WishGranted. One month ago, fate separated us on the
L. I went through a lot to find you, and I won't let anything
separate us ever again!

Even after a ZzzQuil sleep, I don't feel any better about Grant's flash mob. The public disaster flooded my nervous system, dragging me right back to that childish place of Old Micah. In that moment, it didn't matter how much New Micah helped people believe in fairy tales again—or made Grant believe his curse was broken—once everyone's phones came out to record us, Baby Boo-Boo reigned.

I can't even look at my mural—or rather, the black curtain that conceals it. To satisfy my curiosity, I dig out my sketchbook and attempt to draw the event. The best parts of it, anyway—Grant's glorious effort to woo me and celebrate our first month together. A kingdom watching while a gallant tailor performs a romantic serenade.

After five minutes of watching my pencil wave lazily across the page, my dread is confirmed: I've lost my inspiration. For whatever million reasons pinging around inside my head, I don't want to capture this moment as a chapter in our fairy tale. If I were still anonymous, maybe I'd feel differently. My creativity always flowed better that way.

The question I can't shake is: How would I have felt about the flash mob if it wasn't interrupting Elliot's date?

I can't be totally sure the answer is "Amazing!"

So far, my anniversary post hasn't distracted people from the fiasco at the festival. Every comment under the post is slamming me and Grant, slamming Brandon, slamming my dad for not stopping it sooner somehow, or some question begging us for more tea about how it all turned out once the cameras stopped.

*Happy anniversary to us!*

Dad's woes are not just confined to Instagram. When I emerge, unshaven and ZzzQuil hungover, Dad paces the living room on a call while Maggie munches breakfast at the kitchen island. Dad's call has been going on for an hour; I could hear it through my door. He ended up earning his radio station a call from the Disney attorneys after all, just not for saying "eat to the beat." It was for the far more obvious violation of playing a famous *Little Mermaid* song over the airwaves, in its entirety, without permission. It took his station all night to convince the Mouse that he didn't play it; it was his train wreck son's train wreck boyfriend playing it at full volume near their speakers.

"Thank you for understanding," Dad says with a chummy laugh—the kind he uses when he's furious but can't show it. "I'm glad to hear your nephew's an Instaloves fan. Never a dull moment around here."

Dad flares his eyes at me. Not in the mood to be blamed, I quickly pack my satchel with snacks to take to Grant's dorm. Maggie casually dips carrot sticks in hummus. "If I were you," she whispers, "I wouldn't argue with him today. Just say sorry and head out."

A planet-destroying eye roll takes over me. "It's not my fault I got surprised with that flash mob! I tried to be invisible for Elliot!"

Maggie frowns. "How's he doing?"

"*Bad.*" I angrily chomp one of her carrots. "Hannah says he's fighting with Brandon more than ever, and pictures of that"—I choose my swears carefully with Dad nearby—"damn song went everywhere, so his boss saw him at the Taste after he had called out sick from work, which I convinced him to do, so now he got a write-up."

She winces and dips another carrot. "So you're basically ruining his life."

"Not on purpose!"

"But on accident?"

"Yes."

"I'm sure he doesn't blame you. Why don't you just go down to Audrey's and apologize?"

*"No."* I readjust the buckles on my satchel to avoid her all-knowing stare. "Someone will see me and make a fuss. Elliot will end up getting in trouble again somehow. He needs that job."

"Yeah, Hannah told me." Maggie's hand falls on my bag to hold me in place. "Do you really think suddenly ghosting him is gonna brighten his horrible week?"

Maybe Elliot can't thrive here. Maybe it's a good thing he's focusing on his future.

Grant is focusing on his future with this program.

The only person treading water is me. Two rooms over, my mural is gathering dust under a tarp, my artistic vision disintegrating by the day. When I come back from Grant's, I'll devote the afternoon to resuming work and getting my Art Institute portfolio together. I'm not setting myself up for failure next year when Hannah leaves to write in New York, and Elliot leaves to be a small-town vet . . .

The entire next week, I avoid Audrey's like one of my old Instaloves. No meetups with Elliot—just texting to make sure he's okay. It's time for us to focus on our relationships. It sucks, though. I even miss his jokes picking at me about being a silly little Richie Rich.

We'll get that time back once things have settled down, and he's in a better place with Brandon. He won't be able to do that with me hanging around, making Brandon furious and jealous.

They're already working on it: A quick peek at Elliot's Instagram showed me two happy boyfriends swimming together at the lake. They're backstroking again! It's quite a thirst trap. Elliot's chest hair is matted in a long, dark stripe down to his sopping wet suit, which clings so tightly to his thighs, he's got a visible—

Frantically, I slap my phone off. What am I *doing*? Elliot was just so vulnerable after the Taste debacle, and I feel so guilty about it, I'm over here peeping his pics just because I feel bad for him!

Either way, I'm just glad he and Brandon are rebuilding things.

That weekend, another exciting First happens when I get brunch with my boyfriend's friends. Me, Grant, and his program cohorts—those flash mob characters now in day clothes—share the best, biggest sticky buns in the city.

"I was *not* prepared to see Grant in a Prince Eric shirt!" giggles Bethany, a darkly tanned white girl in braided pigtails who was behind the Witch's cloak. A banquet table of cohorts—queer and straight—raise their coffee mugs like beer steins to salute Grant's sublimely wonderful chest. His curly head digs into my shoulder in mock embarrassment, and waves of laughter free my mind of any jagged thoughts I ever had about the flash mob. Neighboring tables shoot us death glares for how heartily we're laughing, but none of us care.

It's everything I needed.

Except there is a slight echo behind my laughter. An empty *ting*. I know what it is: Elliot needs this boisterous friends' brunch more than I do. He'd love this. I should've invited him.

I stuff the depressing thought away as a freckled young woman (wearing sunglasses indoors) leans across two people to snare my attention: "So, Micah, you're teaming up with Grant on his Knight Princess design? The two of you could really draw some huge crowds to the show."

"*Wow*, hard sell," Grant says, nervously shredding empty sugar packets.

As "*huge crowds*" echoes ominously in my head, the young woman throws up apologetic hands. Glancing around the table, I suddenly feel as if I have everyone's undivided attention. No more coffee being slurped. No more bacon being chomped.

Just a dozen sets of eyes trained on Grant and me.

"Crowds?" I ask, taking Grant's fidgeting hand. "Isn't the end-of-year show just for you all, like the Institute people?"

Grant clears his throat and sits straighter—business time: "No, uh, what Hartman is trying to say is the end-of-term show isn't just a culmination of our program; it's a networking event. A once-in-a-lifetime opportunity. The show will be this big production that's open to the public. In past years, they've gotten some heavy-hitter designers to show up and scout talent, some influencers, a lot of angel investors. Design students are allowed to bring outside artists onto their teams. It happens all the time. It . . . could be really cool."

In pin-drop silence, Grant turns to me with a hopeful expression.

"So." I turn to my watchful audience. "You want me to use Grant's and my big internet thing to really juice up interest in this year's show to make sure as many Big Deal Folks as possible show up." I hold a piece of bacon between my teeth like a cigar. "Is that right?"

No one blinks.

Grant closes his hand over the top of mine as an innocent look crosses his face. "If that's . . . okay with . . . you?"

Being with Grant has already changed Instaloves so much. I haven't loved what our Wish Granted exposure has done to my creativity, but this could turn things around. Being a hugely advertised part of Grant's show could be my ticket into the Art Institute on my own terms, with my own portfolio and vision.

Me! In that historic building, sharpening my painting skills and finally cracking the code on how I can take my passion for Instaloves to the next level through massive, epic pieces.

I crunch my bacon and say, "Sure!"

Once more, mugs are raised to the sky. Three cheers for Wish Granted—*hip, hip, hooray*! Grant's classmates descend into excited chatter, made even more joyful by the fact that I've agreed to a thing they apparently conspired to lure me to brunch to ask. This "spontaneous idea" spilled out of Grant fully formed. A taste hits my tongue like bitter coffee. I actually don't think it's a bad idea— it's probably exactly the artistic jump start I've been waiting for to help me get into the Art Institute. I just wish he'd asked me in private, one on one, so I wouldn't have felt so boxed into a "yes."

"Let's start it off right," Grant says, spinning our chairs around. "Selfie with the group! We can post it to Instaloves and announce that Wish Granted is partnering on something big for the Art Institute. Tag the school and the main faculty, you know? Get them involved."

I almost fall off my seat from so much information at once. I agree with the picture, and even though it's savvy promotion, I would've preferred to workshop it together privately first. I could've given my own ideas about how the Knight Princess promotion fit into Instaloves.

I can't believe how quickly I regret agreeing to this.

The promotion doesn't stop. As the week continues, Grant has one bright idea after another about how we can tease our fans about the Knight Princess. We stop for frozen hot chocolates; he takes our picture and asks me to post it with the hashtag #WorkingDate. When I pop over to his dorm for lunch, the first thing he does is switch on his ring light. He even turns the elevator up to my penthouse into an Instagrammable moment.

"Ooh, let's tag your dad!" Grant glances up from his phone with an oblivious smile. "Do you think he'd share it? Is he on TikTok? He'd be hilarious doing that."

"Um . . ." I should get an Oscar for how well I wipe the look of horror from my face.

I just want one date with Grant that isn't livestreamed!

By mid-July, I insist we stop promoting the thing we're working on and actually work on the thing we're working on. Grant's roommate is spending her design show crunch time with her own boyfriends, so we commandeer his dorm room into a make-shift drafting studio while we finalize the ultimate design for the Knight Princess. This location is convenient for when we have to work late—it's also convenient for when we want to touch each other's butts.

Both of us slob around his room in sweats from yesterday, so neither of us is looking or feeling too amazing, which helps us focus on the design. Grant waves me over to his desk to behold the finalized design staring back from his Surface Studio:

The Knight Princess slaps energy back into my body.

He somehow managed to blend his original, gender-fluid fantasy character with the dozens of other pieces of scratch paper lining his walls—even mine.

"You used my tiara helmet!" I clutch my chest.

Grant beams from his desk, and I bury a kiss into his two-day scruffy cheek. "It's still not *final* final yet," he groans. "Our Wish Granted promo is raising the stakes on what people are expecting. This is my chance to stand out—*our* chance, I mean—and we can't disappoint. It should feel bigger. This is just . . . good. We need a gasp."

I trace a studying finger along the edge of his design. "From good to gasp . . ."

We stare, hypnotized, at the sketches until the puzzle pieces hopefully connect. The figure in the design looks great, but there's a vacantness to it. I wish fashion sketches had backgrounds to make them pop. Something to ground the look and give it flavor.

Where is the Knight Princess physically? What's around them? *Who's* around them?

A castle? A ball?

*Dancers . . . In a castle . . .*

"AH!" I yelp, clutching Grant's arm. "What if the Knight Princess was just part of a bigger piece? A piece I've already started?" I clutch fistfuls of my hair. "I can't believe I'm saying this: my mural."

This is it. This is how I finally get down to business figuring out my vision. I'm not going to let my art keep languishing in the dark!

Grant's eyebrows leap in surprise. "You've never even let me see your mural," he says. "This is gonna be seen by . . . everyone."

"I know, I know." I slap my hands to my ears and pace the room. It's miles out of my comfort zone, but this *is* the idea—the New Micah push I need. "I'll get over it. My mural is unfinished because it's this swirling background of fairy-tale figures, but it's missing a center."

Grant stands as if I electrocuted him. He grins. "So my design is all center with no background. No vibe."

"Put them together . . ." I hook two fingers.

"And they're one," Grant finishes. "It's us."

Grant yelps with delight and hurls himself at me. His bigness presses me tightly against the window—a safe firmness, like I'm a swaddled baby—and we kiss. I'm so happy he hasn't been shaving. His scruff is even scratchier than our first night together.

Everything feels correct again. The universe provides.

"The Knight Princess can be a living statue!" he says, alive with creativity. He paces the room, his shirt completely unbuttoned. "It's a performance piece, not a runway. We'll open on your mural. People think it's just a painting. A very great painting, but no one knows the Knight Princess is alive in it. Then . . . they leap out."

"Gasp?" I ask, grinning.

"Gasp!" he yells.

Grant and I clasp hands—our old connection sparkles. My idea has fixed everything. Grant and I will become even closer. His design becomes bigger. I get a ready-made portfolio into the Art Institute. Best of all, this forces me to finish my mural because we'll need it in . . .

Three weeks.

Oh. Well. I just have to finish something in three weeks that I haven't been able to complete in years and then show it to my dream art school, or else I ruin my boyfriend's dreams and my own.

No pressure.

## Chapter 19
# THE BELIEVER

A falling sensation follows me all the way from the Art Institute to Audrey's. I swore I would avoid the café to give Elliot space, but I desperately need chai, and I miss my friend. He always gives me so much courage, and I need it more than ever.

My mural is waiting at home, laughing.

*You're not a real artist, Micah. Not like Grant. You have no vision, babe.*

Elliot will ground my thoughts, like he always does.

When I reach Audrey's, however, he isn't up front. His chipper co-worker says he's in the back mixing mocha syrup—it could be a while. Luckily, I didn't come to Audrey's alone. Coming here was Hannah's idea, as she lured me with the promise of finally meeting Jackson, her super-secret boyfriend. It turns out Jackson is exactly the person I needed to hang with: a chill, no-stakes straight guy who doesn't know a thing about me or my work. At the café, Jackson is a little tidier than when I spied him in the park. He wears a tightly slicked-back ponytail (likely some intervention on Hannah's part to improve his unveiling). His clothes are still black and plain, but they're less torn up than the others. He stirs seven sugar packets into a small coffee and leaves the wrappers scattered around the table, as if wherever he goes, he needs to make a little garbage-y nest around himself.

Next to him, Hannah sits nervously, ankles crossed. *Desperate* for this to go well.

What she doesn't know is that Jackson has already endeared himself to me with how he put Hannah at ease during the Taste.

"I'm pretty into manga, I guess," Jackson says, throwing back his coffee. "But, like, everybody is, so that's not anything too special about myself."

Fidgeting, Hannah leans in. "Jackson draws Naruto perfectly on his folders."

"Oh, you draw?" I ask.

"Kinda," he says.

"Ever go to Rhapsody in You? They've got the best color selections."

"Nah, I'm not an artist. I just use a Bic, whatever's lying around."

Hannah leans in again, much more restless than last time. "Jackson's cousin is a key grip on movie sets. He said he can probably bring Jackson on as a PA."

Jackson sputters a laugh into his hand. "Why'd you just say that out of the blue?"

"Well, he did!"

"Yeah, but what's that got to do with anything?"

"Isn't it what you want to do?"

"No, actually. Sometimes they'll make a Batman here, and I thought it would be cool to do a Batman, but . . ." He laughs, but it's not at her. He shakes her hand like he's trying to wake her up. "You're being kinda weird tonight. Being a little weirdo?"

Hannah mutters, "No, I'm not bein' weird," as her rigid armor slowly drops. They smile at each other, and it brings her to life. She turns to me. "I've been wound up about you two meeting. I want you to like Jackson. Just tell me you like him, and I can calm down."

I raise my hands in surrender. "I *really* like Jackson!"

She snaps her fingers. "But actually, or because I made you say it?"

"Actually literally! You two are super cute. He's cool. Let's hang out more, please."

Grinning, Jackson hops up and says, "Too much praise! I'll be right back, going to piss."

He kisses Hannah. "I love how you don't skip any details," she says.

As Jackson leaves for the restroom, I lunge for my friend's arm and give her the good news: "He really likes you!"

Covering her eyes, she whispers, "He has no plans. Like, none. College applications, dreams, goals, nothing. I don't even think he's taking the SAT?"

"In that case, let me call the FBI."

We smirk at each other until she breaks into an embarrassed

giggle. "I'm serious. What do I do? I know every millimeter of my dreams: three kids—two girls, one boy—by age thirty-four, as soon as my third bestseller goes into its paperback run. Where's he fit into all that?"

I pull her into a tight hug. "I don't know. Until you do, just keep being worshipped by a cool guy who really cares that you're comfortable and being yourself."

A golden glow rises in Hannah's cheeks as she sighs wistfully. "If I must."

My own advice of "just be cool and see how things play out" is immediately put to the test as Hannah and Jackson get ready to leave: Elliot, his hair sweat-glued to his forehead, emerges from the back room's swinging saloon doors clutching an obscene vat of mocha syrup.

My body relaxes when I see him. It's been way too long.

Elliot sets down the mocha tub with a grunt. When he glances up, we lock eyes. For some reason, I immediately duck behind one of the café's Parisian-style pillars in a pathetic attempt to hide. Because we aren't in a cartoon, everyone—including Elliot—notices.

Jackson guffaws. "Your friends are great!"

Hannah pats my shoulder, whispers, "It's still the same Elliot," and waves goodbye. "Gotta catch a train to Orland Park." She sends me a sidelong glare at the mention of this deep, deep suburb.

Whatever their excursion is, it's for Jackson, so I keep my eyebrows where they are and ask, "Who's in Orland Park?"

"Just some buddies of mine," Jackson says, cracking his back.

"They made up this zombie tabletop game, and the lovely Hannah Bergstrom and I agreed to be their beta testers."

She curtsies to Elliot and me, who are both stunned. "Yes, boys," she says, "this city gal is off to the burbs to roll dice with sweet Hobbits." Jackson grins from ear to ear. He doesn't mind this descriptor at all. They kiss. "We all have our own fairy-tale journeys."

Is my own dating advice rubbing off on Hannah, queen of relationships??

After Hannah and Jackson depart, Elliot delivers the mocha syrup to his fellow barista, while I simply stand here, leaning against the pillar I tried to vanish behind.

Do I leave? Does Elliot even want me here?

"I'm taking my thirty early, okay?" Elliot asks his co-worker, who tells him to have a blast as she transfers the mocha into a dispenser on the bar. In one smooth motion, Elliot slides underneath the counter and unties his apron. He flicks back his damp hair and smiles. "How about some chai?" It's weird to see him smiling, as if our last face-to-face interaction didn't feel like pure agony. I nod because forming words is suddenly impossible. Elliot pokes my belly, forcing a giggle out of me. "Come on, don't be chai."

With that single pun, the heaviness of our festival fiasco leaves my shoulders.

He's not mad at me! And it looks like his job is safe. The one thing that isn't safe is his relationship. "Brandon and I have barely spoken since the Taste," he confesses over a large chai.

The words land like a knife in my chest. "I'm *so* sorry. Grant is, too."

"I know. He called before you got here."

"Really?" I ask. Elliot nods. Another stone lifts off me. I'd really love it if Grant and Elliot could be friends.

"You got a good one." Elliot gazes deeply into the swirling chai, as if it holds some mystical answers. "I don't."

"I promise, I can make it better—"

Elliot glances up, a new darkness in his eyes. "I don't want it better. I'm done."

One stone leaves, another knife enters.

*Don't say you're done with Chicago.* Please *don't say you're done with Chicago.*

"He told me he settled for me," Elliot says. "That I wasn't worth giving up *Olympic training* for, not even for a day." He sips while I marinate in my shock that Brandon could be so cruel. "He took it back later. Said he didn't mean it, that it was just the stress of the training and the embarrassing festival, blah, blah. I don't care."

"But you two just went to the lake," I say, confused. "I saw it on Instagram. It was such a cute picture, you two swimming again!"

Elliot laughs hollowly. "Micah, you fell for the oldest Instagram trick in the book. Post an old picture from when you used to be happy so no one can tell how . . . *not* you are."

"Shit," I groan. Of course—they looked almost too happy in that picture. My chest in flames, I shake my head. "Well, Brandon's wrong. You're worth giving up everything for."

Elliot inhales sharply, as if my kindness is more painful than Brandon's insults could ever be. He sweeps his arms like he's wiping a slate clean. "Can we change the subject? My relation-ship is in hospice, and I'm covered in syrup. Talk about anything else? Please?"

"Uh," I say, searching, "I'm going to be in Grant's show."

Grinning devilishly, Elliot snaps a finger gun. "Grant told me. Your mural. That's exciting. You obviously immediately regret-ted saying you would. Am I right? You only have a few weeks to finish it. You hate yourself, yes?"

ALL THE WEIGHT LIFTS OFF MY BODY.

How does Elliot always understand everything?

"Yes!" I moan, collapsing dramatically onto the table. "Give me a time machine. Let me go back and un-say that I'd do this!"

"Relax. Sip." He slides the chai closer, which I drain of its syrupy-sweet dregs. "Answer honestly: Why has that mural been sitting up there under that sad old curtain for so long?"

Why don't I have as strong of a vision for it as I do (or *did*) for Instaloves?

Normally, I'd dodge the question or say there were a hundred reasons why. Except Elliot and I have been so nakedly honest with each other—so relaxed in this café with this perfect latte and these perfect, warm string lights—that I'm not scared of his judgment.

"I don't like it," I admit.

"That is honest." He chuckles. "Why?"

"I was fourteen when I sketched the idea. It's childish. It's about fairy-tale romance, but the way a little kid thinks of it."

Elliot's mouth plummets open. "Come *on*. You don't believe in fairy tales anymore? You're living one."

I bite my nails as I attempt to articulate the truth to Elliot—and myself. "I'm living a fairy tale, yes, but it's . . . different. There's messy dimensions to it now. The picture-perfect mural in my room just feels fake."

Elliot taps a finger to his lips. "Your Instaloves sketches were fantasies drawn from reality. They were real people, right?"

In less than a few taps, he brings up a scroll of old Instaloves posts—blasts from the past. My Intelligentsia crush, reimagined as a magnificent bird-prince of a sky kingdom (to match the sparrow tattoo on his wrist). After weeks of Grant treating Instaloves as our own personal publicist, it's refreshing to hear Elliot cut right back to the soul of why I draw.

I reach over to Elliot's phone to scroll through the next few posts.

The proximity of our hands to each other sends a crackle of static up my arm.

"They were real," I say. "Reality made into fantasy."

Elliot scoots his chair closer. His bare knee is an inch away from mine. "Those figures in your mural were just invented. Nobody real?"

"Yeah?" I swallow hard, trying not to feel his knee hairs prickling mine.

Elliot springs up, his break finally over, and *my* break from sitting so close to him can begin. As he pulls on his apron, he says, "Okay . . . So. Start the mural over."

My single, barking laugh cuts through the café's soft piano music. "I can't?!"

"Why not?"

"I only have a few weeks!"

"You drew Grant on the train in ten minutes. When you're into it, you make it happen."

The room begins to tilt. This doesn't make any sense. I can't just ball up this artwork I've been working on for years and whoosh up a new one over a few weekends.

Can I?

"Clear your schedule tomorrow," Elliot says, tying the back of his apron.

*Don't look at his butt in those shorts. Don't look at*—all right, I looked. Damn. How he doesn't knock over syrup pumps with it, I'll never know.

I breathe myself back to calm. I've had a long week of feeling weird about my boyfriend, and Elliot is just a cute guy I care about who cares about me.

"Okay, schedule cleared," I say, hoisting my satchel. "What are we doing tomorrow?"

"I'm taking you around the city," Elliot says, slipping behind the bar counter. "Bring your sketchbook. Bring two. Plenty of pencils. You're going to get inspired."

"I can't take up your whole day," I splutter.

"I'm not working," he says. "And I have a boyfriend I really want to avoid." His eyes twinkle. "Also, I want this mural to look great for selfish reasons."

I approach the bar, closing the gap between us. "Oh?"

Elliot spreads his mocha-splattered arms in a grand pose. "Meet the Knight Princess."

Okay, now the room is fully upside down. "WHAT?"

"When Grant apologized for the Taste, he told me his model flaked. I'm the right measurements"—he slaps his rear—"it's a paying gig, and he said he promised you he'd make it up to me, so . . . I'm your star. This is a three-way project now!"

Phrasing, Elliot. Phrasing.

I can't believe Grant got Elliot a paying job that's not dealing with customers. That could prevent him from leaving the city! And it's something we can all work on together. We can all thrive! No one has to lose.

I'm flying.

## Chapter 20
# THE MURAL'S MUSE

The next morning, I pack two sketchbooks and plenty of pencils for my day in search of faces to inspire my mural characters. It needs to scream Wish Granted and be a unifying backdrop to ground the Knight Princess. While the morning L trains rush above me, my penny board vibrates with thunderous energy—the same energy that brought Grant and me together in an unforgettable collision.

The train started it all. The mural should be a train.

I stop my board underneath the rails. Through sweating fingers, I type out my concept into Notes: *The mural will be one long train, populated by dozens of fantasy characters inspired by the people of Chicago. In the center will be Grant's Knight Princess gown, worn by Elliot.*

I squeeze my phone with unrestrained glee. The power of

this idea—and to collaborate with the two boys I care about the most—has energized my spark for this mural like nothing before. Elliot is right—the more I bring my Instaloves spirit into my mural, the more "me" it's going to feel. Whether it's pencil or paint doesn't matter. The idea drives everything.

We have a kingdom to create.

Elliot and I begin our search for realness at—where else?—the Water Tower mall. In Nordstrom, we sneak through rows of discounted spring wear, on the trail of a salesclerk he believes "has a vibe." As Elliot parts the clothing racks to let us sneak, all I can focus on are his fingers, which are surprisingly long and elegant for short boys like us. Even more shocking are his nails—manicured nail beds and flawlessly sharp tips. For someone who makes a thousand drinks a day, there isn't a speck of dirt to be found. Impressive.

Glancing back, Elliot smirks. "Staring at these?" he asks, flashing his claws like a cat.

I stifle a nervous giggle. I *hate* being caught staring. "I thought food service was murder on a manicure," I whisper. "That's what Hannah told me."

"It is if you don't keep it up." Grinning, Elliot flexes in his tropical tank top and kisses his manicure. "I do my own nails. I can do yours too sometime, 'cause . . ." He sneers at my fingers, which I don't need to inspect to know they are chewed, frayed, uneven, and paint-crusted. Elliot tsk-tsks while shaking his head. "All that money, and you with those grubby digits. Maybe a little less yacht, a little more styling?"

Laughing, I flick Elliot's shoulder. "You're hired. Now, can we get back to work?"

"Oh." He smiles and waves me closer. "This is the guy I saw. Menswear salesman, kinda looks like he could be a coachman or a palace guard?"

I launch myself on tiptoes to peer over the rack at our quarry—a trim, imperious young white man in a loudly patterned suit waits on a customer. Laughing, I crouch back down. "I've sketched him before." Elliot juts his head toward me, awash in confusion. "He's Instaloves Boyfriend number 71! He sold my dad a Varvatos suit."

Elliot gasps with recognition. "The Old West gunslinger!"

He remembered a sketch I did last Christmas? I'm lost for a response. I'm too flattered that Elliot has been this long-term Instaloves fan before we even knew each other. Back when I would tell Hannah, *"Oh,* Elliot *said the funniest thing today? Hmph!"*

We abandon the salesclerk—the mural inspirations must be independent of my Instaloves. "After all," Elliot says, "there *are* more interesting people in the city than just the ones you want to date." He nudges my ribs, and I shake my fist.

Every time he teases me—and I tease back—my stomach tightens.

It's reckless to come so close to flirting. But who's to say gay friends can't flirt a little bit without it turning into this big deal?

He's cute and wearing an adorable, skin-revealing outfit today. The only thing that me looking at him proves is that my Gay is still working. Me finding him cute is an objective fact, not an opinion or some crush.

Even if we never find inspiring faces today, it will have been worth it just to have a chill day with Elliot where he doesn't have to stress about his awful job or boyfriend. Also, to have a day where I don't stop every block just to capture another Instagrammable moment with Grant.

Luckily, we don't wait long before inspiration strikes Elliot again.

"Her!" He points at a woman outside the three-story, brick-and-glass Eataly building. The woman—a street violinist—is draped in a flowing, scarlet frock and matching wool infinity scarf. She serenades Eataly's patio diners with a jumpy tune—lively but serene.

*A player for the court.*

My face alight, I drop my satchel onto a shaded bench across the street and sketch the woman. The mood is exquisitely captured: a medieval-robed woman in jangling jewels strums a lute for guests of the king. It took only five minutes.

*"That."* Elliot excitedly taps my sketchbook. "Exactly that!"

This could work. Another dozen like this, and I'd have my whole mural!

I pull Elliot into a victorious embrace. The bare skin outside of his tank top is cozily soft, like a heated blanket. I should hug him more; this is nice. While he's in my arms, I realize this is the first time I've let someone watch me sketch something from scratch. I wasn't embarrassed. I didn't even think about it.

That's Elliot's gift—putting people at ease.

Or is it more than that?

All I know is that in Elliot's presence, my creative vision has emerged like a damn phoenix from the ashes!

The afternoon flies by in a blink as Elliot and I cross the river toward the parks, spotting one inspiration after another. Each new face I sketch makes the next one easier to spot: an elderly couple crossing the bridge becomes a Still Happy Ever After; a couple helping their toddler clean her spilt ice cream becomes a family of swamp ogres; a group of skateboarders becomes a trio of leather-winged, punk fairies.

When we reach Millennium Park, a literal pumpkin coach travels past us, as if Cinderella herself were on her way to a ball. The enormous, cream-colored pumpkin—roped in fairy lights—sits atop a horseless, old-fashioned motorcar. Inside, a mother and her two daughters squeal with delight, snapping selfies and capturing the curiosity of the entire street—Elliot and me most of all.

"*Wow*," I gasp, staring jealously at the family as they ride by. "How come I've never seen these before?"

"They're all over the place!" Elliot says. "It feels like it was invented just for you."

"Seriously!" I clasp my fingers together and turn to Elliot. "Let's rent one. It'll be great for the sketches!"

Elliot glances away and laughs bitterly. "A bit romantic, no? You should get it for you and Grant."

I want to roll my eyes, but not at Elliot. I'm annoyed with myself. Grant would love a romantic carriage ride in one of these things—as would I; it's both of our styles . . . If this were our first date night when the whole world was just us. Back when I was just Micah—and he was just Grant—holding each other after escaping the rain and sharing our worst fears. Surrounded by art. Back when the art was bigger than us, not us trying to be bigger than the art.

My throat aches with the memory and how long ago it feels.

Today, Grant would only see this carriage as great publicity for Wish Granted.

"Did I . . . step on a land mine?" Elliot asks, wincing.

I shake my head as if being startled out of a dream. "Huh? No. I was just thinking about the pumpkin carriage and how cool it would be to ride it at night with all the lights on. I'll ask Grant, sure!"

He smacks my arm, looking worried. "I'd love to go! I wasn't trying to shit on it. It would probably be so much fun, just . . . After my big meme, I don't know. Your fans might see it and get the wrong idea?"

I groan. "My fans? Don't worry about them." I smack Elliot's shoulder and am met with another pleasant surge of softness. This entire day has escalated into a game of smack-smack-smack with us. It feels like the safest way of touching each other when I get a sudden urge to hold his hand or hug him again.

It's *not* because I'm crushing. He's just a huggable guy, like how you see a puppy and want to pet them. His shoulder might as well have a sign that says SMACK HERE FOR WARM AND SOFT. Besides, he always smacks first.

"Tell you what," Elliot says with another smack, "if Grant doesn't want to ride the big pumpkin or you can't find time, we should pick a good night and rent it."

YES.

Elliot would be the perfect friend to ride in the carriage with, because when I do it, I want to be laughing, not livestreaming the whole thing. I can already feel the wind rushing through my hair as we ride the coach through a twinkle-lit summer city night.

At our next drawing stop, Crown Fountain, two towering monoliths stand opposite each other. Filling the entire surfaces of the monoliths are digitized faces of real people, as high as a three-story building, watching, blinking, and spitting. From unseen hoses, water arcs outward into the crowd from their giant, digital mouths. Kids run around screaming as they try to avoid the water blasts.

"*God*, I want to get wet so badly," Elliot moans, fanning himself outside the fountain.

"Phrasing." I chuckle.

Elliot runs, whooping, toward one of the faces (the kids have temporarily clustered near the other—no need to freak out their parents). Yelping with delight, he collides with the spray and then shakes himself like a puppy until his hair sticks out every which way.

I sneak a quick picture. I can't help myself.

The moment is captured with shocking clarity: Elliot, beautifully alone, beams while the sunset brilliantly catches falling water droplets.

I'm already sketching Elliot before he sloshes back. "Refreshing!" he booms. "Try it!"

"I'm good. Besides, I'm on to my next doodle."

"Ooh, yeah? Who?"

My hand sweeps over the paper with wide, deep strokes of charcoal. The image materializes in minutes. Elliot peers over my shoulder at the unfinished picture: a large stone face spews a waterfall from its mouth. Beneath it, a short, huggable sea creature—a water sprite—dances along the falls like a magical, homosexual surfer fish.

Elliot squats next to me—cheek to cheek—for a closer look. He's dripping down my back—mercifully cool after our day baking outside. "That is one thicc fish," he says.

"So stupid," I snort, smacking his hand.

"Look at that little mama! Is that me?"

I nod, my cheeks on fire. I don't want Elliot thinking I drew his body in a way he doesn't see it, or, like, in a sexualized way. He's got curves . . . so that's how I drew him.

But it doesn't seem to bother Elliot. In fact, he can't stop smiling at my work.

"I look happy," he says flatly.

"You deserve to be," I say on a shallow breath.

A soothing, prickling feeling sneaks up my neck. It's a throwback feeling to my lovelorn, thirsty days at the dawn of Instaloves. It has nothing to do with Elliot; I always get tingly and weird when a cute boy peeks over my shoulder—whether it's at my sketchbook or my phone. Who *wouldn't* get a small rush when someone cute brings their bare skin a centimeter away from yours?

The tense air between us shatters as Elliot claps to pump up our energy. Yanking my arm, he chants, "Where to next? Where to next!"

Anywhere, it doesn't matter. I just want this to keep going.

On the grassy hill leading out of the park to the street, a young, dark-skinned Black mother in a *Nubia & the Amazons* comics T-shirt kneels next to her six-year-old son. He whispers in her ear. "That's a good idea," the mother responds. "Ask her!" The mother's voice is loud and reassuring—too loud for her son, who glances around to make sure no one is eavesdropping.

For his sake, Elliot and I avert our eyes.

The mother walks her son to the older white woman manning a Sabrett hot dog cart. The vendor's grandmotherly hair is tightly curled and pearly white, and she's decked out in red Chicago Bulls gear. With a combination of delight and plummeting nausea, I remember where I've seen her before: she sold me Andy McDermott's hot dog.

Seven hundred lifetimes have passed over the last two months.

The vendor mists herself with an electric fan and leans down to the boy: "What would you like on your dog, sweetie? Plain? Mustard? Run it through the garden?"

The boy puffs his chest bravely, as if calling upon hours of training on how to speak up to strange adults. "Um, Mrs. Sabrett . . . ?"

The boy's mother and the vendor share a smile. "It's *Ms.* Sabrett, darling." The vendor taps the Sabrett logo on her cart's umbrella. "There's no mister. He's out of the picture. What can I do for you?"

"Um . . . I want to get a Cinderella pumpkin car. Where do I go?"

Elliot smacks my arm and whispers, "It's a little you!" He holds up two pinching fingers. I smack him back. A lightness spills over me.

Good for this kid. It's not easy being a little boy and asking for a princess thing, no matter how cool it looks. I used to be terrified to bring up fairy-tale stuff to anyone outside my family. If I was in a store and saw something princess related, summoning the courage to ask for it was a long, interior negotiation.

After the hot dog vendor supplies the boy with directions to the pumpkin carriage house, he thanks her and yanks his mother away to find his fairy tale. A faint melancholy drags on me like a weighted coat. *Good luck out there*, I silently wish the boy. *Fairy tales exist, but the real things aren't always what you expect.*

Grant and I are still a fairy tale, but after this day with Elliot, I'm more confused than ever. Would a fairy-tale boy not pick up on my signals that I'm really freaked out by all this publicity? Would a fairy-tale prince spend all day with another cute boy and barely think of his boyfriend?

I don't even particularly miss Grant right now, which feels awful, but it's so good to laugh. It feels like an eternity since I've laughed this much without an uncomfortable moment spoiling things. And to be understood without having to constantly explain why I'm feeling a certain way, why I don't want to take that picture, why I don't want that flash mob.

This is the first time I've thought of Grant all day, and immediately, I want to take a Sleeping Beauty-sized nap.

Before leaving, I sketch our newest subjects; the silver-haired, Bulls-merch-clad vendor becomes a jubilant fairy godmother, conjuring hot dogs in the air that swirl around a pumpkin carriage. Beneath her, a baby mouse dances with a mother mouse.

Thanks to Elliot, my mural is going to be brimming with genuine joy.

Back over the bridge in River North, we're lured onward

by the intoxicating aroma of caramel corn. Even the air outside Garrett Popcorn is sugary sweet. The line bursts out of the storefront and continues down the sidewalk, as if the popcorn were a celebrity making a rare public appearance.

"Such a tourist trap," I mutter.

"Some stuff is worth getting trapped for," Elliot says. The lightheartedness in his voice punches me in my throat. His relationship is on life support, but you'd think he didn't have a worry in his mind. If I were in his position, you couldn't pry me out of bed.

His optimism holds a mirror up to mine. All those messages from strangers about how I make them believe in fairy tales again. They don't know about my doubts. My second thoughts. They didn't hear me just now, callously muttering to people what suckers they are to wait for the greatest popcorn ever forged by humans.

When did I stop being that little boy fascinated by a Cinderella pumpkin? My first thought wasn't *Wow, so magical*, it was *Ugh, my boyfriend is gonna want to ride this for weird publicity reasons*.

"Well, twist my arm," I ask. "Want to get some popcorn?"

He turns with a surprised smile. "Actually . . . food isn't a bad idea. I have another tourist trap in mind, if that's all right with you?"

"Let's get trapped. It's a d—" I break off before the word spills out. "Uh, let's go!"

I cannot *believe* I almost said *It's a date*! My panic over the near slip feels like a horse kicked me in the chest, but I can't tell you how many times I've slipped up and said *"Okay, bye, love you"* to a teacher or Wi-Fi repairman because that's how I hang up with Hannah.

If Elliot is the friend I think he is, he'll make fun of me for almost saying *date*. He *loves* jumping on these invitations to pick at me. And I love it.

But by the time we stop for lunch, the jokes never come. Maybe he didn't notice?

If there were a nuclear war in Chicago, you can believe that Pizzeria Uno would remain standing amid the rubble. Uno's is a darkened tavern inside a converted, brick firehouse—a deep-dish staple from an era before things like "windows" or "lots of space" was a thing people factored into their restaurant designs. On the plus side, Uno's offers plenty of privacy where I can cozy away from the world and eat my feelings.

"What did you think of me before we met?" I ask, across the booth from Elliot. "Like, when I was just the guy Hannah talked about."

"Ah," Elliot says, taking a gleeful sip of Pepsi. "The great Micah Summers. I thought you must be a good guy. You know, she's obsessed with you. I was just trying to come in a close second."

*"Please."* I slap the table before serving us another slice from the pan. "You're all she talked about the whole spring semester. Elliot and his animals, the little Disney Princess."

Elliot grins as he nibbles a toothpick. "You were probably like, 'Who's this ho?'"

"Yes."

Elliot laughs so loudly, other customers turn around in their booths. "Okay, don't worry. You're always going to be Hannah's main character. I'm the one who comes in on season three."

I jab my tomatoey fork at him. "Hey, those are some of the best characters."

"Ooh, a fan favorite!" Elliot spirit-fingers down his face like a waterfall.

"You're already the favorite in the Wish Granted show. Honestly, I wish I was in this show *less*."

Elliot waves away my concern. "Your mural is gonna be amazing."

My stomach flips after another bite. "It's not that. I just wish I had my sketch account back. It was a safe space to go when I felt overwhelmed, and now it's become this marketing thing." Silence falls as I slosh my straw around in the crushed ice. "I wish I could still post anonymously. As soon as I dropped that picture of me and Grant, Instaloves became about . . . us, getting good 'press' . . . I don't know. I haven't posted an actual sketch in weeks. It's all been promo."

Elliot keeps his face politely neutral. "So if I could wave a wand and make you anonymous again, what would you draw? More crushes?" He chuckles.

"No." I laugh. "Honestly, today was so much fun . . . I want to keep drawing this." As the words spill out, they feel like deep truths, but so, so simple. Like I always should've known this. "People. Everyday fairy tales. That's my real vision. And I want to use Instaloves as a portfolio to study painting at the Art Institute, push myself to get stronger at painting, and take my vision to a larger canvas."

"Have you said any of this to Grant?"

I swallow hard. "It can wait."

Wincing, Elliot chews the tip of his straw. "As someone about to become brutally single, I strongly urge you to say the little things that you're feeling before they become the big things that you're feeling."

We catch each other's eyes across the booth, both of us falling briefly silent.

*Brutally single.* It sounds awful. I don't want that for either of us. All I want is to circle around in the booth to hug him—and my brain is screaming at me to do it—but strangely, I'm frozen.

Elliot smiles—almost sadly—and sloshes around his own crushed ice. He glances up. "I'm gonna miss Chicago. This pizza just puts me in my happy place. So many people complain that it's not really pizza, it's a casserole—like each person who says that thinks they're the first one who came up with that line. So what if it's a casserole or a pizza? It's sauce, it's cheese, it's hot. Whatever it is, it's yummy."

Friend or fan favorite, Elliot is no secondary character: whatever he is to me, he puts me in my happy place. I can tell him anything, and he just gets it.

I cannot lose him.

*Please, universe! Let Elliot become the main character in some lucky boy's story, so this star-in-the-making can be appreciated and worshipped—and I can stop worrying if he's going to bloop out of my life.*

Because now that Brandon is gone, what else is going to keep Elliot here?

## Chapter 21
# THE LITTLE WORRIES

The end of July is here, and the show is only a week away.

Because of our looming deadline, dates with Grant have become quick lunches and even quicker rolls on his twin bed before he heads back to the workroom. The Knight Princess has graduated from design to construction, so the days of Grant and me locking ourselves away in his dorm to create and fool around are gone. All business has moved to the Art Institute's cavernous design workshop, which we split with a dozen other cohorts. It isn't romantic—it isn't even chill. In fact, the closer we get to the show, the more intense vibes everyone gives off:

Eyes narrow over sewing machines. Short, aggravated breaths huff with each scissor cut.

In this space, hanging around Grant makes me feel like a third wheel, not an active artistic contributor. It burns, remembering my day sketching with Elliot. I got to be me, not some supporting character whose only function is to signal boost the show from my famous account.

*Dummy, you have a mural to finish. GO DO THAT.*

I just wish I could work on it next to Grant and feel that collaborative rush again.

"Okay, I'm taking off!" I kiss Grant's ear as he hunches over a table measuring different lengths of chain mail.

"Good luck!" Grant says, glancing up. "Oh, hey, we haven't done an Instaloves today. Maybe you can take a picture of the workshop door and post something like 'One week left!' You know? 'Ooh, what's behind this door?' Tease something? You're better at the captions."

My smile freezes.

All today, I wanted to post one of my citizens of Chicago sketches, be creative and real again and begin my pivot away from exclusively Wish Granted content, but of course, Grant has more promo in mind. Photos that don't have a single thing to do with my artistic point of view. My grid used to be so eye-catching, and now it's just a hodgepodge of selfies and CLICK MY LINKTREE FOR TICKETS.

Where did my vision go?

I had this huge creative breakthrough with Elliot where I finally crystalized my vision—bringing reality into fantasy—but there isn't an inch of room for that now. Grant is so focused on his show, he's sucking up all the oxygen in the room. He's definitely prioritizing his artistic point of view, so why am I not fighting for mine?

As I watch Grant tinker away, blissfully unaware that a storm is brewing in me, Elliot's words of wisdom echo through my mind: *Say the little things that you're feeling before they become the big things that you're feeling.*

That was two weeks ago. Not only have I failed to bring up the little things to Grant, I'm also worried they're no longer little things.

Yet once again, my courage fails, and I post a picture of myself next to a goddamn door.

Shoving out all unkind thoughts of Grant and Wish Granted, the only thing I allow to take up real estate in my mind is this mural. The ticking clock has made my art come alive. After my pizza night with Elliot, I took my city sketches back to my room and basically didn't stop painting for two weeks. It felt like coming home.

The old, discarded mural was rolled up and tucked away in my closet with the rest of my childhood things. No longer boxed in by my original, dusty ideas, I transcribed sketch after sketch into a living, breathing kingdom aboard a magical train: the fairy godmother conjuring up hot dogs, Maggie and Manda as lawn gnomes in matching outfits, and Elliot as a joyous water sprite dancing up waterfalls.

Elliot was right: drawing the fantasy out of everyday life is my superpower.

To my mother's horror, I've been averaging five hours of sleep a night, but it's impossible to rest now that my motor has finally been switched on. My woes about Instaloves disappear. Even my painting anxiety is manageable. The painterly strokes don't look slapdash—my colors lie across each other with spectacular harmony. I don't hesitate selecting hues; razor-sharp instinct now guides my hand. While painting remains more laborious than sketching—each detail needing inner negotiation before I add it to the muslin—I'm up for the challenge.

My sophomore-year painting tutor wouldn't even recognize me!

I need to make sure she gets an invitation to the show.

With only a few touches remaining, I send updates to Elliot and Grant—but *only* to them because they're part of the Knight Princess creative team. I zoom in on Elliot, the thicc water sprite, and text the group about his mural cameo. Which I immediately regret.

Omg which character am I? Grant texts.

Oh no.

Blood abandons my head, and the room starts to tilt.

*How* could I not put Grant in the mural? Boy 100? My prince, my boyfriend?

I've never painted faster in my life. No time to fret over choices or second-guess, I don't even sketch an outline first. *Swoosh, swoosh*, I lead with indigo, forming a large, swooping back in a vacant patch near the right of the train. My shaking fingers open new canisters of royal blue, gray, and bronze. In under fifteen minutes, Grant becomes a larger-than-life prince—the Beast—waltzing with another prince—me, sloppily detailed but kept in shadow.

Why the Beast? Well, anxiety flooded my brain, shutting down complex thought, so the only idea that arose about Grant was his feeling of being cursed.

I text Grant's inclusion to the group, along with a lie about my delay being because I stepped away for lunch. After four tortuous minutes of no response, Grant texts: BEAST??? How dare you? jk I love it! I look hawt. You're so good at this!

Finally, I breathe.

I need a lunch break, after all. I skip out to make soup and lock my door behind me. In the three minutes it takes to micro-wave a bowl, Maggie and Mom have crept almost entirely inside my room.

"Stop!" I order, balancing my scalding bowl of French onion. "I locked this door, how . . . ?" A key sits jammed into the handle. My glare shoots directly to Mom. For my sixteenth birthday, she promised me I could have my own lock where no one else had the key.

She glances away guiltily, muttering, "It's my house."

"Then you owe me a new birthday present."

The next day, on a stormy Sunday afternoon, the members of Team Wish Granted meet for the official relocation of my mural to the Art Institute. Grant, Elliot, Hannah, and Jackson gather around the kitchen island to pick at the deli tray my mom ordered. Outside my room, Maggie meets me in cheeseburger-patterned pj's and freshly showered hair. She cradles Lilith, who plops uncertainly in her arms like a furry Koosh ball. "I can't let you go," Maggie reassures the cat. "There's people moving stuff; you'll get underfoot."

Lilith glares sourly at me, as if she knows I'm the reason for all of this. I give the good girl a little scritch, very rare to achieve except when she's being held. "Manda okay?" I ask. Maggie's girlfriend is currently saving a street space for the moving truck that'll take my mural to the Institute.

Maggie winces as she flips wet hair from her eyes. "She's fiiiiiine. She just gets stressed out holding spots, like she's gonna get in trouble."

"I'm sorry!" I double-check my pockets to make sure I have everything I'll need to leave from here. "We're coming now!"

"She'll be okay!" Maggie pulls me into a sharp hug, Lilith moaning as she smooshes between us, and whispers, "So proud of you. I've never seen you work so hard at something."

"Thank you!" I whisper. "You're still not getting a peek at the mural."

"You little *shrimp*!" She pushes away from the hug and, with a final smile at my closed door, huffs, "Happy for you, though."

We air kiss, and Maggie and Lilith return to their room. On my way to the kitchen, I can't shake the smile from my face. My mural is finished. It's going out into the world. And everyone I care about is here to help.

We roll the mural up like a carpet and slip it into a sealed bag. It isn't until the largest helpers—Grant and Jackson—try to lift it that we realize just how heavy the mural is when it's compacted. While the Institute expensed Grant a small moving truck to transport it, the mural still needs to be shuttled downstairs.

Our penthouse elevator is too small, so it needs to be navigated twenty flights down out of the emergency stairs.

The journey out of my home is treacherous, not only because of the mural's bulk, but because of the bitter barbs people keep flinging at me:

"I promise I'm not looking!" Mom says. "Should I hide in the laundry room?"

"Oh, *now* I'm part of Team Wish Granted?" Hannah asks. "Now that there's grunt work to be done?"

The only person who minds their business is Jackson, who is earning major brownie points with his confident directions pivoting the mural around corners. Whenever he speaks, I want to throw Hannah a thumbs-up.

Their connection is beautiful.

The things they whisper to each other when no one's looking, the small touches to each other's wrists and smalls of their backs. With a surge of nauseous nostalgia, they remind me of Grant and me on our prologue date at Le Petit Potage. When he kept touching me—not sexually, just tiny touches, like we were strange animals exploring each other.

Those tiny touches around other people haven't happened much lately.

Is it my fault? Have my bitter thoughts about Instaloves subconsciously stopped me?

*Little problems become big problems, Micah.*

In the emergency stairwell, we have eighteen stories to reach the street. The mural's journey is also complicated by our extreme height differences. Grant and Jackson are quite tall, while teeny

Hannah, Elliot, and I struggle to keep the bag from touching the floor.

We look like a seesaw.

Chuckling, Grant elbows Elliot. "We could use Brandon's height right about now."

Next to me, Hannah tenses. The stairwell goes quiet for a brief, dreadful second, and in that moment, I already know what Elliot is going to say: "Yeaaah, I dumped him Tuesday."

Over the top of the bag, I watch Grant's eyes widen. "Oh God, I'm sorry."

"Elliot, I'm sorry, too!" I shout from the back.

My hands are slick with sweat. I can't believe I'm finding out this information when I'm a million miles away from Elliot and can't hug him. He must not have told me because he didn't want Grant and me feeling bad that we firebombed his relationship's last chance at survival.

"Thank you both," Elliot says, stopping at the bottom stair to catch his breath. "I don't want anyone feeling bad. This is a *good* thing, it was a long time coming, and your anniversary show was cute. Any cool person would've thought it was a hilarious misunderstanding. The fact that Brandon didn't"—he exhales loudly—"told me everything I needed to know."

Elliot's words aren't reassuring. Grant and I exchange worried, guilt-ridden glances.

"Who are we talking about?" Jackson asks.

The stairwell erupts with gales of relieved laughter. Hannah really scored with Jackson.

Good cheer returns as the five of us hustle my mural through the lobby and into the moving truck that Manda has kept idling outside. "Oh my God," she says, leaping out in French fry pajamas to match my sister's burger ones. "Like seven cops have come by. No one answered their phones!"

"So sorry!" I say, pulling out the moving truck's rear ramp. "Twenty stories down a tight stairwell with this beast. I'm never painting at home again."

Grant high-fives Manda and says, "Thank you! Go get high. Eat some Crunch Berries."

On an anguished exhale, Manda says, "Don't mind if I do!"

After she flees, Grant takes over driving. The others hoist my mural into the carriage before leaving separately. Finally alone, I join my boyfriend in the passenger seat. He doesn't start driving yet—he just turns to me with a lit-up expression and his phone's camera already open. "Ooh, a selfie where we tease us bringing a mysterious art piece to the show?"

Grant snaps a picture of me with the biggest frown.

Little worries became big worries.

*Say something, Micah!*

"I need Instaloves back," I say, my throat dry with fear. My stomach flips as Grant's brow crinkles in confusion. "I thought I was okay doing promo for the show, but . . . Instaloves is for my art. I know my vision now. And I really think it was supposed to stay anonymous."

Grant stares, unblinking. "Okay . . ."

"I'm sorry—"

"Do you regret telling people I'm your boyfriend?"

His tone dipped so sharply into darkness, I'm momentarily

speechless. "No. Selfies of us are just personal life stuff. I just . . . I don't want to put any more Wish Granted promo on my page. I need my own artistic space—"

Grant flinches, like I've punched him in the heart. "So you do wish I was a secret?"

"That's *not* what I'm saying—" I try to get the words out as Grant squeezes the steering wheel.

"Just tell me I'm smothering you, Micah. You don't have to come up with all of this stuff about you wanting your own artistic space—"

"Grant, you're not listening to me, and *that's* the issue!" The frustration leaps out of my chest. I couldn't control it. Physically incapable of facing me, Grant stares at the moving truck's steering wheel. I breathe myself calmer. "I don't want you to be a secret. I want . . ."

But my brain has flooded. I don't have a clue how to finish the sentence.

"What?" he asks.

"I want Instaloves to be my own thing separate from Wish Granted. Okay?"

Grant shuts his eyes to squint back a rush of tears. With a dull thud in my chest, I realize all he heard was "I want to separate Micah from Grant."

"This is my only chance," he whispers. "You've always stood out. I never have. You're the only reason people are coming to my stupid show and looking at my stupid little costume."

There it is—the truth.

The old wound behind every promo post and every forced selfie.

He thinks he's nothing without me.

I brush wetness from his eyes and pet his precious cheeks. Where is that smiley, confident boy I met on the train hoisting bags of books with ease and taking my breath away with his dimples? I thought he was this immaculately cool and collected star. How could he not trust himself to stand on his own?

He got into the Art Institute before I even thought to try!

"You did something I never could," I say. "You got into this program as a high schooler. You're killing this. You're enough."

Grant can only shake his head. He refuses to believe.

"We can keep promoting," I say. His pink-stained eyes open. "But after the show is over, I'll get back to my sketches. Okay?"

With enormous strain, he smiles and nods. Meanwhile, I can't help but feel I put my heart out on the table, only to have Grant not listen to a word I said. My worries filtered through his pain, his paranoia that I'd ditch him like all the others, leaving both of us unsettled.

## Chapter 22
# THE CAGE

Thunder cracks the sky on the drive to the Art Institute. Gloomy clouds hang overhead, but droplets don't start to fall until the last stretch before the auditorium. Two of Grant's cohorts save us a spot on the rain-soaked curb behind the building.

Grant and Jackson lift each end of the mural while the rest of us race ahead to open the rear entrance. Giggling turns into delighted shrieks as the rain falls harder. I hurl myself against the auditorium doors, letting Grant and Jackson hustle my artwork inside. Soaked but out of the rain, I laugh hysterically against the double doors until I turn . . .

I'm an inch away from Elliot. His shirt and hair are plastered to him.

Droplets fall from his nose onto me; that's how close we are.

He smells sweet and fruity . . .

He's as startled as I am to find himself so close. Thankfully, he breaks our trance when his attention turns to the vast auditorium ahead: "Whoa."

I can't stop myself from gasping. I haven't been inside the auditorium before, but I was expecting something like a janky high school stage. This is like Broadway meets New York Fashion Week: a stunning white runway extends from a proscenium arch with VIP seating on either side and attached stadium seating beyond. The capacity must be in the thousands.

Elliot points at the eternally long runway, which shines like glass. "That's what I'm gonna walk down?"

I point at the stories-high scrim behind the runway. "Yep, and that's where my mural goes."

"We got this." Elliot throws me a triumphant, wet smile, which I return as we grip each other's hands. Confidence whooshes back into my heart.

But only for a moment.

"We ready?" calls a bass-y voice that makes me jump.

Grant waits across the room with a blank expression. His joy from running through the rain has extinguished.

"Yep!" I separate from Elliot without looking back.

*It was an accident, it was an accident, it was an accident.*

Half an hour later, Hannah and Jackson leave for dinner and Team Wish Granted collaborates in the darkened theater. A stage manager, makeup stylist, art director, and show director huddle together several stadium rows above Grant and me. The director calls out various lighting and technical cues until he's satisfied with the exact shade of pink for our piece.

Fairy-tale pink.

Other than the music, Grant barely has an ounce of say in the show's direction, but these decisions are best left up to professionals. Since the director acknowledges Wish Granted is already the most publicized part of the show, he's placing us at the end to make sure no audience members take off early. Other pieces—runway, performance, and art installations—have been deliberately scheduled to build up momentum to us: the grand finale.

The physical realization of the tech rehearsal turns the electricity in me up to eleven.

Fairy tales in our world. Art meeting reality.

Luckily, Grant seems to have forgotten all about Elliot's and my accidental touching. The rehearsal's bustle of productive energy has plastered a wild grin onto those dimples. I wrap my arm around his chest and pull him tighter. "I'm sorry," I whisper, not knowing why. For touching Elliot's hand? For dumping my worries on Grant so close to his very important show? Whatever the reason, *sorry* is the only word that swam to the surface.

Grant moans happily and rests his head on top of mine. "I'm sorry, too."

He means it. Once this show is over, we'll get those tiny touches back.

At last, the big moment comes: Elliot is called to the runway.

He's changed out of his wet clothes and into dance pants and a pastel tank top—very eighties workout video. The choreographer marks Elliot through the steps—my sweet barista moves with incredible energy! He's not even performing yet, but his natural movements are so fluid, I'm reminded of how gracefully he'd juggle four lattes at once.

Grant can't close his mouth, he's so awed. Neither of us was expecting our friend to hit it this hard out of the gate.

Forget whoever dropped out. Elliot is no shoddy replacement.

I remain in the audience while Grant joins Elliot and the choreographer on the runway. Since the previous performer was a professional dancer and Elliot isn't trained, they've reduced the moves to a few simple variations. Nevertheless, he wows everyone. With grace and ease, Elliot throws his entire body into the character of the Knight Princess, which begins as a frail and frightened creature and ends with the runway-stomping moves of a jungle cat.

Gentle but fierce, and Elliot nails it.

He's thriving without Brandon. Obeying his instincts. Savoring moments. Leaping boldly into the unknown. Free and unencumbered.

Oh my God. The idea pops into my mind, fully formed.

"Um, Grant?" I shout from the dark.

Grant, Elliot, and the choreographer shield their eyes against the lights and mark their stopping place. "Everything look okay from back there?" Grant asks.

I grab a sketchbook and pencil and then sprint down the aisle to the runway. The show lights are so strong, I pinch the sting from my eyes when I reach them. "Three-minute break," the choreographer says, collecting his water bottle. "Your group only has another hour before we load in the next team."

Elliot and Grant step closer into my three-person huddle.

The closeness is almost too much. One spicy cologne, one sweet one.

*THREE MINUTES, MICAH, JUST SPIT IT OUT.*

"Grant, you still don't feel a hundred percent about the skirt, right?" I ask.

He shifts uncomfortably next to Elliot, his eyes darting between us, like I'm spilling dirty secrets. "No, I do. The rainbow train completes it."

I take Grant's wrist with a calming hand. *Tiny touches.* "The rainbow train is great! But you said you wanted to make it bigger, showier? Give it a twist? Would you have time to add one more concept to it?" Elliot winces, and Grant grows redder by the second. "Your statement with the Knight Princess is that people don't have to choose between the knight box or the princess box."

"Right . . ." Finally, Grant's fists unclench. Intrigued, he leans closer.

Elliot follows our movements like he's at a tennis match.

"What if there are no boxes?" I explain. "The boxes are traps. A cage." I open my sketchbook to a blank page. Grant and Elliot peer over my shoulder as I sketch the new skirt: a birdcage. "The skirt cage is a continuation from the armored bodice. I know this might be a *bit* of work, but . . ."

Grant closes all distance between us. He grabs my shoulder,

a smile scorched across his face. "The rainbow train hides inside the cage."

"*Yes.*" With another few pencil strokes, I complete the image. "Bustled, the cage is closed. A box. Unbustled . . ."

"The rainbow train spills out of it?" Elliot adds, eager to be part of the excitement.

Grant puts his hand to his lips. Thoughts race behind his eyes.

"Is there time to make it?" I ask.

"There has to be, because *that* is the idea!" he says. He throws those wonderful arms around Elliot and me. Neither of us are complaining.

At last, we're a creative trio!

Our allotted hour with the choreographer ends far too quickly, but the three of us are too lit with energy to worry about the performance. After we're shuffled out of the auditorium, Elliot and I follow Grant into the dissipating rain outside and through the quad where our story began. A poster for the end-of-term show remains pinned to the activities board—who knew back then that this show would bring us all together?

We leave Grant in his design program's studio space when it becomes clear he has several all-nighters ahead of him constructing the birdcage skirt from my updated concept. The show is in six days! Not that Grant minds—he barely speaks as he slices a sheet of elastic material into new strips of armor for the birdcage.

My idea has ignited his mind. An artist can't think of anything else once their mind has been set ablaze. Just like Elliot did with my mural, the inspiration arrived when it was time.

We make good partners.

At least, creatively we do.

I can't escape the nagging feeling that I confided a terrible fear to Grant, and he centered himself until I took it back. But there's no time for this Classic Micah Overthinking now—we're all overstimulated and under-slept.

"Micah, would it be cool if you walked me home?" Elliot asks.

Before even looking at Elliot, I look to Grant, who's already looking at me. Although still hunched over his worktable of elastic strips, he stopped all work the moment Elliot opened his lips. "Fine by me," Grant says, eyes moving back to his table. "I'll be busy all night, no fun to be around."

There's that dark tone again.

Elliot twiddles his fingers, as if suddenly embarrassed he asked. "It's just a few blocks, but it's dark out, and I've got dance leggings on. Never know who's out there, ready to beat up a little F-slur."

Out of the corner of my eye, I briefly admire the outline of Elliot's short, hearty (okay, thicc) legs in those tights.

"I'd be happy to," I say, kissing Grant goodbye. His return kiss is colder than usual. It makes my heart shiver. We just had the most exciting creative experience of the entire show, and Grant gets weird at the last minute over nothing.

Is this how it's going to be?

Before shutting the studio door, I take one more look at Grant at his workstation, beautifully broad-shouldered. I don't know why I looked back.

Something feels different.

Later, Elliot and I walk silently, comfortably, through a nearly empty city toward his dad's pizzeria. The night is warm but foggy. Familiar skyscrapers rise into the night, but vanish halfway up into the dense mist, as if a wizard has made the tops magically disintegrate.

"You were a star tonight," I tell him.

"You don't have to make me feel better about my breakup," he groans. "I'm *okay*."

"I got that birdcage idea watching you dance."

He glances over, eyes narrowed.

"I'm serious. You got thrown into something new and messy, and you just flew."

Elliot laughs to himself. "Lil' ol' me?"

"Hey." I tap his shoulder. He's still in his tank top. When my hand connects with his cool, bare skin, I briefly forget what I was going to say. "How does it feel to do a job that's not Audrey's?"

Elliot scoffs. "It didn't feel like a job. It didn't feel like me."

"But you were great!"

"That's not what I mean. It just felt like . . . I was somebody else up there. I've done so many coffee shifts, my muscle memory just does it." He mimes pouring espresso shots and pumping syrup into invisible mugs. "Even on my days off, in bed, my hands will just do the motions. It's weird. So when I was onstage, doing something physical . . . my body finally remembered it wasn't making coffee." He exhales. "I was *finally* present in a new place."

Good for Elliot. He needs this win.

A neon slice of pizza buzzes in the window of Little Parisi's, which I've somehow never heard of, despite it not being too far from my home. One story above the shop, a wall-unit air conditioner hangs outside of a darkened window. Is that Elliot's room?

"Oh, did you finally get AC?" I ask.

"Nope! It's broken." Elliot throws a middle finger up at the unit. "Landlord won't fix it until the building gets a full rewiring."

I'm too exhausted to say anything but "Ewwwwwwww."

As usual, Elliot shrugs it off. Through the pizza parlor's window, a man with a thick, dark mustache hands slices of pepperoni over the counter on flimsy, grease-soaked paper plates.

"That's Stuart," Elliot says. "My dad. We have a first-name-basis thing."

Elliot waves through the window. Stuart—identical to his son, just with twenty extra years and a mustache—waves back and breaks into a smile with oversized chipmunk teeth.

Adorable.

But when Stuart spots me behind the neon slice, his smile disappears. "Oops," I say.

"He's just busy," Elliot says with a twinge of humiliation.

"He doesn't want you out on the town with some strange guy."

"You're not strange! I've"—Elliot avoids my eyes—"talked about you."

Elliot, so cute in his tank top and tights, suddenly looks like an adult. Grown-up, like a professional Broadway performer. No apron to make him look hunched and small. He stands straight. Without burdens.

"What have you told him about me?" I ask, not meaning to whisper, but . . . here we are.

Elliot stares with the wide, vulnerable eyes of a trapped animal. A fawn.

I don't know how it happened, but we're standing close again.

If he kissed me, he'd be too close for me to stop him. I take his hand. *Tiny touches.* Stuart is distracted with customers. He can't see how close I am to his son. Dangerously close. Elliot leans even closer— another inch and our lips will meet. It's not like with Grant, where he stoops to kiss me. Elliot and I are identical heights. A match.

Kissing Elliot would require no thought. Every single cell in my body is screaming for closeness with this boy. They demand it. Electricity flies off my cells like cattle prods. There's no inch of me that isn't awake and begging me to come closer.

Kissing Elliot would be as easy as my hand soaring across my sketchbook, knowing what I want to draw before my brain does.

My brain is definitely slower than my hands right now too.

My hands say, *Reach for him. Kiss him. You want this more than anything, and so does he.* But my brain—always late, says, *MESS. Messy! Please don't! Please wait!*

Elliot just looks so strong and beautiful in the lamplight.

I would take such good care of him. He'd take good care of me, too.

I have to kiss him . . .

The universe is pulling us together. Fighting it would be like fighting the tide . . .

*This isn't the way it should happen! There's no fairy tale about cheating!*

"Did you get it?" a voice whispers across the street. "Did you *get* it!"

Like startled rabbits, Elliot and I snap toward the voice. In the dark, beyond a parked car, two teens watch us. Their faces are obscured by hooded sweatshirts, but one detail is brutally clear: they're pointing phones at us.

"Getoutofherego!" one of them shouts, and they scramble out of sight . . .

Along with pictures of me and Elliot.

## Chapter 23
# THE DEPARTURE OF THE SQUIRE

The internet is a casino. Occasionally, if you're lucky, you win big. For an even luckier few, it might even change your life. The rest of the time, it mostly just ruins you.

That's me today, the ruination part.

A picture of me and Elliot—centimeters away from kissing—has struck Instagram and TikTok like a meteorite. How could I be so out-of-control stupid? We were out in the open. Even before Wish Granted, everyone in the city knew my name and face; after Wish Granted, it became profitable to track my every move and capture every screwup.

Well, this was a screwup, and it has been captured.

What was I thinking, getting that close to Elliot? Grant had been pissing me off with his clout chasing and ignoring my fears when I voiced them. Elliot and I have spent the last month vibing off the art we were making, excited conversations we were having, and he was *listening* to me. Maybe I'd be more comfortable sharing details of my relationship online if Grant were more receptive to what the attention does to me. From the minute we started hanging out, Elliot covered his eyes when he saw I was working, checked in with me, and knows that it's not about what other people's attention can do for Wish Granted but what we can do for other people.

Bring the fantasy out of reality. Remind them that nice surprises are always possible.

Elliot and I share that.

In the electric glow of his dad's pizza place, Elliot looked . . . I don't know . . . I just wanted to be closer. I feel like I wanted to kiss him—and he wanted to kiss me—but we're just two victims of loneliness. Elliot is rebounding *hard* from Brandon's neglect, and Grant has been seriously devaluing what I'm telling him about my art. Plus, I've been overworked and under-slept getting this mural done, so I absolutely cannot trust my impulses right now.

But now there's photo evidence of my latest impulse, so I've been FaceTiming with Grant for hours trying to explain what the hell I was thinking. We're both still in bed—me in my room, him in his dorm. His eyes are beet red from crying, his curly hair is tousled and tangled in knots, and he's whispering so his sleeping roommate doesn't hear.

Whispering for hours. It's impressive.

"If you want to dump me, Micah," he hisses, "I'm begging you to please just wait until after the show this weekend, because I have no bandwidth left in my body."

"I don't want to dump you, Grant!" For some reason, I'm whispering too, even though I'm alone. It just seemed like good manners to whisper with him.

On the FaceTime, Grant grips his head like he's trying to pry out his troubling thoughts. "This curse on me . . ."

"There's no such thing as curses."

"So you believing in fairy-tale endings and the universe bringing people together is normal, but I say I have a hex on me and I'm the one making stuff up?"

I sigh into my sleeve. I'm losing strength. This argument isn't even about anything anymore; it's just him going on about how he always knew this curse was going to pull us apart.

Maybe he's right.

Not about the curse, but what if my fairy-tale stuff is just as ludicrous to measure my life by? Grant is Boy 100. My Cinderella. Two months later, we're arguing over FaceTime about hexes and I'm almost kissing another boy.

Some fairy-tale ending!

What I know is that I have a very real boy on the phone who cares about me, and I'm losing him. "I *promise* you that picture is not what it looks like," I say. "People got bored of us being happy, so they had to invent this crap to stir things up. I do not want to kiss Elliot."

Yet the only words ricocheting through my brain are *kiss Elliot.*

*Kiss Elliot.*

"It doesn't matter," he says. "The picture looks like you want to kiss him. Everyone thinks I'm a loser about to be dumped, and my show is gonna become this big letdown mess." He pinches back a headache. "Design schools are coming to scout . . ."

My lip begins to quiver. Even though he *just* made this about optics and his show versus what's really in my heart, I hate seeing him so frantic.

This show is his dream, and I know how high stakes it feels when something threatens your dreams.

I'm putting a stop to this now. The internet doesn't get to decide what my life is and isn't.

After we hang up, I open Instaloves and post a candid of three creative boys at play—Elliot, Grant, and myself, backstage at the Art Institute, laughing while we work on the Knight Princess. One of my new favorite pictures. This is one of those "keep forever until it's faded and yellow, and we're old and gray" life-defining photos.

And it's going to serve an important purpose.

I'm going to set the record straight.

In the caption, I clear the air:

Hey, #WishGranted fans! Let's talk. This is me and Grant working on our major project we're unveiling this Sunday at @artinstitutechi. The other person in the photo you may also recognize. This is Elliot, one of my best friends and a key collaborator in the Wish Granted project. He ran all around the city helping me find Grant back when I only knew him as Boy 100. We're just friends. The picture going around of us is two friends hanging out. Nothing more. And whoever who took it is just trying to make trouble.

I take a breath and reread what I've written.

It's not enough. I have to be clear. Unequivocal. Or Grant will never believe me. I keep typing: Elliot is an amazing friend, but I have NO romantic feelings for him whatsoever. It's a shame two queer boys can't be friends without people thinking they're secretly hooking up. Grow up. Bye.

I close it with a peace sign emoji and send it into the world. If Instaloves has turned into a publicity machine, let it start doing some good.

I throw my phone onto the bed—to get that lying thing away from me. I pull out my *Little Book of Firsts* and write the truth: *First Time I Almost Kissed Someone Else: 7-31-22* and *First Time I Lied to My Fans: 8-1-22.*

After dotting my *i*'s, I fling my *Little Book of Firsts* across the room. It smacks against my hamper, and I bury my face in my hands. Furious at myself.

I'm not overworked, under-slept, or "just pissed at Grant." I like Elliot. I wanted to kiss Elliot then; I want to kiss him now. I want to kiss him because of what I know about him, not because of the fairy tale I imagined about him—like with Grant. Elliot listens to me, knows me, steels my spine, and is just plain fun to be around. But Elliot is caught in this nightmarish breakup, might be leaving town soon, and probably doesn't even like me like that. He's such a good person, he just makes everyone feel as valued as he makes me feel.

Dammit. What the hell did I just do?

*"I have no feelings for Elliot whatsoever."*

Biggest lie of my life.

♡  ♡  ♡

As Monday folds into Tuesday, Wednesday, and Thursday, it's clear that Elliot—as always—is the first one to be hurt. The first one *I* hurt. He hasn't texted. He won't respond. I deserve it. Not only that, but my Instaloves post has only poured gasoline on the fire. I've learned that what's currently happening to Elliot is called the Streisand effect: tell the internet to ignore a story, and it will only amplify it and give it validation.

Just call me Babs, because my post is Streisand-ing EVERYWHERE.

The same blogs that covered my relationship so splashily last month are now doing hit pieces on me as just another deluded, privileged celebrity brat. They're doing full profiles on "Just Who IS Elliot?" that make him look like a broke striver trying to scam himself inside the Summers empire, whatever that is. Worst of all, this didn't even ease Grant's fears. Queer media sites have been doing nonstop funeral pieces for my relationship:

## Wish Un-Granted

## The End of the Fairy Tale: Anatomy of an Ex–Power Couple

## Micah Summers: The Wrong Example

Hard not to take that last one personally. Apparently, I'm a filthy cheater, propping up insidious gay stereotypes and setting a dreadful example for the legions of baby tenderqueers who want to be me and Grant when they grow up.

Me and Grant . . . He hasn't stopped acting cold to me since the post. That's *when* he chooses to respond to my texts at all.

Last but not least, Elliot has disappeared from everyone's lives.

"He's not responding to me, either," Hannah says. "Not since yesterday morning."

In the Bergstrom family's tropical kitchen, Hannah, Maggie, and I mope on barstools, each of us with a beach towel tied around our wet bathing suits. Not even an afternoon plunge in our building's pool could turn my mood around. So many frowns. Hannah is worried about Elliot, and Maggie is worried about me—or at least, respectfully joining the somber mood of the room. She looks the glummest, though: while Hannah and I are in shockingly hot-pink swimsuits, Maggie wears her Wednesday Addams, 1920s black bathing costume that she bought as a goof but later fell in love with for real.

If only I could be the weird bathing costume in Elliot's life.

Hard to see how that's remotely possible at this point.

Hannah nuzzles Red Velvet's wet dog nose while we peck at her mom's coconut cream cake. The cake is doing nothing to muffle the plummeting elevator shaft of emptiness inside my chest right now.

Nevertheless, I devour the cake mindlessly.

Maggie slices off a piece of just cake, no frosting, like a serial killer. "I'd like to speak on behalf of Elliot, a fellow Always-Hated-Social-Media person," she says, securing a second beach towel over her shoulders so her bathing costume top doesn't drip. "Elliot is being the Other Woman'd by the internet, and just reading these comments—that have nothing to do with me—makes me want to hide under my covers and rip the Wi-Fi out of my wall. So give him time."

"I haven't been reading the comments," I say miserably as I scoop Maggie's discarded frosting.

Maggie pulls another *yikes* face, which I don't appreciate. "Let's just say if I were Elliot reading those comments, it would not make me super excited to take your call."

I slam my fork against the island, startling the little Pomeranian. "But this wasn't my fault! I hate all of this as much as Elliot does."

How many ways can I explain that I just want my old relationship with Grant, my old friendship with Elliot, and to do new art with them both?

"Hmm," Hannah says, wiggling a fork inside her mouth as she thinks. Red Velvet struggles in her arms to reach the precious frosting.

"What?" I ask. Hannah sets her fork down and fiddles with her silicone swim cap, which contours perfectly to her head. She doesn't need to adjust it. She's avoiding saying something. *"What?"*

"You tell him," Hannah says to Maggie, who looks away shamefully at her plate. "You're better at this."

"Better at what?" Maggie asks. "Being a buzzkill?"

"Tough love." Hannah kisses Red Velvet's head and avoids my desperate eyes.

My stomach sinks. The last thing I need after this hellacious week is tough love. Yet not wanting to hear what Maggie has to say has never stopped her before: "You hurt his feelings, Micah.

You're a dummy for not realizing that post wouldn't do a single thing but hurt Elliot."

"But I didn't—" I start to say.

"And you did it to make Grant happy—a noble but useless reason."

I don't talk back. The walls inside my brain close in tightly. She's making a point.

"Of course I want to make Grant happy," I say. "He's my boyfriend, and that picture was of me almost kissing someone else."

"But Grant can't be happy, Micah," Hannah says, clinging to poor, overstimulated Red Velvet. "He's got too much stuff he hasn't dealt with yet. All he cares about is what the internet thinks of him, and that's not gonna go good places. Even after you destroyed Elliot's reputation for him, he's still icing you out."

The frosting has turned bitter on my tongue.

I need water.

"I just wanted to clarify . . ." I say weakly.

"Clarify what?" Maggie asks. "That Elliot means nothing to you? Is that even true?"

My sister is x-raying me to death. The shock of humiliation shoots up my back as if my swimsuit suddenly vanished.

How could she know I like him? Is it obvious? Does everyone know? Does Elliot know, and he feels too sorry for me to push me away?

Maggie unwraps the towel from her shoulders and pats the rest of her hair dry. "He just lost Brandon," she says. "And instead of leaving things alone, you pointed all your fans his way. Whatever you really feel, that's only gonna get him shit."

Tough love it is.

I tagged Elliot in that awful post. I recommitted myself to a boyfriend I'm not even sure I want anymore, but that doesn't matter because nothing is ever going to happen with Elliot anyway! He'll leave town—too nice to ever turn me down—and my relationship with Grant will wither until I'm back where I started, sketching unrequited crushes. With a plummeting fear, I realize I'm going to end up sketching Elliot forever, long past the time when he's started a new life for himself as a small-town vet— with a small-town husband who isn't me.

I can't lose Elliot.

"So how do I make it right?" I ask the room, hoping Hannah, Maggie, or the universe will respond promptly with an easily executable game plan. I'm even open to taking tips from Red Velvet at this point.

We chew silently before Maggie speaks again. "First, you have to admit that you and Grant may not be working."

My hands clench to hold back my tantrum. "But you and Manda fight!"

Even though I've already admitted it to myself, there's something about saying it to other people that feels wrong. Admitting failure.

Sighing, Maggie ties the colorful beach towel around her head, in stark contrast to her Industrial Revolution ghost-child one-piece suit. The image is so bizarre, it almost cheers me up. "Manda and I have been together a long time, and we resolve our fights in an hour," she says gently. "We don't keep punishing each other. You and Grant have been together for a month and change. This is the time everything's supposed to be magic."

There's no more cake. My shoulders won't unslump.

Hannah reaches across the island to squeeze my hand. "I'm so sorry," she says. "But Maggie's right. Jackson and I—"

"OKAY, I GET IT!"

I rip my hand away and leap off the stool. Red Velvet scrambles out of Hannah's arms and flees to her safety closet. Maggie and Hannah watch me standing over them, my chest thrumming with rage. I can't sit here anymore and let these two people in perfect relationships lecture me about what a dreadful boyfriend I turned out to be.

I've waited too long to say this, from the loneliest, darkest pit of my stomach: "I'm so glad you're both full of advice for me." I turn to Hannah. "And for your incredible new relationship that worked out, when mine didn't. I'm so happy Jackson is this great guy. You deserve it—"

"I *do* deserve it!" Hannah stands. She looks at me, stern but controlled. "And *you* deserve it, too, but you fell in love with someone else, someone better for you!"

I crumple onto the stool, as deflated as a spent Capri Sun, and let myself finally admit the truth: "*Duh*. With Grant, I see myself being great. But with Elliot"—I sigh at the lost cause—"I see myself being good. Kinder. Stronger. My art is better with him. We look at the world the same way." My heart beats violently against my chest. Yeah—being with Elliot would be great, but it'll never happen, so I've wasted my breath confessing this. "Now what the hell am I supposed to do?!"

Maggie reaches for my hand, and Hannah steps toward me,

looking heartbroken, but I pull away. I run from Hannah's apartment and into the elevator, but these stupid mirrored walls keep reflecting my lying, cheating, bad-friend face over and over.

Thankfully, the penthouse is empty of anyone who'd bother me with questions, so I quickly hustle into my bedroom. Waiting for me on my bed are two identical cardboard boxes. My mom must've brought the mail in and determined they weren't from unhinged fans.

When I open the flaps on the first box, my stomach hits the basement.

The universe isn't done playing games with me.

The box isn't from a fan—it *is* a fan.

The industrial-strength fan I bought for Elliot. One for me so I can dry my mural, another for Elliot to withstand these city summers.

It's still summer. And I can still make it up to Elliot for that post.

It's not about what I need, it's about what he needs—and he needs a friend.

♡ ♡ ♡

The Uber to Audrey's Café is taking forever. Each breath weighs a trillion pounds, or is that just because of the large, awkward box sitting on my lap?

This will be my first time seeing Elliot since I realized . . . everything.

By the time I reach Audrey's, the sun has dipped below the

skyline. The warm string lights are already lit over the patio. Pleasant jazz piano drifts from the propped-open doorway. Most heavenly of all, however, is the boy leaning his hip against the espresso bar.

Elliot.

He's on the customer side, in street clothes, his work apron draped over his wrist.

For the first time in a week, my exhausted face cracks into a smile. Best of all, when I poke his shoulder, he smiles back. Before saying anything to me, Elliot asks his co-worker to make me a dirty chai. The nostalgia of this moment crushes my heart, as if somehow wishing hard enough caused time to rewind to before I'd messed everything up for us.

"One for the road," Elliot's co-worker says as she hands him my chai.

"Thanks, Ani," Elliot mumbles, sipping his own coffee.

"Got my hands full," I say, gesturing to the fan with a large, sweating grin.

"I noticed!" Elliot smiles—smaller than usual—and gestures me over to the armchairs next to the unlit fireplace. The greatest spot! The little table where we deciphered the riddle of Grant's jacket.

Simpler times.

"Is that the fan you said you canceled?" he asks.

"I totally forgot to cancel it!" I drop the box carefully at his feet. "It showed up today, and I had to get it to you. I hope you like it."

"Thank you." Elliot doesn't look at the fan again. He's not

being cold, exactly, just . . . cautious. As if he just emerged from surgery, and every move he makes must be done carefully or he'll tear his sutures.

"We've been looking for you everywhere," I say.

"I'm here." Elliot chuckles hollowly.

"Are you okay?" I ask. "I'm sorry about that post. I really thought I was helping."

Elliot doesn't blink. "Don't worry; I'm barely on Instagram. How's Grant?"

"Eh. Let's change the subject."

"Okay." He laughs, almost bitterly.

"Elliot, I wanted to ask you something." Finally, his expression brightens.

*Ask him, Micah. Ask him if he really wanted to kiss that night?*

I can't. Not now. Elliot needs support, not my pressure, and I still haven't figured out what I'm doing with Grant.

Chickening out, I clear my throat and search for a new topic: "Uh, with everything going on, I'd understand if the answer was no. Are you . . . still planning on being in Grant's show?"

Like a balloon bursting, Elliot darkens. He downs his coffee in two long sips. "Micah," he says. "Micah, Micah. Yes, I'm still planning on doing it."

My entire body exhales. "Great. Because I've loved doing this show with you—"

"I'm not finished," he growls. Elliot actually growled. I stiffen as he gazes with hard, wounded eyes. "Micah, you got me in trouble with your fans, and on top of that, I had to read in a post—not from you personally, in a *post*—what I mean to you:

nothing. No, worse than nothing: your helper mouse. Then you come down here with your pity gift that I told you embarrasses me, ready to solve my problems, telling me you want to ask me something important, and it's about your show?"

I freeze as if Elliot were an oncoming car. "I'm—I'm sorry."

He blinks, his eyes soft. Even hurt?

An exciting—yet unpleasant—twinge shoots up my chest. Did Elliot want me to ask about the kiss? Is he disappointed I didn't ask? Could he . . . want what I want?

Yet in a blink, his sweet eyes toughen. The room goes cold.

"You're sorry?" he asks, his voice reaching deeper registers than I thought possible. "Sorry for telling your fans how little I mean to you? Sorry for the truth?"

Shit. He might like me, too.

Breathlessly, I try to interject, but he stands, bumping his chair loudly as he does. I check behind me. If that awful manager is here and catches him making a scene . . . "I'm so tired of being your runner-up," Elliot says, wiping his hand through his tangled hair. "I was Brandon's runner-up and it gutted me, which you *know*."

I've lost all power over my body. I sit, immobile, like a decommissioned robot.

Goddammit. All I want to do is blurt out that he's not my runner-up, that I want him to be my number one, but it feels wrong to talk over him when he's this upset. My brain won't let me speak.

*Why* didn't I just tell him the truth? Or have I already messed up so badly, it wouldn't have mattered?

Elliot whips his apron onto the floor. I flinch. "When we almost kissed, it felt incredible because I knew it wasn't just me who felt it," he says. "I was ready to just have my crush in secret forever, but then you got close. I knew I wasn't imagining it."

He covers his face. As badly as I want to, I don't reach for him.

He likes me. I like him.

WHY ARE WE FINDING THIS OUT NOW? DOES THE UNIVERSE HATE US?

"I was too depressed to get out of bed or reach for my phone," he confesses. "Too depressed to go to work. I didn't even call in sick; I just ghosted. You said you called? Texted? You know where I live. I didn't leave my bed until this morning. You could've found me anytime."

"I'm sorry," I whisper. "Just . . . please. I don't want you to get in trouble at work, so . . ." I fan my hands downward for him to sit. If he gets in trouble or loses this job, that's it. He'll leave Chicago, and even if I somehow fix things between us, it won't matter. We'll have missed our chance.

But Elliot doesn't sit. He just laughs. "Are you listening? I ghosted my shifts. My manager fired me."

As if zapped by a cattle prod, I scramble out of my chair. "No! Where is she? I'll explain what's going on."

"Explain what? That I'm obsessed with somebody else's boyfriend, and, and, and . . ." Elliot becomes lost in his train of thought as he clutches fistfuls of his hair.

"Elliot, what if I wasn't . . . ?" *Someone else's boyfriend. What if I wasn't someone else's boyfriend?* SAY IT. "I wish I'd never made that post!"

I reach for Elliot's hands, but he backs away. It's ten times worse than the train doors slamming shut between Grant and me.

"Tell your fans," Elliot says. "Tell Grant. Just don't tell me unless you're gonna do something about it because *this* "—he gestures to me—"is messing me up in a major way." Elliot chucks his cup into the trash but leaves his apron on the floor. "I just came in for my last check. See you at the show."

I don't say anything. Everything out of my mouth makes things worse.

Elliot angrily picks up the fan box. "I'm only taking this because I still live in hell." With that, he leaves Audrey's Café— our place—for the last time.

This was our last chai.

He doesn't work here anymore.

Chapter 24

# THE BALL

The morning of the end-of-term show, Grant decides he doesn't feel weird about me anymore and FaceTimes me to celebrate our impending success, as if no one's life has been ruined. While he's already showered and shaved, I'm barely poking out of my covers. I have not moved from this spot in two days. Forty-eight hours since my fights with both Elliot and Hannah, my floor is littered with ghosts of DoorDash past: liters of Pepsi, tins of caramel corn, deep-dish pizza boxes, Audrey's cups—everything I used to share with Elliot.

As if consuming any of these objects would magically summon him back into my life.

Dozens of spent tissues everywhere. Disney movies on a loop.

I feel nothing.

That believer child I used to be is gone. The damaged boy I turned out to be disgusts me.

Otherwise, my room is blank. My art supplies are at Grant's studio. My mural has already been shuttled to the Art Institute. The bedroom wall where it used to hang lies blank and barren: this is my life when stripped of art.

I never bothered to fill it with photos or happy memories.

A realization crept up on me slowly while I was painting Elliot and Grant into the mural, but it didn't click for me until everything blew up: I've treated them abysmally. With each swipe of my brush, I felt it. I've been playing with them like paint colors. Flourishes on the mural of my life.

Certainly not real people I could hurt.

I played around with imaginary boyfriends for so long, it didn't occur to me that a real one would require real responsibility. Real stakes. When you love someone, you open yourself to the possibility that you could hurt them just as powerfully. I learned that too late.

"Get your ass dressed!" Grant happily sings over FaceTime, lusciously shirtless, but I can't enjoy a moment of it. He's bouncing around in his bed, as chipper as a songbird. I wish so badly I could be back in his bed, feeling the way I felt that first night we slept together: scared but certain that I'd be safe with him.

He's so happy. But I'm not.

"I'm gonna get dressed soon," I say. "Still got plenty of time."

"Woo!" Grant toasts his coffee mug way too close to the phone. "And I know you'll make it cute—you always do—but we just found out there's going to be a red carpet!"

Good God. More Instagrammable moments. When I feel like a demon.

"Do they usually do red carpets for the show?" I ask.

"There's sometimes a big to-do with fancy clothes, but they're kicking it up a few notches because of all the hard work we've been doing promoting this!" As Grant cheers again, I let out a forced "woo-hoo." He winces. "I know you said you'd be okay with one more Wish Granted promo on Instaloves . . . for the show?"

I nod dully. At least he remembered something from that conversation. "Yeah, I'll—I'll find something to post."

Relieved, he grins. All dimples. "Amazing. Also . . . if it's okay, could you please, please, *please* ask your dad if he can share it to give us one final boost?"

Before this moment, I couldn't think of anything I'd rather do less than post some *Believe in the Magic of Love* nonsense to Instaloves. But after talking to Grant, I realize there is something worse: asking my dad to give it a boost.

Grant signs off with a juicy kiss to the screen but hangs up before I gather the energy to return it. I lifelessly repost an old Instaloves photo—Grant and me at the immersive gallery—and rework the caption to promote tonight's show, making sure to tag all the right people, and then text it to my dad with no explanation.

He'll figure it out.

An hour later, I crack open my door to embark on my most heroic quest yet: getting more OJ. As soon as I step into the hall, I'm met with laughter from another room. Like a hunter on safari,

I shuffle soundlessly past Maggie's open door to avoid detection.

Inside, Manda lies on my sister's bed, her head on a pillow next to Maggie, who sits upright and plays with her girlfriend's hair. They watch an old standby—*Parks and Recreation*—and laugh at the same intervals.

In sync. Peaceful. Happy.

Like a miserable, spurned Gollum, I watch them with the deepest envy.

A frown I'll wear forever.

I thought I knew everything. Any chance I could get, I'd make fun of Maggie and Manda and their boring ol' same ol' Netflix nights. But they aren't bored. They're joyful.

I'm rotten.

And I would sell my left lung if I could just have one boring movie night with Elliot while we laugh and I play with his hair.

My heart sinks. I thought of Elliot, not Grant. He's who I want to be with. But break up with Grant? How? Impossible. Could we stay friends? *How?* He'd feel so betrayed. Triple cursed.

I promised him he wasn't cursed. I *promised.* Was I a liar? I believed it then. My feelings for him weren't different then. How could I want someone else but still feel awful about losing the one I'm with?

Back in my room, the sun lowers as rapidly as in a time-lapse photo, but my self-pitying ass remains in bed. Knocks come and go at my door, various people wanting to feed me, confirm details about the show, or just confirm that I'm still alive.

"I'm good," I say, face half in my pillow. "Just figuring out what to wear."

Half an hour later, there's another knock but no voice comes. The door opens on its own. The gangly boy who enters—impossible as it seems—is Jackson, gala-ready in a sparkling black suit, bolo tie, and long hair piled in an updo. Someone (or him) has applied a gorgeous smoky eye.

"Sorry to barge in," Jackson says. "Hannah says she does this all the time, and it's cool?"

Still in my depression pajamas, I pull my covers to my chin. "Yeah, it's cool."

"Uh, I was sent to get you. Make sure you get dressed for your big night." He twirls his fancy self in a circle. "Remember: *this* is the high bar you've gotta meet."

I laugh wheezily, my first in centuries. Yet like a roller coaster, what comes up must come down: Hannah sent her boyfriend to get me, not herself. "She didn't want to see me?"

Jackson makes a cutting motion across his throat. "She didn't know if you wanted to see her. It's your big night. You got way too much going on. She didn't want to bug."

"She can always bug me," I say, my heart lifting. "Can you tell her that? Like, lifetime hall pass to bug me, push me, tell me when I'm being a jerkoff."

Jackson shoves his hands into his fancy pants pockets. "Does that lifetime hall pass extend to me? If I may?"

"Oh. Sure." I was not expecting *everyone* to have an opinion on my life choices, but why not? Grab a stone and start chucking, good sir!

Jackson emits a long, uncertain squirting noise before saying, "You need to cut yourself a break, like, right now."

I recoil as if he just spit at me. Give myself a break? What kind of lie . . . ?

"From what I've heard from Hannah," he says, "and what I've seen around here, you're a good friend. Clever. Passionate. Understanding. Grant is super fun and artistic. Elliot is pretty much the best. But the three of you . . . you know, you've gotten into a little car accident. None of you are bad, so just . . . get each other's insurance info. Get back on the road."

No one is bad? We each deserve love, just maybe not with each other.

Could it be that simple?

"Stupid metaphor?" he asks, squinting.

"No!" I say. "I just . . . I feel so terrible, and Elliot is so mad at me. And I have so many shitty feelings about Grant, but also great feelings . . ." I search Jackson's face pleadingly. "I want us all to be okay."

Straight as ever, Jackson merely nods. "Get dressed, go to the show, and make it okay."

Jackson's honesty brings out a smile in me.

He's right. Whatever goes down, I owe it to both my boys to show up tonight.

With enormous effort, I throw off my covers. Jackson returns downstairs, and I agree to meet him and Hannah at the street. I dress in the show outfit I selected weeks ago: a black cadet jacket with silver tassels on the shoulders and a high, rigid collar that swallows my entire throat. A long, silver chain drapes exquisitely across my chest. The mirror reflects the prince I hoped I was but may never be.

*Fake it for one more night, Micah.*

My slender, steel-toed dress shoes echo through my empty house as I exit the building to find Hannah matching Jackson's visage beat for beat. They're the jazziest couple Chicago has seen since the last roaring twenties. Gone are Hannah's cute pencil skirts. Instead, she wears a sparkling black-and-white tube dress that ends in a waterfall of fringe just above her knees. She wears a silver-quilled fascinator and the same smoky eye she obviously gave Jackson, only hers is as silvery as stardust.

"I'm speechless," I say. "You've taken my speech."

Hannah throws me a chef's kiss. "That high collar, Micah."

Jackson gives me a grand, rather nerdy bow. "Your Majesty."

At this compliment, an urge to run back under my covers wallops me. "Please," I groan. "Right now, I feel about as popular as the Royal Family."

Giggling, Hannah brushes lint from my shoulders. "You'll have to mess up a lot more before you get to that point, darling." Meeting my eyes, she smiles until I do. At the same moment, we both say, "I'm sorry."

"You don't have to be sorry!" I clutch my chained chest.

She hugs me. Pulling back, she throws me a wink. "Enough about me. Let's support Grant. Let's see Elliot be beautiful. Let's celebrate your mural finally, *finally* leaving your room."

With a head as heavy as concrete, I nod. She's right. Our three hearts may be broken, but tonight is still a significant, defining moment for me, Elliot, and Grant.

At least we have that.

We Uber to Millennium Park and walk the rest of the way to the Art Institute. The surrounding area will be too much of a publicity zoo to get close. Purple curtains of twilight beautify our warm summer's evening walk along Michigan Avenue, the lake and park stretching forever on our left. While Jackson leads far ahead, I turn to Hannah. "You look stunning."

She takes my hand. "I'm so happy."

"Jackson's a really great guy."

"He's such a weird little wiener."

We walk in silence, except for the clip-clop of Hannah's heels and the lapping of the lake against the high bearing walls. She leans into the crook of my neck, and the grip around my heart finally loosens . . . It then triple-tightens when the Art Institute appears around the next corner. On instinct, I squeeze Hannah's hand.

"What is it?" she asks.

The truth rises out of me like a squall, but I keep to a fierce whisper: "When I first did this walk, it was when I was trying to find Boy 100, and . . . Elliot was with me. We found Grant here, together. Elliot still liked me. Grant was so happy to see me. I'm never gonna see that look on their faces again."

"Shh, shhh, shhhh," Hannah says, petting my cheeks.

"Hannah . . . I have to fix my head. Elliot helped me see that what I do best with my art is find the fairy tales in everyday people, but these boys aren't fairy tales. Nothing about this has gone smoothly." I pause to catch my breath, but Hannah doesn't interrupt. She watches me with deep focus. "I messed things up because"—an exhausted chuckle escapes me—"I've been afraid to let things get messy. I think I need to start saying what I feel and see what happens."

Hannah laughs softly and takes my hand. "I would like to see that."

At the Art Institute, a red carpet spills down the front stone steps. Powerful lights beckon a procession of town cars toward the palace. It's one of the most elegant, expensive-looking things I've ever seen. All that Wish Granted tagging paid off—Grant was right about that, at least. Red carpet interviews begin the moment I'm swept into a sea of people with VIP passes. On sight, two Art Institute representatives snatch me from the crowd and hiss, "We're running late. Grant will meet you."

In an instant, I'm separated from Hannah and Jackson by a force as powerful as the tide: publicity. Through endless, massive light stands, Grant's professors and classmates appear in their own gala looks. Every major designer and design school must be here tonight, because nobody missed a stitch on their outfits.

Despite my churning stomach, I'm pushed onward by one excitable Institute employee after another.

Pushed where? I have no idea. I'm assuming someone will eventually get me where I need to be, or at least let me die on the steps, trampled into a fine pulp.

Then a familiar, comforting voice drifts through the air.

I see them. My heart lifts like I've been drowning and found a lifeboat.

My parents.

Mom wears a chic black pantsuit, while Dad peacocks in a black-and-white floral-print suit with intentionally visible bespoke stitching. A throng of interviewers have caught them. "I'm not an art guy." Dad laughs. "When I heard Pablo Picasso, I thought he was a Sox outfielder."

Mom swats him with her clutch. "So corny, Jeremy."

Dad waves sheepishly. "All right, all right, not my best."

The media pool swarming them roars. They eat it up, always have. Mom and Dad know how to play to the cameras when they're together, a little comedy team. Everyone loves it . . . even me, I hate to admit. Here at my lowest, it's unspeakably comforting to watch them ham it up and feel like a child again.

They're a power couple who knows how to make publicity work for them, not let it sink them like I did with Grant. He deserves someone who could be up there joking with him.

"Kidding aside," Dad says, "we couldn't be prouder of Micah. Don't know where he gets it from—I'm a goony jock, she's an egghead—"

"Hey!" Mom swats him again but then shrugs. "Yeah."

The press—and me—can't help but laugh along.

"But he's a wonderful kid," Dad says. "He's a true sensitive soul . . . and super shy." As if sensing my presence, Dad's eyeline shifts from the press to me. "Which is why he's been hiding behind you this whole time. Micah, man of the hour, get up here!"

Whooping, Dad waves me toward him. Mom applauds. The cameras turn.

Somewhere from behind, hands push me forward.

Dad pulls me into a side hug. "Yeesh! Making me stand up here, talking about art."

In the shadows beyond the media pool's microphones,

Maggie and Manda wait in black cocktail dresses, which—upon closer inspection—are emblazoned with golden champagne bubbles. Warmth settles over my heart. Even with formal wear, Manda found a way to print food on their clothes. I wave them over to us, but Maggie draws her arms across her chest into a big *nope* X.

We Summers children did not inherit the publicity gene from our parents.

"Micah, this is your first live Instaloves project," a voice calls from the lights. "Are you and Grant the next Summers power couple?"

"Woo!" Mom yelps on a single clap. Her clap cracks my heart in half. I have no way of knowing, but I think I just flinched on camera. Everyone must've seen it.

I can't let Grant down again, not on his big night.

"It'll depend on how tonight goes," I say, with a dash of my father's twinkling eyes. "But I'm thrilled you're all about to see what Grant has created. We've been working with an incredible model. His name is Ell—"

But a swell of cheering drowns out Elliot's name.

Grant has materialized at my side, standing almost half a foot taller than usual thanks to his heeled, dark leather riding boots that hug his enormous calves. "Hey, babe," he whispers before kissing my forehead. He smiles for the eruption of cameras that have now formed such a tight circle around us that even my father, the king, has been cast out.

Grant is breathtakingly handsome dressed as a renaissance fancy man. His barrel chest puffs out a crushed-blue-velvet jacket with a frilly undershirt. A single, matching blue ribbon is fastened in the curls of his midnight-dark hair.

I adopt my mother's "Oh, you!" tone as Grant answers question after question with effortless warmth and humor. He's a natural.

How could anyone so larger than life think he's nothing without me?

♡ ♡ ♡

As Grant and I enter the subterranean hallways of the Art Institute's dressing rooms, he stops in front of me. His mask has fallen slightly—nerves are creeping up on him. "Are you okay?" he asks. "Your FaceTime this morning, you looked . . . not like yourself."

*Lie, Micah. Build up his confidence. Don't make this about yourself. It's not fair to him.*

"My sleep is all over the place," I say. "But I am great. This show is going to blow them out of the water." I give his chest little punches, which brings out those dimples. "The Knight Princess is finally here."

Grant gives my hand a princely kiss. "We did it together."

If anything, from the outside, we look the part.

Deeper into the dressing rooms, everyone's red carpet confidence has fallen away like dead skin. Outside, it was all smiles and sound bites, but down here, away from the press, a monstrous collective anxiety has consumed them. Students and their teams grip pins between their teeth as they make last-minute adjustments to garments. Their models grip wire racks to brace themselves as they're jabbed by stray needles.

My stomach itches with an odd tickle. I wish I could make such frantic, eleventh-hour touch-ups to my mural, but it's already locked in place onstage while the theater fills with my closest loved ones and every judgmental designer who's ever lived.

*No aborting this mission now, Micah.*

When we arrive at our dressing room, the Knight Princess outfit sits gallantly upon its mannequin beside a trio of makeup mirrors. At the end of the row of mirrors, waiting alone, is Elliot. He smiles.

I finally breathe again.

Elliot plucks two Audrey's to-go cups out of a tray and delivers them to us: "Iced Americano for Grant. Dirty chai for Micah."

I can't stop beaming. "Elliot . . ."

But I stop myself from saying, *You came!* That's what got me into trouble with Elliot in the first place, assuming he would bail or let people down, as if he's ever done that in his life. As if that's not the exact thing people keep doing to him.

In a blink, the sun goes away. Elliot passes me, his eyes cast downward. My smile falls. I turn to Grant, but Grant is already watching me. He is stung.

My stomach twists.

Grant saw everything: my genuine joy to see Elliot, Elliot's aloofness to me, and how that beat the smile from my face. He's already done the math in his head.

"Where do you want me, boss?" Elliot asks.

"Um . . . we'll get you into makeup." Grant, coming to,

searches the makeup mirrors for someone he can't find.

"Oh, Kris is right behind you!" Elliot points.

A green-haired girl excuses herself as she slips into the room with her own Audrey's cup. "Ready to get pretty, Elliot?" she asks. "Prettier?" Kris and Elliot giggle as they retreat to the mirrors, leaving two sad sacks in the doorway.

The silence between Grant and me hardens, and time stands still. My summer with Elliot flips through my mind like pages in a book:

*Elliot, dancing in the fountain as his relationship fell apart.*

*Elliot, hitting the runway with beautiful, graceful steps, fearless and free.*

Elliot was free on that stage because he'd done what I couldn't do—ended a relationship that was no longer serving him or Brandon.

Waiting on the other side of breaking up with Grant is that freedom for both of us. And I'm not doing his nerves any favors by acting weird and prolonging this.

I tug on Grant's crushed-velvet sleeve and ask, "Hey. Want to go somewhere to talk?"

Grant stares blankly at the Knight Princess before whispering, "Yeah."

The hallway of dressing rooms leads to a set of stairs. Once we're backstage, Grant and I wander through a curtain of ropes and pulleys like condemned men. There are a few scant stage-hands racing back and forth, but we're otherwise alone. Grant, so beautiful in his princely fineries, looms above me. Before I can speak, he cups my face with strong, graceful hands and lowers a kiss to my lips. My limbs turn rigid. My terrified lips don't kiss back.

It's agonizingly brief.

"Wow," he says. "I know I'm your first boyfriend, Micah, but . . . have you ever kissed someone who's fallen out of love with you?"

A tear races down my cheek. I can't do this. This is worse than any horror movie.

"No," I squeak.

"It's the emptiest feeling in the world." His bass-y voice tightens with a knot. "I wouldn't recommend it."

On a deep, courageous breath, I say, "We have to break up."

As much as we both expected it, Grant looks pile-drived to the stomach.

My nerve breaks. I can't let him think I never cared about him. Launching onto my tiptoes, I clutch Grant's face and kiss him.

He was right.

It really is the emptiest feeling in the world.

"I'm sorry," I say. "I'm so, so sorry. Can we please stay friends?"

"No," Grant says.

I flinch like he stuck me with a needle. No matter what happened between us, even though we were falling apart, I still love Grant. That wasn't fantasy.

"I don't want to never see you again," I say. "Being with you—working with you, falling for you—changed me. I don't want to miss watching you soar. I still believe in you—"

"*Micah.*" Grant's frilly chest piece rises and falls on his deep, loud breaths. "Quit trying to hold on to me. I was never your prince."

"You were!" I insist, my hands flailing helplessly. How can I make him believe?

"I wasn't. You were just mine." A pained moan escapes me. Sucking in another breath, Grant lumbers away through the maze of ropes, becoming a silhouette in the dark.

"Please—" I start to speak, but Grant's shadow stops.

"Micah," he says, "give me a head start back to the dressing rooms. We've still got a show to do."

I feel naked backstage.

No friends. No boyfriend. No Elliot. No art. No sketchbook. No sounds but the clamor of people filing inside, ready for me to show them what I've got.

What was the universe's plan for putting Grant and me in such a meet-cute situation, only for it to end here, unglamorously in a pile of wreckage beneath the Art Institute?

My collar is choking me. I can't breathe.

I pry open the clasp and accept giant gulps of air.

*Please*, I beg the universe. *Please make sure Grant is okay. Let him find someone soon. Someone who will truly love him. I don't want him to be alone.*

I exhale a single, choppy breath, and finally, my hands stop shaking. It's been longer than three minutes. Time for the show.

One painful step after another, I rejoin the living in the dressing room hallway. Each person I pass—stagehands, lighting grips, stage managers, hair and makeup crew—sips from an Audrey's Café to-go cup. Their names have been written on the cups in the same slanting cursive—Elliot's handwriting.

He brought coffee for every single person.

My brain can't comprehend that level of goodness.

Whenever he'd bring me a dirty chai, I thought it was a special thing he did for me, but it's so much more than that. This is just what Elliot does: he takes care of people.

And shelter dogs.

And wannabe princes in search of their vision.

Through the dressing room doorway, Elliot has his face applied. Hope begins to grow inside me like a stubborn blade of grass breaking through the frost. I'm frightened. I'm exhausted. I feel like pure dumpster garbage. But looking at Elliot melts all those dreadful feelings away, as if they were never there.

I would be the luckiest prince in the universe if he'd only look back at me.

Less than an hour later, I'm in the dark again with Grant. Except this time, we're not in the dark about our future together. He and I are seated beside each other in the VIP seats along the runway reserved for designers and the highest-profile scouts. The seats were predetermined for us, but even if we had the choice, Grant and I wouldn't sit apart. The story of the night will not be what happened to Wish Granted; it will be about the creative triumph of me, him, and Elliot.

The dressing room tension between us is gone. Everything between us is gone.

This right here, this moment seated together, is the closest he'll ever want to sit to me again in my whole life. The enormity of it threatens to capsize my head. Why didn't I do this before, when he and I could've had time to process and lick our wounds?

Mentally, I transport myself back to my bedroom, find the *Little Book of Firsts*, and write *First Breakup: 8-6-22.*

At last, the auditorium goes dark—a blessing—and the squall in my head finally quiets.

Wish Granted is the last piece in the show, but everything that comes before it contains truly gasp-worthy creativity. Bold fashion patterns, ingenious marriages of music and light installations, and captivating performance artists. We all whoop and cheer. Grant gives thunderous standing ovations to every piece, and I join him.

In these fleeting moments, we forget our doomed romance and simply catch the magical fever that can only be found when creatives watch other creatives unleash their true potential.

The stimulation in my veins is undeniable.

I want more. I want to be part of this world.

Finally, it's our turn. The lights go out. The air crackles. A light piano tune fills the room, sounding like the patter of rain against a window.

Grant stiffens next to me, and I bite my lip in anticipation.

In the dark, a whip cracks and a flag unfurls. A soft pink lights up the stage, and the audience takes a breath as one. My mural wraps around the stage wall—an L train bustling with a vibrant fairy-tale kingdom. Fairies, princes, princesses, kings, queens, jesters, dragons, mermaids, and mice. The city we call home reimagined as a place where magic can happen.

The footlights make my mural glow with a three-dimensionality I couldn't dream of.

Elliot stands in the center, still and flat against the canvas. Part of the design itself. His face is painted like an elegant bird queen, textured feathers of red and blue surrounding a winged, black bandit eye mask.

A goddess from another realm.

Grant spun literal magic out of his sewing machine—that birdcage skirt looks like it weighs two hundred pounds, but he made it lighter than air so that Elliot's movements could be as fluid as possible.

Grant is an unbelievable artist. Even if I didn't know him, I would say this piece is objectively the best in the entire show.

The piano tune changes, joined by an orchestra of strings—like a bistro in Paris, Grant's music selection is exquisite. When the music changes, the Knight Princess emerges from the painting. As the mural springs to life, the audience applauds with delight. Elliot glides along the runway as cautiously as a fragile animal discovering a new world.

We did it.

Grant's design. My illustration. Elliot's performance. Working in harmony with each other as we never did in our own lives.

The thought presses on my heart like a boot: I could've been doing art like this all along, but I was so worked up about people seeing it imperfectly, I chickened out. Elliot encouraged it out of me, created the environment where I could thrive.

Watching Elliot move like a swan is almost alien: someone I thought I knew inside and out but have only begun to scratch the surface of. There's oceans of Elliot still to explore.

*Please. Please let my story with Elliot not be over.*

The fragile animal onstage is no longer cautious. He picks up speed, races to the end of the runway, and as he moves, he spins. Spins. Spins again. With each spin, there is a crack of pure color, until the rainbow train rips free of the armored cage. The billowing curtain unfurls into the air, swirling around Elliot like a ribbon dancer, like a sorceress commanding light itself.

In the auditorium, every flash in every camera blows up at once.

Elliot did it. He's a star.

I love him.

This isn't some new development. I've loved him for a long time. Since the very first quest. His mere presence summons the best in people. His warmth neutralizes all my fears—and I have way too many. I want to do the same for him. That, I can't be afraid to tackle. We can be wonderful.

Elliot strikes a final pose, and the lights go out. The audience roars.

When the proscenium lights fade up slowly, a standing ovation has already begun in the VIP section and stadium seats rising into the dark. Hundreds—thousands—applauding. Grant claps along, gentlemanly, for the rest of his cohorts' pieces, but he doesn't notice what I do: everyone who is standing is looking at him.

Not at us, not at me—at Grant. Grant Rossi, the designer of the Knight Princess.

"It's you!" I say, shaking his arm—that beautiful arm I'll never hold again, but for the best reason in the world. He startles when I touch him. Not angry—confused. We meet eyes, probably for the last time. I nod. "It's for *you*."

His face opens like a sunrise. *"Me?"* He turns to the audience, bewildered.

People in gowns and fine tailored suits surround him with applause, whistling, hollers of *"Bravo!"* and *"WORK IT!"*

"Get up and take it," I whisper, poking his side. Grant leaps to his feet, and the cheers intensify. He can't even smile, he's absorbing so much at once. He's enough. He's always been enough.

But there's someone else out there who needs to be reminded of how great he is. I have to find Elliot *now.*

I sprint toward the backstage stairs, knocking into audience members' knees as I fly. I'm not wasting another second. No more messing around, no more cameras or Wish Granted nonsense; I just need him.

The house lights rise as I'm halfway to the stairs.

I can see Elliot in flashes through the billowing backstage curtains. He hikes up his train and descends the stairs to the dressing rooms.

"Micah, stunning work!" a voice cries from the aisle. I blow past them. Next, a group of well-dressed people jump into the aisle, blocking my path. Whoever they are, they're all smiles and reaching hands. More strangers cluster around them, and my path to Elliot closes.

They hurl questions and praise. I mutter, "Thank you, thank you," but it does nothing to dull their excitement. With one final push forward, the wall of humanity separates enough to let me pass. I break into a sprint backstage, through the maze of ropes where my first relationship died, and then hurl myself down the stairs toward the dressing rooms.

"Elliot!" I yell, bursting into our dressing room. Kris shuts the clasps on her makeup tackle box and finds me, red-faced and panting. Elliot isn't here, but the Knight Princess gown rests haphazardly on the mannequin. The rainbow train lies bunched on the makeup counter.

Startled, Kris says, "Sorry. He left."

## Chapter 25
# THE SEARCH FOR THE SQUIRE

The roar of people celebrating a successful show sounds dull and miles away on the steps of the Art Institute. Outside, the city is dark and empty. Cars whoosh by along Michigan Avenue. Wherever Elliot went, he is long gone.

My stomach shrivels into a raisin, and a wave of over-excitement saps my limbs of strength as I dial his number: straight to voicemail. *Please call me, Elliot.*

I text him instead: **Elliot, are you still here?**

I really need to talk to you. I'm sorry about everything.

I broke up with Grant.

Every text struggles to send before turning green. That dreaded color: Unavailable Green—as if the message itself failed to thrive and died on the vine. Like, maybe if my message were a little better, more substantial, more exciting, more apologetic—if I'd tried harder—it would turn that lovely iMessage blue. The color of connection.

But this green does not mean *go*.

My connection to Elliot has severed.

His phone is out of battery. *No, Elliot would never be so unprepared.*

He's in a bad signal area. *No, he's in the same area I am, and I'm at full bars.*

He's turned off his phone. *Yes, that's it! He wants me to leave him alone.*

Alone.

All I can think of is that he wants me to leave him alone. His wounded face in Audrey's returns to me—he wanted me to say I loved him. He told me he wanted to hear it, but not until I'd closed things with Grant and was ready to do something about it.

No more fear. No more second-guessing.

It's time to finally tell Elliot how I feel. The rest is up to him.

My body sways with seasick nausea. My story with Elliot didn't arrive as a classic fairy tale, but nevertheless, our story is one now: the prince who realizes who his heart truly belongs to . . . only too late. The True Loves Lost fairy tales always have this moment—before the prince embarks on a final, daring quest for love. I'm living it right now.

*You've been training for this your whole life, Micah. Go get him.*

In my pinched, steel-toed dress shoes, I flee through downtown and don't stop until I reach the neon glow of an electric pizza slice. The door to Little Parisi's has been propped open with a brick, probably to tempt in customers with the aroma of melted mozzarella. Or more likely, to tempt in a cool breeze. A wall-unit air conditioner hangs above the door with a flap of cardboard Scotch-taped over the face reading DO NOT TURN ON.

The land that air conditioning forgot. It's Elliot's home, for sure.

The air is thick inside the long galley pizza parlor, so much so that I instinctively shield my face the moment I enter. Stuart, Elliot's father—with his *Bob's Burgers* mustache—sweats as he hands slices on paper plates over the counter. A swarm of miserably hot customers bolt out of the place the second they grab their food.

Already stifling from my run, I peel off my jacket and unbutton my collar as I wait behind the last customers, a father and his tiny, whining son. The father fans himself uselessly as he orders.

Stuart blinks through sweating eyelids as he listens to him order, but it's difficult to concentrate—he keeps glancing over his shoulder at me.

Something about Stuart's expression presses my insides flat.

As if he knows why I'm here . . . and the news isn't good.

After the man leaves, balancing two plates on top of each other as he tugs his sobbing child out the door, Elliot's dad exhales loudly. He digs into an ice chest beneath his feet—the remaining flecks of ice slosh around inside a sea of melted ones—and pulls out a dripping, long-necked bottle of Pepsi. "Mr. Summers, if you're not gonna order a slice, do you mind if I throw this back and sit a bit?"

"Sure, go ahead," I say.

He chugs it, second after second, glug after glug, and finally sits at one of the tables. He points angrily at the seat across from him. I know right away to take it without questions. "Yeah, you're not here for a slice. You're too good for it."

"Mr. Tremaine, I'm—"

"How about you let me talk for a bit? I got a few things to say."

His exhausted glare silences me. No rebuttal or fight comes to my lips. Guilt surges through my brain, sizzling and popping like bacon grease. So many friendly faces—Elliot, Grant, Stuart—have looked at me tonight with hurt, betrayal, or misery. A dark mirror of the interactions we used to have.

"Elliot talks about you so much," Stuart says. "Do you know that? He was unhappy for so long, and then he meets you, starts having these adventures with you, and it was like I had my son back again." Tears glaze his eyes. He bites his lower lip to stop himself.

"I love him," I blurt.

Stuart's expression brightens. "Did you tell that to Elliot?"

"I, uh . . . didn't realize it until tonight."

Stuart's entire body deflates. "I couldn't make his show. How did he do?"

In my mind, Elliot's gown unfurls like golden light. "He was a star."

He smiles without strength. "So you're here looking for him?"

I nod. "I need to find him. I need to tell him how I feel. Do you know where he is?"

Both our chests rise and fall under the swelter of this dreadful heat. No wonder it wore Elliot down. Stuart and I stare without blinking. We both love Elliot—his absence fills every molecule of this building—but I don't like the beaten look on Stuart's face.

"Elliot needs a change," Stuart admits. "He loves animals—animals help. For his senior year, he's going back to my sister in River Valley. She's got a farm with horses and sheep. It's always been good for him."

There isn't an ounce of water left in my body. My lips could blow away like dust.

Elliot—gone.

"When?" I say with a squeak.

"Midnight train tonight out of LaSalle Station. He wanted to stay in town long enough to do your show." Stuart can't look me in the eyes anymore. "He left here a little bit ago. We already said goodbye."

Midnight. Tonight. In little more than an hour.

When the clock strikes twelve, the magic is over.

Now is the time to toughen up. This final quest isn't over yet—if anything, this is more serendipitous proof that Elliot and I are living in the unbreakable, unshakable sequence of a fairy tale come true. I will find him before midnight.

He'll stay.

"Where is River Valley?" I ask.

"Far, far away," Stuart says, mopping his forehead with a wad of napkins. A group of young guys stroll inside, laughing loudly, one of them dribbling a basketball. As soon as they cross the threshold, they shout, "WOOOOOO! It's hot!"

Stuart welcomes them flatly with a "Hello, gentlemen" and retreats behind the counter.

As the ballplayers confer with each other about what toppings they want, I actually feel the seconds vanishing through my fingers. I have until midnight. Would Elliot want to see me? Could I convince him to stay?

I have to try.

*Courage now, Micah!*

As I'm about to reach fresh air again, the last ballplayer in line snaps his fingers like he just remembered something important. "Hey—Prince of Chicago!" His friends turn around, pointing happily. "Whoa," one of them gasps. "The King's here, too!"

I glance up from my belly button and almost have a heart attack.

Outside Little Parisi's, a black stretch limousine idles along the curb. Leaning against the car is my dad, still in his bespoke suit fineries but with the collar undone. Beside him is my mother, Maggie, Manda, Hannah, and Jackson. They've all been waiting for me.

I almost detonate with affection for each one of them.

"Micah, you ran off before anyone could congratulate you," Dad says, smiling. "I was gonna say that's bad form, but Maggie and Hannah told us something else might be going on with you. They had a hunch you'd turn up here."

My quest to find Elliot just got a whole team of squires.

# Chapter 26
# THE COUNSEL OF THE KING

Inside the limo, my dad's curated playlist of Smashing Pumpkins and Earth, Wind, and Fire thumps while disco lights strobe through the car, which is normally spacious but currently crowded with my entire family, Manda, Hannah, and Jackson—every person I care about in the world.

Almost every person.

Grant is still at the Art Institute, heartbroken but hopefully being rightfully lauded for his showstopping design. Elliot is probably already at the LaSalle train station, about to leave my life forever. But if we can find him first—and I pour my heart out—there's a chance that won't have to happen.

Before I can tell everyone that I'm not okay and have extremely little time left, I realize I don't have to. My mom exchanges worried glances with Maggie and Hannah: they know something's wrong. They were expecting to be cheerleading my mural victory all night, which I can't believe I have zero interest in now that I'm on the worst ticking clock of all time.

"What's wrong?" Mom asks, patting my hands.

Every face in the limo is on me as I huff panicked breaths into my lungs.

"Did you break up with Grant?" Maggie asks. I only have the energy to nod. While my parents moan sadly, Maggie grips Manda's hand and they both smile at me like proud moms. "Good for you."

I want to thank her, but I might start crying, and there's so much more to lose tonight.

Jackson wraps his arm around Hannah. My best friend hasn't spoken since she showed up. She looks terrified. We lock eyes across the parallel seats while hot-pink disco lights swirl across our grim faces.

She knows.

"When did Elliot tell you he was leaving?" I ask her. Silence falls inside the limo.

"After I got out of the show," she says, strangling her tension out on a cocktail napkin. "He emailed. It was long. He must have scheduled it to send as soon as the show wrapped."

"When it would be too late to stop him."

She nods, and Jackson squeezes her tighter. I shut my eyes and try to catch my breath.

He doesn't want to be stopped.

I didn't even get an email goodbye. He probably has nothing left to say to me.

*NEVERTHELESS, MICAH. YOU HAVE TO FIND HIM AND TELL HIM.*

A large, loving hand falls on my neck. I open my eyes to find Dad, fear etched across his face, but he's activated—leaning forward with the focus and energy that won him an Olympic medal. "Something's going on, kid," he says. "Lay it on us."

As if granted permission, I finally blurt everything: "I was dating the wrong boy, and the right one—Elliot—is leaving Chicago permanently, tonight, in an hour, unless I can find him."

Giving no one an inch of daylight to interrupt, I launch into a speedy recap of this hellish night: dumping Grant, my true feelings for Elliot, how I let it all blow up, and Elliot's imminent departure from our lives. I speak so quickly that emotion doesn't sneak into my voice until the end, when a cacophony of heaviness falls from my mouth: "I hurt the person I love by making him think I didn't love him. And if he leaves, I'll never be able to fix that mess."

The truth I've been avoiding all night.

The horrific possibility of losing Elliot tonight. I'll never be able to tell him how I really feel. I'll never get to be with him, for real.

Dad doesn't speak. Not defeated like Elliot's father. Not worried like Mom.

Calm. Thinking.

"First of all, come here," Dad says, the leather seats squeaking as he leans forward to wrap a tight hug around me. Mom throws her arms around both of us. Then Hannah. Soon, six pairs of arms cocoon me in the world's greatest embrace. Dad breaks the hug first, followed by the others as they sit back, leaving only Hannah to give me one final squeeze. She needed this almost as much as I did. Dad pats my damp cheeks and says, "I'm gonna do everyone's least favorite thing and make this about sports, but just stay with me, okay?"

The limo party tenses and nods as one.

"Okay," I agree.

Dad doesn't break from my eyes once as he says, "Life is full of game moments and not-game moments. You're in a game moment right now. On the ice—in the game—everything gets shut out, every other thing going on in your life. There's only you. The clock. And the game. You're in the game."

"Okay."

"I lost your grandma right before the best game of my life. I made a choice to be in the game because that was my space where I hadn't lost her. In that space, I didn't even know a mother. I went somewhere else. You're following?"

"Yes." The world focuses all around me. Dad's words work on me like magic. I'm in the game. Even though the rest of my family watches us just inches away, it's only me and him.

"Finding Elliot is your game, and you have an hour," Dad says. "Every single time I made a mistake on that ice, I was rushing. I wasn't breathing. I wasn't present. You need to find him before midnight. Not just that, you gotta unscrew the pooch with him, too." Dad pauses to inhale quickly, calmly, like he's taking a sip of air. I copy him. The short, deep breath lightens my head. "You don't have time for mistakes. So breathe. Focus on your goal."

Elliot's laugh fills my head.

Possibility fills my heart.

I can do this. No fear, no fear, no fear.

"So this Elliot . . ." Dad leans back into his seat. "You're telling us he's The Guy?"

I clear my throat. "If he'll have me . . . he's The Guy."

Hannah glances at me, grinning through her glistening eyes.

Dad laughs. "You made fun of me when I confused Elliot for your boyfriend, but that just shows you how I always know!" Maggie and I groan, but Dad merely claps his hands, satisfied at being right once again. "Now, I got this party limo for the family . . . but the party can't start because the family is missing someone."

*The family is missing someone.*

Elliot. As much a part of my family as Hannah or anyone else.

That's what I want more than anything.

"Micah, it's your game," Dad says, slapping my knee. "What do we do?"

Fire wakes up my heart and lungs. My energy bar fills completely.

I'm in the game.

Whatever I do, it has to mean something to Elliot.

*Elliot dances through the spitting fountain, a magical water sprite.*

Something personal. Something that's us. Something I can arrange in less than an hour.

*"It's a little you!" Elliot whispers, laughing about the boy outside Millennium Park.*

I know what to do!

"Micah?" Dad asks, bringing my focus back to the limo. "Should we go to LaSalle? How can we help?"

Glowing from ear to ear, I say, "There's only one person who can help me."

## Chapter 27
# THE KINGDOM HELPS

The park. Back to the beginning, where I couldn't ask out Andy McDermott—where I first asked the universe to help me find Boy 100. Less than a minute later, Hannah would text me to come to Audrey's Café. She said Elliot would brew a chai latte that would make me feel better. *"Prince Charming after all, huh?"* he said. It would be the first of many times Elliot caused courage to flood the anxiety out of my veins.

Now here I am, outside the park, my family and friends in a limo behind me, facing the one person left in the city who can help me get Elliot back: the hot dog vendor.

"What kind of dog can I get you, sweetheart?" asks the woman with curly gray hair beneath her Bulls cap. The fairy godmother in my mural, who will hopefully become my fairy godmother for real. Next to her, a thirty-year-old man crosses his arms and observes me sourly underneath an identical Bulls cap. He's never been at this cart before, but I assume he's here now for the vendor's safety, as Millennium Park is pitch-black this time of night and nearly empty except for a few passersby on their way to a train stop.

"She asked you what you want, friend," the man snarls.

My back stiffens at the man's tone. I've been staring too long, but I have absolutely no idea how to begin asking this *mess* of a question.

Clicking her tongue, the vendor narrows her eyes at the man. "Don't mind my son. I asked for protection, not scaring away all my business!" They sneer at each other before the vendor returns sweetly to me. "Ooh, you look fancy! That limo for you?"

Behind me, my family waits inside the idling limousine along with Stuart, who closed up an hour early to ride with us.

I check my phone. It's 11:11.

*Make a wish, Micah.*

"Sorry, I don't have time for a hot dog," I say.

"Then beat it," the man says, his scowl amplified. "Take your party bus with you."

The vendor casts another dark look at her son, and I step closer. "I need your help. A few weeks ago, I saw you give a kid directions to find the Cinderella pumpkin cars that drive around here. I don't have time to explain, but it's *extremely important* that I rent one of those pumpkins tonight, right now." The vendor and her son blink silently. "Please. Someone really important to me is gonna leave the city forever at midnight. This pumpkin meant something to both of us during a really bad time in our lives. If I can get it and pick him up before midnight . . . maybe he'll stay."

My heart pumps furiously.

With one last deep breath, as if it were my last shot, I add, "It's true love."

The vendor's startled expression softens, a rosy hue rising in her cheeks. "I'd love to help you, angel, but the people who run the carriages are gone for the day." Before I can have a devastating heart attack that my plan is over before it starts, the vendor pats down her Bulls windbreaker. "Unless . . ." A heavy-looking key ring emerges from her jacket. My breath stops. Giggling devilishly, she turns to her son. "Watch my cart!"

"Ma, no," he says, snatching the key ring.

"Damian!" She and her son snip at each other in rapid Greek as they play keep-away with the keys. Failing to reach her son's height, she turns to me pleadingly. "A few of us in the park keep spare keys for each other, in case of emergencies. We help each other out." Angrily, she swipes at the keys again. "And I've always wanted to drive that pumpkin!"

"You don't even know this kid!"

I grit my teeth. The carriage is so close, so *possible*, but with all this bickering, I'm going to run out of time. After a minute of these two jumping around in their Bulls gear, the vendor finally slaps the key ring out of her son's grip, and it clatters to the sidewalk.

I clutch my chest, almost faint, as the vendor dives for the keys. With that, the vendor leaves her son in charge of the cart and leads me toward the final step of my Final Quest.

It's about time I asked this magical woman her name.

"Margaret Kastellanos!" she says, sliding open the gate to the carriage house after disengaging the alarm. The carriage house is a small stable behind the park that was apparently converted into a warehouse once the public finally turned against horse-drawn carriages. With a satisfying *thwap*, overhead lamps snap on one at a time, illuminating the pumpkin in the middle of the room. The carriage is a mostly open-air skeleton of beams in the shape of a pumpkin, its ribs roped in lights not yet activated. Like it has slept here ever since Elliot and I saw it, waiting for me to finally show up.

Margaret wastes no time hoisting herself into the driver's seat outside the sphere, and she begins fiddling with switches. My fingers close around the cool steel cage. I pause one last time and ask, "You're sure it's okay we take it?"

"I already texted the carriage owner!" The pumpkin's rear engine sputters to life. "Oh, she was *jealous* when I said who I was helping. Wanted to race down here out of bed in her nightshirt so she could take you herself. No time, I said." Margaret chuckles nastily as she flips a final switch, and the thousands of twinkle lights wrapping the pumpkin burst to life, filling the warehouse with a white, scorching glow. She leans back. "Well, get in! Clock's ticking!"

My phone reads 11:29, which jabs a knitting needle into my heart.

I hurl myself into the back seat, and Margaret hits the gas.

We soar with the speed of a jacked-up go-kart, probably slower than a car, but the wind whipping through the open-air vessel makes me feel like I'm flying. The pumpkin doesn't slow down as we pass the curbside hot dog cart and limousine, where everyone has piled out onto the street to wave and holler. Hannah whoops the loudest, jumping in place next to my mom and dad, Maggie, Manda, and Jackson. My best friend screams with joy and records the moment on her phone.

In a blink, they're behind us, and Margaret merges into the general flow of Michigan Avenue traffic. It's difficult to keep up, but Margaret doesn't take her foot off the gas. Cars pass us on both sides, some angrily, but most people are cheering out of their windows. They don't know me or why I'm in a pumpkin going as fast as I can to catch a train, but whatever the reason in their minds, we're a bright beacon of fairy-tale joy.

I fight the urge to close my eyes. My excitement and anxiety are clashing in an epic battle inside my stomach.

11:36. Elliot's train is already boarding. But we're going to make it.

I text Elliot one more time: **Please don't leave. I'm coming to the station right now!**

A desperate hope . . . but one that pays off. The text sends blue.

His phone is back on! I bite my lip. No typing bubbles yet, but he's getting my messages.

Through the trees, the digitized faces of Crown Fountain continue spitting into the night. I lean forward, gripping the pumpkin's skeletal cage so I don't topple out onto the Magnificent Mile. I want to see Elliot dance in that fountain again. I'm going to join him next time. I should've joined him then. I was afraid. Always afraid.

Please, please, *please* let me see him one more time.

Next on our left, the Art Institute comes and goes. The lights have turned low, and the street outside is no longer jammed with a media circus, but remnants of the red carpet remain as cleaning crews hustle under work lights to remove it. My lungs ache. It's like they're removing the ruins of Wish Granted.

Someday soon, when I'm there on my own terms for my *own* work, hopefully thinking of the Art Institute won't burn so much. Still, I know I'll never forget Grant or what he woke up creatively in me.

Margaret turns sharply from Michigan onto LaSalle. Elliot's train leaves in twenty-one minutes. Memories flood my mind, threatening to drown me. Memories of all my perfect days with him—Dockside Shirley, chai, pizza, popcorn. *"Such a tourist trap,"* I said. *"Some stuff is worth getting trapped for,"* Elliot said.

I should've told him then. I could've stopped him then.

No more fear.

*"Fear is a trap,"* Elliot told me on our first quest. I was worried about meeting Grant, what I would say to him, what he would think of me, if any of it would work. I repeat this advice to steel myself against the same questions about Elliot.

I check the map. We're only a few blocks away.

Maybe we'll even see him on the street.

My heart is going to detonate inside my chest any minute, but I use my supernatural psychic powers to will it to behave until I find Elliot.

In the distance, the train station appears. Eighteen minutes left. This is it.

I believe.

## Chapter 28
# THE STROKE OF MIDNIGHT

**11:44. I'm not too late.**

I don't wait for the carriage to fully stop before leaping to the street. My steel-toed shoes land with a sharp tremor that courses up my back, but nothing can stop me. "Thank you, Margaret!" I shout, scrambling up. "I've gotta catch him, but I'll be right back!"

"I'll be right here!" she hollers. "GO! GO!"

The reddish-brown marble halls of the LaSalle Street Metra Station echo with the distant sounds of lonely footsteps. If you're taking the train this late at night, odds are good you're doing so alone.

Like Elliot.

*Elliot, you're here alone, but I promise—no more lonely nights for you. For either of us!*

During the day, there's an overwhelming bustle in these corridors. A barrage of humanity rushing to catch a train or racing off one to make it to work. The Chicago Stock Exchange shares a wall with the station, so these trains always carry the air of stuffy, grand, *old money* importance. Brokers traveling from suburbia simply *must* make it to the floor on time or the financial fabric of society will come undone!

Not tonight.

I hear footsteps but see hardly anyone at all.

There's no one rushing, except for me.

My lungs feel like someone has taken a cheese grater to them. Stinging, shallow burning prevents me from taking full breaths as I stop to survey for Elliot. As I do, my shoes squeak on the lobby floor. A lanky maintenance man looks up from his mop bucket. I look down. I've left a dark shoe mark on his newly scrubbed floor.

"Sorry," I pant through breathless lungs before traversing around his cleaning.

I'm here!!!! I text Elliot. Once again, it turns blue but with no response. No typing.

I don't let the bad thoughts in.

Elliot is in this building.

I sprint the rest of the way through the lobby to the train platform. My lungs are still rebuilding themselves—breath by painful breath—so I keep myself at a brisk jog, despite my brain's insistence to GO, GO, GO, NOW, NOW, NOW.

The LaSalle platform is partially covered, but otherwise open to the elements. Retro music drifts ghostly distant out of unseen speakers overhead. Alannah Myles's "Black Velvet" carries away dreamily in the warm, night wind. A Lip Sync for Your Life song—definitely how it feels for me at the moment. Rows of long, fading silver carriages wait like bullets ready to be fired—ready to send Elliot away from here forever. A digital clock reads 11:48 above future departure times. There's only a handful of passengers scattered around, but none of them are Elliot.

Cruelly, I keep expecting one of them to turn around and—*gasp*—find my sweet barista dancer. Yet each time it isn't him, it's like Donkey Kong is squeezing my heart.

I run, huffing more abnormally by the second, along the length of the scheduled midnight train. The first few open portals are empty. No train attendants. Not even many visible passengers. From the outside, I press my face against the passenger windows—germs be damned—to make out the faces of people already curling up in their seats for a long nap. He's not there, from what little I can see through the glare of my own reflection. I'll never find him this way. I need an attendant.

Finally, one appears at the farthest doorway—an older gentleman in a refined maroon vest with one foot on the train, the other on the platform. He grips a handle on the doorway and lets his body gently, playfully swing. A man who is terribly bored with little to do.

Perfect!

"Have you seen everyone who's gotten on this train?" I ask, opening my camera roll.

"Hrmmm?" the attendant asks, waking from his sleepy hypnosis.

I show him the picture I took of Elliot running through the spitting water at Crown Fountain. "This guy, Elliot, he's booked for this train. Have you seen him? Is he here?"

My breath suspends inside my lungs while the man strains to get a closer look. He shakes his head. Chuckling, he says, "No one that young on this train. Sorry."

I can't tell if I'm distraught or relieved he hasn't seen Elliot.

This is the train. Where else could he be?

"Thank you for your help," I tell the attendant.

"Thank you for your help," I say over and over, each time closer to a panic attack, to each new attendant as I race from doorway to doorway, even to other trains. No one has seen Elliot.

He's not here yet.

There's eight minutes left. Maybe he's running late.

But Elliot has never, ever been late or kept me waiting.

I ignore this immutable fact. He's doing a big move. Things happen when you move. You get behind schedule. Things get left behind.

*Like me. I'm left behind.*

I wait for him. I take a bench seat, breathe steadily, check my phone exactly one hundred times for a text that hasn't come, and wait. Elliot and me, in Audrey's Café, is all I want right now. I'd do anything, sell anything, to get back to that little table in Audrey's when Elliot still thought I was the coolest person in the world.

That's never coming back. How could I let this dream get away? I already had everything I wanted.

11:58.

No one has come through these doors.

My phone has no texts from Elliot.

I bite my lower lip so hard I might gnaw it off and force myself to shoot my last shot.

With my head still on a swivel for Elliot, I text him with a trembling thumb:

Elliot, I'm in the station, about to watch your train leave. I wish so badly that you aren't on it. But if you are, I wish more than anything that you get your happy ending. Even if it isn't with me. You're going to be the greatest vet in history, even if I'm not there to watch it happen.

I take a deep, agonizing breath and finish the text:

A weary world deserves a little dreaming. And no one deserves it more than you.

11:59.

I send the text.

With one last call for passengers, the train leaves.

## Chapter 29
# THE END

Midnight has come and gone. With it go my hopes, dreams, faith in magic, and—most importantly—patience with myself.

*Burn this into your mind, Micah. You didn't have to lose Elliot, but you did—forever—because you're a frightened, timid mouse. You faced your dragons too late. If you really knew fairy tales, you'd remember that time runs out on magic. The clock is everything.*

The carriage turns back into a pumpkin.

The Beast's last rose petal falls.

The sun sets on Ariel's wish.

I'm too late. The curse of loneliness is permanent now.

There's only one train left in the station. Nothing but tracks and a few lone Metra workers. Emptiness is everywhere. Elliot must have gotten on an earlier train, or no one noticed him get on the one that just left. Or he's somewhere in the city and simply too over my crap to answer me back. I hate that version most of all, because it feels the most real.

"Micah?" asks a comforting voice. I turn to Margaret, Bulls cap perched on top of her tightly curled gray hair and wearing the kindest smile I've ever seen. She touches my shoulder. "The train left. What are you still doing here on this bench by yourself?"

"I . . ." Words strangle inside my throat. Tears break on my next syllable. "I can't get up."

"You can't?"

"I can't move." I shake my head. My legs feel like they're filled with concrete. They refuse to budge. If I get up, I'll have to walk out. If I walk out, I'll have to tell everyone I failed.

"Sure, you can get up," Margaret insists.

I shake my head harder. "I can't get off the bench."

"No tears." She pulls me into a hug with a whiff of Liz Taylor's White Diamonds perfume, my grandma's favorite. As she pats my back, I crumple further. "No tears. Let's get you up."

Standing is dreadful, but I do it anyway. Margaret makes it feel at least one percent possible. Her warmth but stern confidence commands me to instantly do as I'm told. Right now, when I'm this lost, that's comforting. I trudge back through the halls of LaSalle Station with my jubilant fairy godmother.

"It was so nice of you to help me," I say after clearing my throat.

"Forget all that!" She waves blood-red nails, and another whiff of White Diamonds collides with my nostrils. As we descend the escalators outside, the omnipresent light from the pumpkin carriage rises from the street below.

Oh God. We're about to make a *far* less triumphant journey back in this thing.

*Watch out, Chicago! Behold, the devastated boy in his dazzling pumpkin carriage!*

When the escalator spits us onto the street, my family's limousine is parked with everyone waiting outside. A sandbag drops on my heart for each loved one I'm going to have to tell about Elliot. But as I turn to the pumpkin carriage, I realize I don't have to tell them about Elliot.

Elliot is already here.

Waiting for me, one foot on the pumpkin carriage step, in crisp, white linen Dockers and matching button-down with the sleeves rolled to his elbows . . . is the boy I've been searching for. A boy as bright as sunshine surrounded by the twinkle lights of the carriage. The image is so perfect, so romantic, I'm terrified I'll ugly cry right here in front of everyone we know and ruin the whole moment.

"Elliot," I say, more wind than sound. Air gasps back into my lungs so quickly, it becomes harder to breathe than when I thought I'd lost him.

I close the distance between us as carefully as if the road were glass. My fingers close around his—and his gaze doesn't leave mine. In the glow of the coach lights, a watery sheen sparkles across his eyes. This is as emotionally risky for him as it is for me.

"I'm sorry," I say.

"I know," Elliot says—not quite smiling, but not quite upset.

"I broke up with Grant."

"I know."

More neutrality. Terror ascends my chest like warriors scaling a castle wall.

How does he feel? Is he happy to see me? I'll never know for sure unless I make the jump, and this time, I'm jumping first.

He isn't here for apologies or to talk about my breakup. Whatever made him get off that train, I think he's here for one thing only—the fairy-tale sweep.

"I was too scared to do this until now," I say, grazing my thumb rhythmically across his palm. He doesn't flinch. He watches me carefully, as if he can't trust me yet to say the truth. But I'll prove to him that I can. "Before I really knew you, I sketched ninety-nine boyfriends but never found the right one. I wished for the universe to send me Boy 100, the one I knew I'd fall in love with. I assumed it was Grant, but I was wrong. When I made that wish three months ago, the very next boy I saw . . . was you. You were Boy 100."

Elliot chews his lower lip. He's desperate to keep his expression neutral, maybe to hold on to his anger, maybe to see how much more I'll say. But his glistening eyes, shimmering like stardust in the carriage lights, tell me everything.

*Say it, Micah. Finally.*

"The boy with the perfect hands," I say, pressing the back of his hand to my princely lips. The tiniest gasp escapes him. "I love you, Elliot. I've been falling in love with you more with each moment I'm with you. If it's not too late, would you please stay and be my boyfriend?"

Speechless, his lip trembles. A few steps away, Margaret watches us eagerly. Only Hannah is as close, our mutual best friend's hands clasped over her mouth. To everyone else's credit, they know to keep their distance.

Unable to breathe, I watch Elliot.

Slowly, his lips form a smile. "I love you, too," he says.

Breath returns, but this time, it's my heart that stops. He loves me. He loves me back!

Elliot rustles his adorably shaggy hair, which will never, ever look tidy, no matter what. "When I moved to Chicago last year," he says, "I didn't think I'd fall in love. I didn't think anything was gonna happen to me. Ever. Then I started following this cool art Insta, all about fairy tales and believing you could be loved, even if that felt far away." He smiles. "Then I met the artist. And you gave me a whirlwind summer. You were the best parts—and the worst parts." He chuckles, but my laugh is *much* louder. "Even when I was falling out of love with Brandon, I felt happy and safe . . . because I was with you."

"Same!" I shout, almost shaking with excitement. "I feel exactly the same."

"But," he says, his jaw stiffening. "I love you, *but* . . . I need you to do something."

"Literally anything."

"Nonnegotiable."

"I will skydive out of a plane screaming your name. I will wrap my arms around the moon—"

Grinning, Elliot reaches out his perfectly manicured fingers and presses them to my lips to hush me. "I'll never interfere with

Instaloves, but you need to tell your fans to leave me *alone*."

"Done," I say into his fingers, stifling a relieved laugh.

He removes his hand, and his eyes narrow. "Tell them you were wrong."

I raise my hand in a solemn pledge. "So wrong."

He steps closer, less than two inches from me. He wets his lips, and I wet mine. "Tell them you love me."

Quieter than a whisper, I say, "I love you."

Without warning, at long last, I kiss Elliot. Light from the carriage engulfs us. I can't see anything—can't feel anything—except the closeness of Elliot. He tastes like hot chai and warm oat milk. Out in the dark, beyond the bright lights, my family, friends, and new friends applaud and cheer.

The kingdom rejoices.

I wasn't too late. I really was worthy of love all along.

Elliot presses his forehead to mine, and we spend a long moment staring at each other, our Great Quest finally complete. "How?" I ask, catching my breath. "What made you get off the train? My texts?"

"Well," he says, chewing his lip again. I want to dive back in for another kiss, but my curiosity is killing me. "I was on the train. I promised myself I'd keep my phone off, but I got antsy. I got your messages, but I was still mad. Sorry."

"*I'm* sorry!"

"But then I got this video from Hannah."

Elliot pulls out his phone and plays a grainy clip. Right away, I recognize the shaky POV of Hannah, recording Margaret and me tearing down Michigan Avenue in the pumpkin carriage. The video zooms in on me, and as soon as we're out of sight, spans the limo passengers one at a time until flipping the camera back to Hannah. She leans in close, her smoky-eyed face filling the frame, and whispers, "We're all coming to you! Please. *Please* get off that train, love."

The video stops.

When I look up, Hannah has crept closer to us. Clutching her purse to her chest, she eyes us warily, wondering if it's okay to be part of the moment. "Well," she says, shrugging, "this was too important to leave everything up to you, Micah."

Without wasting another moment, Elliot and I drag Hannah into the most grateful hug of our lives. Hannah wipes a tear, taking half her makeup with it, before skipping back to Jackson near Maggie and Manda at the limo.

Elliot brushes sweat-plastered hair from my forehead. His touch—his intimacy—is something I've been needing for so long, it's almost unbearable. An overload to my system.

"What about vet school?" I ask cautiously, not fully trusting that he's back for good—or rather, not fully trusting that such a wonderful thing has come to me without strings.

Elliot chuckles. "You know, when I turned my phone back on, I also had an interesting email waiting for me from Grant."

Time freezes. Oh God, *no*. "What did he say?"

"It was a forwarded email . . . from someone offering me a job? This designer, Geoff something—I was too stressed out trying to get off the train in time to read it again—but he saw Grant's show and wants me to be the face of his campaign. It's called something like 'Fashion for the People.' I don't know, I need to read it again, but the pay is good. Better than Audrey's, and so is the schedule. I can wrap up my last semester of classes in the city while I save for vet school."

Elliot, a fashion model! It is *everything* he deserves. And Grant really came through for Elliot. Wherever Grant is right now, I hope he feels like a king.

I grab Elliot by the shoulders, as energized as if I could lift us both into the sky, and whoop, "That's amazing!"

When I cup his surprisingly bristly cheeks, he relaxes into me and meets my eyes. "I've got a messy life," he says seriously. "I work a lot. I get in my feelings a lot. I'm not this sweet, flawless person, if that's what you're thinking you're getting with me."

"I'm looking for Elliot," I say. "Whatever comes with that."

He smiles and darts his eyes to the glowing carriage. "You got me the pumpkin."

"I promised you a ride if I ever . . ."

"Decided to stop making my life miserable?"

"I was gonna say 'came to my senses and asked you out,' but yes, same diff." He kisses me, and my head buzzes like it was hit with the rush of champagne bubbles. Once more, I take Elliot's hand. "Elliot, will you do me the honor of joining me in this pumpkin carriage on a victory lap for finishing our magical quest?"

Now it's his turn to pull my hand to his lips. A prince and a prince.

"Our quest isn't finished," he says. "Just getting started."

I'm flying. *Just getting started.*

I hoist myself into the back seat of the pumpkin carriage and reach my hand out to Elliot. He entrusts his rolling suitcases to Hannah and Maggie before rushing back to take my waiting invitation. Budged up against each other, it's even brighter than I remembered inside the coach. Margaret hurries into the driver's seat, and as the golden carriage fires to life and pulls into the street, our family and friends cheer and wave. Like two Cinderellas, we wave back through the illuminated rear window and watch them sink farther away into the dark road.

"I love this thing!" Margaret hollers from the front. "We're gonna see the whole city! Got another hour before it's due back!"

Not quite the midnight *coach turns back into a pumpkin* deadline, but this is a gay fairy tale, so running a little late makes sense.

This time, we get to make our own fairy tale. Our own magic.

I've got my prince, and he has me.

# EPILOGUE

Instaloves is changing—from now on, it won't just be about me and my romance. When I was making my mural for the Wish Granted show, I realized my love for all kinds of people in this wonderful kingdom of Chicago. Fairy tales aren't just about romance, they're about finding the fantasy in everyday life.

That's my art. My mission. My quest.

Instead of big fairy-tale dates, I'm going to sketch the magical little moments that are the DNA of our relationships and our lives.

What's your love story? What do you love most about this city? Or yourself? That's the story I want to tell. Send me your little moments that you'd like to see on Instaloves, and maybe next year, I'll feature you in a sketch. (I'll try my best to get to all of you)! But until then, I'm showing some Happily Ever Afters in my own life.

Just saying hi to three pups at the vet clinic.

Thanks to her boyfriend, Jackson, my best friend Hannah has officially become a gamer!

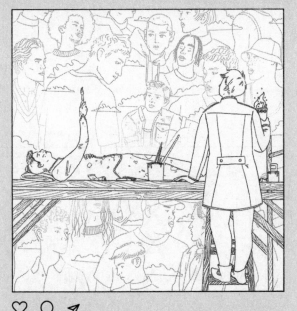

Letting Elliot peek at my next project for the Art Institute (in exchange for chai).

Happy Holidays! My sister made it official. Gross.

(jk love you, sis and soon-to-be sis-in-law!)

A fairy-tale ending that never ends.

# Acknowledgments

Writing about Micah and his boyfriends was a challenge. This is a story of joy, and I was writing it during one of the most turbulent times in both my life and the world's. It was the first year of COVID. It was during the election of Joe Biden and the subsequent insurrection. I had been let go from my job and finding another one turned out to be near-impossible. On top of it all, my husband and I realized we were unhappy where we lived and would need to (yet again) reboot our living situation. There were times when tapping into Micah and Elliot's joy felt like a lie. Writing Grant felt easier—I similarly felt like I was trying to smile myself out of a curse.

But then the funniest thing happened.

Micah saved me. Bit by bit, his joy survived the harsh winds and it kindled joy in me.

A weary world deserves a little dreaming!

It turned out this was the exact thing I needed to be writing at a time like this. And for that, I have some folks to thank. Kelsey Murphy, my editor, always knew the right tone to strike, and she lasered in on what I was trying to do with this John Hughes meets *Amélie* world. James Akinaka and the whole team at Penguin Teen were cheerleaders since day one! *Micah*'s phenomenal low-fi album-esque cover is all thanks to designer Kaitlin Yang and artist Anne Pomel, who also created the stellar designs throughout the book to bring InstalovesInChicago to life! To Kate Brauning and Lynn Weingarten at Dovetail, thank you for these wonderful characters—and for picking me to write them. Thanks also to Chelsea Eberly for making sure Micah made it to the best publisher possible! To Eric Smith, thank you for making sure I took that very important call where you convinced me I had it in me to write a rom-com. Lastly, thank you, Michael Bourret, for your razor-sharp eye.

Thanks to my family, who—even though I grew up hours outside the city—brought me to Chicago frequently to foster my love of art, theater, culture, and cuisine. A queer boy needs to feel fancy, or he'll starve, so this small act kept me going in otherwise low times! Bonus Easter Egg: my parents got engaged at The Art Institute, so when the time came to choose a setting for Micah's grand romantic adventures, I didn't think twice.

Although I used to live near Chicago, that was some time ago, so if I was going to write my big love letter to the city, I was gonna need help grounding Micah. For that, I turned to old friends like Paul Anderson and new friends like Simeon Tsanev.

Being a writer can get lonely. Luckily, I have some of the best writer friends there are, who supported me emotionally and creatively throughout making *Micah*. Ryan La Sala, Robby Weber, Robbie Couch, Sophie Gonzales, Phil Stamper, Caleb Roehrig, Kosoko Jackson, Kevin Savoie, Damian Alexander, Tom Ryan, Alex London, Lev Rosen, and Julian Winters were all enormously helpful (especially Julian, who kindly dropped his lawsuit against me when I changed the name from Micah Winters to Summers). But two writer besties kept my candle burning when it threatened to go out: David Nino, who was vital to helping shape Elliot into the perfect star he is today, would always take my calls (whether he wanted to or not); and Terry Benton-Walker, my twin, who helped me with . . . everything? Life? I really owe him a boat for all he's done for me.

Last, but far from least, is my husband, Michael—my companion in all things, and the inspiration for many of Micah's moments with Elliot. The scene where Elliot instantly bonds with Micah's testy family cat? That was Michael. Like Elliot, Michael knows how to put people at ease, and during the writing of this book, he had to work overtime doing that. Thank you for once again seeing me safely through another book. Let's do more!

STAY TUNED FOR
# CURSED BOYS AND BROKEN HEARTS
## BY ADAM SASS
### COMING SOON!

Grant Rossi is never getting a happily-ever-after. But when he has to spend the summer working alongside his former childhood crush (and biggest enemy) refurbishing his family's run-down B&B—will his trail of broken hearts continue? Or will he find that two cursed boys are better together?